CAIN LAKE

TWO

PHANTOM PAIN

PHANTOM PAIN

CAIN LAKE

BOOK TWO

E-Book: ISBN 978-1-7364107-5-2
Paperback: ISBN 978-1-7364107-4-5

THE DARK 

He wasn't dead—not yet, anyway. A drop of blood clung to his left nostril until the man with the large wrench took another swing. Bone cracked, and blood spattered against the rough-cut lumber partition inside the room. The victim sat in a metal chair—not the folding kind, but a heavy tulip chair manufactured in the 1970s. His hands were bound behind his back with a pair of zip-ties. His elbows were tied to the chair's arms with a thin, pliable rope. His reaction to the blow was merely a wince. His energy to resist or cry out was depleted. He'd accepted his deadly fate hours ago. This is where he was likely to die.

"Still awake?" The man with the wrench asked with a muffled voice.

The assailant let the weapon fall from his hands, clanging loudly on the concrete floor. He didn't want to kill the man in the chair. The blows were only hard enough to hurt like hell but soft enough to keep the prisoner alive. He chose a seventeen-millimeter Craftsman because it was the largest wrench in his tool set. Initially, the beating started with bare knuckles, but the bruises and abrasions starting to form would be evidence of his crime. He needed to ensure no one would suspect him.

The man in the chair faded out of consciousness—the seventh time in two days. A broken tooth fell from his mouth and bounced across the floor.

Cody Savage watched the brutality of it all, helpless to intervene or save the man in the chair. He was an observer and nothing more. He tried to take mental notes; the size and shape of the room, the lack of windows, even the style of shoes the victim and assailant wore. Any little detail that could help him identify the individuals. The light was dim, and the details were vague.

But there was little to view in the dark room. The only light source came from a window—no larger than a pillow—six feet above the concrete floor. A single beam of sunlight cut through the darkness and reflected off the coarse floor, and it was just enough to illuminate the figure in the chair. The hard shadows it created made it impossible for Cody to identify the bludgeoned man. There was, however, something familiar about his face. Cody was sure they'd never met unless it were a random passing on the street or in a local store. Perhaps he'd seen the man in prison. Hundreds of faces came and went during his four-year stay at Dannemora Correctional Facility, and Cody had a knack for remembering most of them. Maybe this guy was a short-timer who spent a month or less living in prison, scared shitless before becoming accustomed to the concrete view.

Everything Cody was witnessing was a mere vision in his mind—a psychic episode of an event unfolding somewhere near Cain Lake. He'd had this clairvoyant ability for over a month and still lacked the skill to control it. Maybe he'd never be able to handle it.

Though he couldn't control his psychic power, he learned to provoke it. Water was always a catalyst for the vision, but fortunately, few people were in danger lately, which made Cody glad.

Cody knew the man in the chair was in danger, just like Darcy Poole had been the previous month. Cody had found the missing girl with his psychic ability, but that was because he could see more clearly where the young girl was being held captive. And it didn't hurt that his dead wife Willa pushed him in the right direction.

Now, he struggled to see. He pushed the sound of the unconscious man's breathing out of his mind and tried to focus on the environment. He remembered Daisy's advice. His girlfriend urged him to focus on more senses than just vision. She encouraged him to listen, smell, and try touching the walls. Cody closed his eyes, although he wasn't physically present, and the darkness swallowed him momentarily. His olfactory senses took over, and he could smell urine and blood mixed with acrylic. The odor was more potent when he stepped closer to the chair.

He paused and listened for audible clues that might reveal their location. A Bon Jovi song played faintly over a radio. His ears picked up a chime somewhere outside the building—a sound similar to a wrench tapping a metal pipe. The noise lacked rhythm—not an intentional sound but happening accidentally.

The man dishing out the beating was a silhouette against the soft glow of intruding street light. He did not speak nor push his victim for information. The assault was occurring without reason or motivation. That was clear to Cody.

After several minutes of no activity, the chair-bound victim lifted his head and spoke what might be his last words, "Who are you?"

The antagonist dishing out the pain, stepped entirely into the shadows. Darkness enveloped him as he spoke with a soft, muffled voice, "I'm nobody. Just a sinner like everyone else in this friggin town."

The vision waned, and Cody departed the nightmare. He found himself back at the beach—back at Cain Lake. Daisy held his head above water as he lay on his back, floating in the calm water. He was grounded to the sandy bottom, his toes sunk into the soft lake bed while she balanced his torso.

Her eyes were as wet as his, "It's okay. I'm here."

The couple stood in waist-deep water. Daisy helped Cody stand straight, causing gravity to pull blood from his nose and run down his upper lip. The tinnitus in his ears made it difficult to hear his girlfriend's words. It sounded like he was still underwater, and she was shouting from the surface. A migraine wrapped around the left side of Cody's head, making the summer sun scorch his retinas. A trickle of blood spilled from his nose, which Daisy wiped away with her thumb and then rinsed in the lake water.

Cody's left arm was numb, held down by the weight of a wet bandage at the end of his wrist where his hand used to be.

They trudged through the cool water until Cody collapsed on his hands and knees.

"What the hell was that?" Daisy asked.

Cody coughed water from his lungs. Full of water, his sinuses started to drain through his nose, diluting blood as the mixture dripped from his chin. Watery droplets of blood fell to the ground, absorbed by the tiny sand grains. Even with the sun beating down on him, he trembled with icy chills as his muscles convulsed. He tried to compose himself to answer her. He'd never had a vision this powerful—this painful— and hoped he never would again. He thought about Jesse Lewis, the Sin-eater, and wondered if this was how he felt when he sensed a sinner.

Cody turned toward the water and sat with his knees bent. His arms wrapped around his legs, keeping his torso upright rather than collapsing on his back.

Daisy sat behind him, wrapping herself like a blanket around his body. She squeezed Cody with both arms to transfer her body heat to his skin. "Are you okay?"

Cody wasn't sure what the answer should be. She bit her bottom lip as he explained what he had seen.

"Do you think it's really happening right now?"

"I'm not sure. It doesn't make sense."

She squeezed him tighter.

"I've got to find him, Daisy, if it ain't too late. I've got to stop the sonovabitch that's doing this."

BOURBON & WATER

He inserted the knife into the soft flesh of the belly and then slowly sliced upward until the blade reached the throat. Intestines and organs fell outward and dangled from sinewy tissue that refused to let go. He pulled the gory mess like he'd done a hundred times before, not satisfied with the job until the body was hollow and clean.

There was very little blood.

Once the dirty work was completed, Jeff Bourbon slid a small wet stick through the gills and mouth. Two ten-inch perch for lunch was the most meat he'd eaten in days. The fish weren't biting yesterday, and the previous day he had been too close to his prey—his real prey—to catch any food. But today, he took time to fish during his manhunt. The fishing in Cain Lake was always good if you had the correct tackle, but Bourbon had nothing more than a wound-up fishing line and a one-inch metal Red Devil lure. The little lure was shaped like the head of a spoon with a broken treble hook on the business end.

Bourbon had found the rusty lure inadvertently while trekking around the massive lake. The hook had lodged into his boot when he stepped on it.

He was skeptical of the spoon's ability to attract hungry fish, which is probably why its previous owner failed to retrieve it from the mud. If the lure were more effective, no serious fishermen would have lost track of its placement. On his first attempt, Bourbon tossed the Red Devil into the clear water and wound the slack onto a short stick of cherry wood. A small perch instantly followed the metal meal toward shore. He laughed at the fish's gullibility and wondered how it could believe this was anything worth tasting. Bourbon contemplated the notion that he was perhaps the gullible one.

His gullibility was that he could catch and capture the Sin-eater, the serial killer that had hidden in plain sight while playing pastor in the local church. Was it possible to apprehend Jesse Lewis? Who the hell knew?

But he wasn't going to give up.

If necessary, he would chase Jesse to the edge of hell and bring him to justice, or he would die trying.

Bourbon hung both fish over a red hot bed of coals, remnants from last night's fire, and let the meal cook. It was painful to be patient enough to cook the fish properly. He wanted to keep moving—keep searching. The only way to catch a predator was to be a predator. He needed to think and act like Jesse Lewis and stay close to the only thing the former pastor loved—Cain Lake.

Bourbon bent some tall green grass over, pulling the stalks inward until a makeshift bed had formed. The morning dew had burned off the top half of the grass, but the lower part still held moisture. It was crude and more suitable for a wild animal but would suffice while he napped in the late morning sun.

He listened to red-wing blackbirds scour the cattails, lay back, and stared at the clouds. Reoccurring memories of the previous month haunted his brain. He thought about how he had misjudged Cody Savage and remembered thinking that Cody was everything he despised in a human. But Cody proved otherwise, joining him to stop a serial killer, saving Annabel Thompson, and sacrificing his left hand to save a girl he'd never met. Bourbon replayed the night they were shackled in the barn when Cody, without hesitation, cut his hand off to save them.

Bourbon wasn't sure he could have done the same. He shuddered, thinking about the pain Cody must have endured.

He wondered how Cody was doing now and hoped he was well.

A dozen or more clouds passed overhead, and Bourbon tried to pretend the ambiguous shapes were something identifiable, like an elephant or Snoopy, but the clouds just looked like clouds to him. His imagination wouldn't conjure such thoughts, and he had to accept that he was getting too old for such foolish games.

He turned the fish that hung over the fire to allow the meat to cook evenly. The smell of cooking perch made him hungrier. He thought about a side dish that would pair well with the fish and decided it was a toss-up between mac-n-cheese and potato salad. He didn't have either, but these were the things you contemplated when isolated in the woods for weeks. Living in the wild was tough. A person could go mad from the lack of social interaction, and Bourbon only had himself to argue with, except the day he spent an hour arguing with a porcupine that wouldn't leave his campsite. Bourbon laughed out loud, thinking about the memory, and realized how much he missed arguing with people—especially Annabel.

He missed her.

When the fish meat began to separate and appear to fall off the bone, he pulled the delicacy from the hot coals and set it aside to cool. "Poor man's shrimp," his mother used to call perch. He preferred the freshwater fish to the saltwater crustacean, although a dash of salt for his meal would have been a nice touch.

When the last of the protein was consumed, Bourbon decided a quick swim to clean up was in order. That was one perk of chasing Jesse Lewis around Cain Lake—easy access to water. He stripped his clothes off and strode into the cool, clear water.

He was knee-deep.

Bourbon was surprised that his legs and arms had some definition he hadn't seen in many years. The muscles had lost some size and strength, but he felt they were better conditioned for stamina. He'd lost eighteen pounds in the last three weeks. He needed to be careful with his diet and consume enough calories to keep up the chase.

Waist-deep.

He felt good and loved living under the stars—free to roam. Some days, he would forget there was a purpose to surviving in the wild and wondered if he'd ever return to his home on the edge of town. Maybe, in some subconscious manner, he was purposely not catching the Sin-eater to extend his time in the dense forest.

Chest-deep.

He lifted his feet from the muck and floated. The lake held him now, supporting his weight and invigorating his body.

His thoughts were interrupted by an awkward sensation. It felt like thousands of tiny bubbles had wrapped around his groin and backside. The bubbles swirled around his belly, and Jeff Bourbon stopped swimming waiting for the bubbles to surface. They did not.

After several strokes, he was back to chest-deep water. He cupped his hands around his eyes to shade the sun gleaming off the surface and leaned toward the water. When he peered into the lake, he realized the bubbles appeared to be lights.

Little blue lights surrounded and swirled around the former sheriff like they were investigating a fresh meal. Bourbon tried to run toward shore, but the water's resistance made him sluggish, and the big man moved in slow motion. He kept pushing through the liquid, digging his feet into the soft clay bottom and leaning forward for momentum. His right foot slipped, and he fell, completely submerging himself. The blue lights flowed past and spiraled around his body. Bourbon panicked, unsure of the little organism's intent.

When he finally broke free of the lake's playful grip, he stood on the shore, watching the blue lights crowd along the edge like hungry koi waiting for a tourist to scatter pellets across the water's surface.

He leaned forward with both hands on his knees to get a better look. *What the hell?* "What the hell are those?"

No one answered. In the wild, you never got answers to your questions; most of the time, you just had to make something up yourself. Nothing clouded the mind more than unanswered questions. But Bourbon knew where the answers could be found. Two people knew all about these little blue bugs that glowed with excitement—Jesse Lewis and Flesti Thaed.

The lights began to dissipate and eventually retreated to the depths. He inspected his skin and couldn't find a single mark that indicated the intruders had a malevolent cause. He brushed himself dry with a small towel from his backpack and redressed in light clothes.

*****

The day was warm and humid with a slight wind from the west, and Bourbon had six more hours of daylight before he'd make camp for the night. The bay where he'd been fishing wasn't ideal for camping, with its marshy shore and craggy rocks that enveloped the east and north edges. It was a forty-yard climb up a steep hill to retrieve firewood, which caused him to overexert himself. So he opted to move a half-mile closer to town for a more suitable location.

He packed up his belongings: Nikon binoculars; a SOG military knife with a six-inch fixed blade; a small frying pan; a hand towel; his toothbrush and paste; and a Gregg Hurwitz novel he was reading for the second time. He had much more in his bag but tried carrying only what he needed.

He scoured the horizon with the Nikon's, looking for smoke from a campfire, movement on shore, or anything else that might hint at Jesse Lewis's presence. He saw only a few boats on the lake and two campfires at the cottages on the other side. The Sin-eater had seemed to vanish, but Bourbon knew he was out there, somewhere.

The Sin-Eater needed the lake, craved it, and wouldn't wander far from these marshy shores.

Bourbon squatted in front of the hot coals where his fish had cooked thirty minutes prior. The red heat had dissipated, and gray ash took its place, but he could still feel its burning warmth. The heat made him recall the last chapter of his life when he was Sheriff Bourbon and nearly died in Jesse Lewis's barn—that night had changed him forever. Cody Savage and Jesse Lewis had saved his life. He felt he owed Cody the world for what he'd done.

But Jesse Lewis? Jesse Lewis could never be forgiven. Jesse Lewis could never atone for his sins and what he did to Annabel Thompson. No, there would be no trial and no jury. There would only be an execution.

Jeff Bourbon's Smith & Wesson would be the last thing Jesse Lewis ever saw.

He poured lake water over the hot coals, which protested with a fit of steam and puffy screams. The steam rose and surrounded the man who'd extinguished the heat, and he inhaled the smell and humidity with his eyes closed, baptizing his body in the fire's convection. He poured the last few ounces of water over his forehead, hoping it would decrease the temperature of his anger, but it only cooled a few degrees.

Satisfied that the fire was too weak to find new life, he started to creep through the weeds that overran the grassy shoreline. He weaved his way along Cain Lake, scaring frogs and turtles lounging lazily atop dead logs, and stopped only when he was within yards of a great blue heron.

The bird was massive up close. Bourbon had witnessed few standing before him in his life. The crane-like creature stood as still a tree stump, watching for a precious meal to swim within striking distance. Finally, a small rock bass darted into the shallows chasing a tadpole. The heron's head lunged downward, like a snake string, and recoiled back to an upright position. The lightning-fast strike was over almost as soon as it began, and the heron was posing with a fresh meal in its bill.

He made it look so easy. *Fuckin' show-off.*

The heron looked skyward, maneuvered the fish head-first toward its throat, and swallowed it. Its hunger satisfied, the blue bird with sleek feathers leaped into the air and took flight with its nearly seven-foot wide wingspan.

Bourbon kept his eyes on the creature, beating the wind with perfectly formed feathers to gain altitude as it crossed the lake in minutes. If only Bourbon were a blue heron. If only he had the patience to wait out his prey and be able to strike with such power and speed. He wouldn't swallow the Sin-eater like the heron had consumed the bass. No, he would gut him like the perch he'd caught earlier.

Fifty yards ahead, movement in the tall grass diverted Bourbon's attention. It moved up and down and then disappeared. Bourbon crouched to hide his profile and pulled his backpack from his shoulders. He reached into the bag to retrieve his Nikon binoculars and began duck-walking through the weeds. He peeked with the binoculars, but the figure in the tall grass was too well hidden now. He lowered the binoculars and raised his model 686 revolver. He stayed low and let the pistol lead the way, pushing grass aside as quietly as possible.

The next time he saw the movement, a large turkey vulture erupted from the weeds, and Bourbon nearly filled the considerable bird with a lead bullet. A second bird, with a wingspan nearly as wide as the heron's, hopped sideways away from the intrusive human. The bird watched Bourbon with coal black eyes staring from its bald red head. Once Bourbon took a few more steps, it took flight and accompanied its mate on a nearby rock. The two raptors scanned the scene, irate with the man who had interrupted their fresh meal.

Bourbon doubled over, nearly regurgitating his fish when the smell of carrion filled his nostrils. He moved to his right, trying to get upwind of the foul odor. It was a one-two punch when he discovered the source of the rancid odor was not an unlucky animal. It was a human corpse.

"Get out of here," Bourbon screamed at the scavengers perched on the rock. The birds ignored Bourbon and would have yelled back if they could. Instead, they watched with keen eyes, studying the interloper, and waited for him to leave. Few animals had the patience of a vulture watching for death to creep up to a victim. Whether perched in a tree or soaring in the sky, the presence of a vulture was quick to sway a man to live. The thought of becoming buzzard food was grossly motivating.

Bourbon removed a medium-sized bottle of peppermint schnapps from his backpack and sipped, hoping the heat of the liqueur would overpower his olfactory sense and cover the smell that invaded his nostrils. Pleased with the results, he knew the minty mask wouldn't last long.

He stepped close to the body and crouched to examine it further. The vultures had torn much of the skin in the abdominal area, going straight for the entrails and organs. The skin was partially intact and peeled away from the rough incision that the bird's beak had created. On one side of the opening, Bourbon could read two alphabetical letters, "SI." On the other side of the abdomen, a third letter was visible through the blood, "R." Neither was the work of a tattoo artist but rather a serial killer. The Sin-eater was still out here, stalking the lake and leaving his signature engraved on his victims.

Bourbon blamed himself for the man's death. He leaned closer, ignoring the smell and the flies, and put himself face-to-face with the bloated corpse.

"I'm sorry, my friend. This should not have happened to you. He will pay for what he's done to you and all the people he's hurt."

The corpse was silent.

Bourbon guessed the man had been killed at night due to the warm clothes he adorned; denim jeans, a tank top, and a gray hooded sweatshirt. The sweatshirt had a familiar design silk screened on the left chest—an oval logo with two canoe paddles forming an X and the words "Lake Life." Bourbon had seen a lot of the townspeople wearing the garment and similar tee shirts in town. The local clothing store sold them by the dozens. The hoodie would have been too warm for a summer day, but nights on the water were cool. A comfortable hoodie was the perfect way to protect yourself from the chilly night air. His feet were bare, an indication that the dead stranger was on a boat or camping nearby. Bourbon checked the pockets— no identification.

He placed a shirt from his backpack over the body, hoping the scent of his apparel would keep the wild animals away, and backed away from the corpse, taking the same path in which he had approached. He'd already contaminated the crime scene enough and didn't want to compromise an investigation.

Once clear, he found a seven-foot-long stick as thick as his wrist, tied a white tee shirt to one end, and then drove it into the soft earth as deep as he could. He reinforced the flagpole with three cantaloupe-sized rocks. It was a makeshift marker so he could find the body again when the authorities arrived.

Bourbon made his way along the shore, leaving the deceased stranger to wait for his return. If he could reach a populated area, then he'd flag down a car and report the dead man's location. He was torn about the decision. If the new sheriff in Stoneville started an investigation, then it could mean his search for Jesse Lewis was over. If they found Jesse, Bourbon's chance of revenge would be over. On the other hand, Bourbon wasn't having much luck tracking down the killer, and the last thing he wanted was another victim.

3

TWO COLD PIGS 

Daisy drove the Subaru Outback into the gravel driveway and parked a few feet from the front porch. She exited the car, ran to the passenger side, and opened the door for Cody to get out. He spilled from the vehicle and caught himself with his right hand to prevent collapsing on the ground. He coughed as Daisy pulled him to his feet and used the car door to support most of his weight. He threw his right arm over her shoulder, and they climbed the porch stairs together. The screen door squeaked loudly as Daisy threw it open and then shut with a loud slam as they moved into the kitchen.

Cody sat at the kitchen table while Daisy retrieved a plastic cup from the cupboard. She turned on the faucet and filled the cup halfway, but Cody refused the drink to avoid further contact with water. Daisy set the cup at the center of the table in case he changed his mind.

"Feel any better?" She asked.

"Yeah—much. But the vision," he paused. "What I saw made me sick. Why is someone torturing that poor man?"

"Did you get a good look at his face? The guy in the chair. Would you recognize him if you saw him again?"

"No. Maybe a little. He was looking down, and it was pretty dark."

Once he caught his breath and his pulse slowed to normal, Cody stood, went to the sink, and stared blankly out the kitchen window.

"I have to find him."

"How? What we should do is call the sheriff or maybe the state police. This is their job."

"Do you really think they're going to search for someone just because

17

I had some psychic vision?"

"Bourbon believed you," Daisy peered out the kitchen window as if Jeff Bourbon was outside listening. Brown eyes stared through the spotty window as if she could see Jeff Bourbon. It didn't work. The neighborhood was quiet, and she wondered when they would see the ex-sheriff again.

"I can find him. Just like I found Darcy Poole." He felt skinny arms wrap around his waist from behind. Even though they were so thin, they brought comfort when they squeezed him, like a heavy fleece blanket on a cold winter morning. He turned around and let the arms squeeze some more. Daisy's hands slid to Cody's arms. She ran her fingers over his muscles. Atrophy was starting to take its toll on the size of his arm muscles, but she didn't care. Her hands stopped when they came to the wet bandage, still soaked from being submerged in lake water, loosely wrapped around his left wrist.

"Let's change your bandage." Daisy pulled away and disappeared from the room. When she returned, she was carrying a small plastic box of bandages and medical tape.

Cody tried to unwind the old elastic bandage from his wrist and arm. A stubborn piece of tape hindered his progress.

"Let me help," Daisy said.

Cody hopped up and backward to take a seat on the kitchen counter. Daisy unraveled the damp bandage. "Any changes in the last few days?"

"See for yourself."

The gauze fell to the floor like Rapunzel's hair after she'd been caught in a rain storm. It twisted and wrinkled, forming a soggy pile on the linoleum surface.

Cody's left forearm was smaller than the right. The color of his skin was pale compared to his suntanned bicep and pink at the end. A grotesque appendage had sprouted from his wrist, growing outward like a short tree trunk. Cody kept the bandage on to hide it from the rest of the world.

"This is amazing," Daisy said.

"It looks disgusting," Cody replied. "Do you think my hand is actually growing back?"

"I do. What else could it be?" Daisy smiled in excitement. "Whatever effect the lake has had on you...it seems to be stimulating this—regeneration."

"What if it turns out to be a lobster claw?" He motioned with his right thumb and fingers like a claw snapping at her.

"Well, Sammy will think you're the coolest guy ever."

"Sammy already thinks I'm the coolest guy ever."

"No, he doesn't." She teased as she wrapped the regrowing appendage with a clean bandage.

"What? Who does he think is cooler than me?"

Daisy didn't even need to think. "Captain America, Handy Manny, those Lego ninja characters, and Alyse. He loves Alyse."

Cody scowled, thinking about Daisy's son. "Yeah, Captain America is pretty cool."

Daisy finished with the bandage and taped the end, "Too tight?"

Cody shook his head. Satisfied with her work, Daisy went to the fridge and pulled out two cold beers, even though she knew it was too early for alcohol. She handed one to her lover, and they sipped the cold brew in silence. The cool Pilsner soothed his dry throat.

"*Dos cerdos frio*," Cody said, testing his Spanish with her.

"*Dos cervezas frías*," She corrected him.

"That's what I said. Two cold beers."

"No, you didn't. You said 'two cold pigs.'" She laughed as they kissed, then clinked their bottles together. "To your new lobster claw."

"What do you think will happen when the rest of the town sees this?" Cody took a long drink of his beer. "I can't hide my hand forever, and everyone will notice. They're going to think I'm a freak."

"No, they'll want to know how you regrew your hand. Then it will be hysteria, and everyone will flock to Cain Lake for its healing powers."

"And if they're affected like Jesse Lewis?" Cody shuddered at the thought. "Cain Lake may be giving me my hand back, but it also takes away. That's what Flesti Thaed told me. The lake gives and takes, there must always be balance."

"I wouldn't worry too much about what she says. She's sounds a little crazy to me. Maybe we better get you to a doctor to examine your hand, in case it's something else."

"No. Not yet, anyway. Let's see what happens. I don't want word of this getting around."

Daisy stowed the medical kit under the sink and gathered the old bandage piled on the floor. Cody stayed seated on the counter, lost in thought, drinking his beer. The image of the man in the chair was burned into his brain, replaying the scene in his mind. There was such a gruesome motive behind the torture that he never wanted to see it again. But he couldn't act like it wasn't happening. If he was going to find the victim in the chair, he needed to incite the vision to return.

Daisy cleaned the kitchen and put away a few dishes from their breakfast. When she finished, she turned to Cody, who was still sitting on the counter. She squeezed his cheeks with both hands and gave him a lingering kiss.

"I have to go check on my mom and Sammy. Get some rest and stay out of the shower." She knew how the water provoked Cody's clairvoyant ability and didn't want him to repeat his experience at Allison Park.

After their goodbyes, she left the house. Cody watched her from the kitchen window as she pulled away and drove out of sight.

He dumped the remaining third of his beer down the sink and rinsed the bottle. The sound of the water made his heart race. He dropped the bottle in the recycle bin and left the kitchen.

His feet moved slowly when he got to the staircase leading to the second floor. One by one, he climbed until he was standing in the upstairs bathroom.

The room was small, with white tiles protecting the sheetrock, and the gray laminated hardwood was cool to the soles of his feet. The smell of soap and a new plastic shower curtain filled the air. He stripped off his clothes and dropped them in a plastic clothes hamper. He reluctantly turned on the water and stepped into the bathtub. When he pulled the shower curtain closed, he submitted to the visions that were sure to come. He knew it could be dangerous, painful, and perhaps deadly, but the tortured and beaten man deserved to be found—alive or dead.

4

JUST JEFF

Jeff Bourbon emerged from the thick flora surrounding Cain Lake 500 yards from the church. The tall white steeple made a significant landmark that could be seen almost anywhere on the body of water. It allowed Bourbon to keep a sense of direction while he hiked in circles. Sometimes, when the moon was bright enough and the clouds sparse, the white church was still visible at night, despite the distance. Bourbon marched west toward the old religious building and then turned north to intersect with Grandview Drive.

Bourbon didn't have to wait long. He heard a heavy vehicle approach with a deep rumbling engine as the driver down-shifted the transmission to navigate the twisting hills of Grandview Drive. Sitting in the driver's seat, Pat Hollis maneuvered his old yellow dump truck over a knoll. Brakes squealed in pain as the driver applied pressure to the foot pedal, and the big truck rolled to a stop for the hiker standing in the middle of the road. The driver's side glass descended into a door with a crudely designed logo that read "Hollis Hauling" in red and black letters. Pat Hollis dropped his cigarette to the pavement as Bourbon stepped around the truck's fender and greeted him by name. Hollis recognized the voice, although it was as rusty as the dump truck's brakes.

"Jesus, sheriff, is that you?"

"I'm not the sheriff anymore, Pat."

"Oh hell, you'll always be the sheriff of Stoneville as far as I'm concerned, Bourbon. What the hell are you doing out here? Camping?"

"Yeah, I decided a little camping and hiking were a nice way to start my retirement. Say, Pat, you wouldn't happen to have a cell phone, would you?"

"Course I do," Pat held up a black Android phone with a cracked screen. He opened the dump truck door and stepped down. The diesel engine kept stuttering, stuck on a word it just couldn't spit out, and doing so through a rusty exhaust pipe. Attempting to escape the noise, the two men chose to step away from the truck rather than yell over the sound.

"Would you mind calling the new sheriff?" Bourbon asked. "I found something he'll want to see." Bourbon described the body and gave Pat directions to its location. "Tell the Sheriff to hike along the shore or come by boat. You can't miss the flagpole I set up to mark the site."

Pat dialed the Sheriff's Department and spoke with a deputy. He reported Bourbon's discovery and relayed everything he'd been told. The deputy assured Pat that they would send someone to investigate as soon as they finished with another matter.

"It's going to be at least an hour," Pat informed Bourbon.

"Jesus. Okay, well...I guess I'll go wait with the body," Bourbon said. "Have you met the new sheriff, Pat?"

"No, sir, I have not. Hassett. That's all I know. Kind of hoping I don't meet him, you know. Your boy—the one you shot—used to give me a hard enough time about my truck, you know?"

"Archer? Charlie Archer?"

"Yeah, yeah, that's the sonovabitch. Always given me tickets for my exhaust, expired truck inspections, and anything else he could fuckin find. Shit, he'd give me a ticket for the color of the paint if he disapproved. Good riddance to him, I say, you know?"

"Yeah, I know," Bourbon agreed. He turned and studied the paint of the truck and partially thought Pat did deserve a ticket for the bright yellow and illegible logo.

A month-old memory played in Bourbon's mind—the night he put a bullet through Deputy Archer's throat. Archer had nearly burned him to death in Jesse Lewis's barn. Archer tried to finish the job after he'd escaped, and drew his pistol at the sheriff. But Bourbon had practiced drawing his gun for years, hoping never to need the skill. His holster had been worn smooth from years of practice, perfectly molded to allow his Smith & Wesson to slip in and out without the slightest resistance. His hand was trained to know exactly where the pistol sat on his hip and how thick the wood grip fit his fingers. His draw was quick and tight, and Charlie Archer learned the hard way never to underestimate the experience of a gray-haired man hellbent and determined.

He hadn't fired the pistol since.

Pat lit a cigarette with a Zippo lighter and cleared his throat, "You need a ride somewhere, Bourbon?"

"No, thanks, Pat. I'm going to hike back to the body and wait there."

"Okay then. I best get going. Gotta get this load of crusher run stone up the road, you know? New house gettin' built on Lake View. I'll be seeing ya, Sheriff. Tell Annabel hello when you see her."

The name stung a little, and Bourbon could feel the anxiety swell within his chest. He wished he could see Annabel. He wished he could tell her 'hello.' But, for now, he needed to keep his distance from his former girlfriend.

"Thanks for the phone, Pat," Bourbon said. He watched the scruffy truck driver climb back into the cab of the dump truck and drive out of sight. When he was gone, the world fell silent again, and Bourbon just stood in the road and listened to nothing. A few chickadees scoured the catkins of a birch tree. Their delicate voices were barely noticeable upon the gentle breeze. A blue jay swooped in and began to caw obnoxiously, disturbing the peace and encouraging Bourbon to start hiking. He spun on his heels, pushed through a thick patch of blackberry brambles that pulled against his clothes and skin, and entered the forest.

*****

Bourbon saw the boat before he heard the motor. It was silent as it patrolled the shore from 100 yards, looking for the makeshift flag Bourbon had constructed as a marker. He waved his arms as someone in the front pointed to the tall flag dancing in the wind. The boat's pilot gave the Evinrude engine a little gas, and the forty-eight-horsepower engine growled as it charged toward shore. The person standing at the boat's bow made a gesture to slow down, and the watercraft reduced its speed.

Jo Hassett stood at the front of the boat with one hand on a holstered pistol. The new sheriff had dark skin, bony shoulders, and wide hips. Hassett helped navigate the little fishing boat converted to a "search & rescue" vessel. It was sixteen feet long from bow to stern and white paint and high-visibility reflective vinyl covered the manufacturer's color. Bourbon had purchased the boat at an auction a few years ago, and it sat idle most of the time, but with a body of water as large as Cain Lake, it was imperative that the Sheriff's Department have a means for searching the lake.

Bourbon watched the boat, and his successor, navigate the shallow water, working around a tree stump and squeezing between two boulders. Jo Hassett stepped off the front of the boat into knee-deep water as the deputy at the controls killed the engine. The craft floated with grace toward shore. Hassett turned toward Bourbon, a shiny badge gleamed in the sun. He wondered if the town had splurged on a new one or if this were just his old credentials recycled.

"Sheriff Hassett?" Bourbon asked.

"Mr. Bourbon? It's a pleasure to meet my predecessor," Hassett replied. She put her right hand forward and gave Bourbon an impressive handshake. Her smile was genuine, with perfect teeth. The contracting muscles that formed her smile amplified her high cheekbones. For some reason, she blushed, but smooth, dark skin concealed the change in her complexion. She'd read up on Bourbon's past and surveyed many of Stoneville's residents. Hassett knew she had big shoes to fill and that the town would never respect her like Bourbon. He was loved and admired. Any sheriff that could attain that status earned her respect.

"I wasn't expecting—" Bourbon began.

"A woman? A black woman?" Hassett interrupted.

Bourbon gave her a playful dirty look, "Someone so young. I wasn't expecting someone so young to take my place."

"Thirty-four in a few weeks. Been a sheriff for five years." She stepped past Bourbon and headed for the flag that beckoned her attention. The plum-faced deputy was still in the boat and stayed behind. Hassett introduced him as David Simpson.

"How's the job so far?" Bourbon asked.

"Good. Great really. I've met a lot of fantastic people. And this is such a beautiful town."

"Mrs. McClesky calling you every other day about her dog?" His playful smile returned.

Hassett's eyes grew big, "Yeah. What the hell? I swear that dog just wants to get away from her."

"Smart dog."

They laughed in unison, and Hassett pushed past Bourbon toward the body in the weeds. She spoke over her shoulder, but Bourbon's eyes were much lower, "I think the department's gonna donate one of those electric fences to keep—what's the dog's name?"

"Mr. M."

"Yeah. To keep Mr. M from leaving the yard."

Bourbon followed Hassett into the tall grass. The two turkey vultures hadn't gone far. They stayed perched in a dead evergreen to keep an eye on the intruders.

Tall grass with sharp edges brushed against their thighs as they walked. The soft wind played with the weeds, making each blade dance in perfect choreography. The smell of clay and cattail pollen was replaced with the odor of decay. It was unmistakable to the two veteran officers who turned west subconsciously so they could approach the corpse from upwind.

Hassett crouched near the body, studying the form visually, recording every inch of the scene to memory, and playing out the suspected scenario in her mind. Bourbon forced himself to stay back, resisting temptation—or habit—to keep from verbalizing his crime assessment.

Bourbon slapped a deer fly on his shoulder, snapping the new sheriff's thoughts. She turned toward him.

"Well? What do you think?" Bourbon asked.

Sheriff Hassett knew Bourbon was testing her. He wanted her analysis of the scene, and though he wasn't privy to the information, she gave it to him anyway.

"Dave," she called to her deputy. "Would you bring up the camera and forensic kit?"

The deputy hurried to the back of the boat and lifted a large plastic toolbox. He sprung over the boat's gunwale with the forensic kit in hand, landing in two feet of water, then reached back into the bow to hoist the camera bag.

Hassett stood and stepped backward until she and Bourbon stood shoulder to shoulder. She was the same height as the tall man and started drawing imaginary lines with her right index finger as if she could see clues. "I scanned the local "Missing Persons" files before I came out. No young adult caucasian males appeared in my search except for Nick Smithers—but he's only five foot three. This man's close to six feet. He died here—alone. If he'd been dragged, his legs and arms would be straight, but the position of the body suggests he was writhing in pain when he died. The weeds around him are mashed and broken. A trail from the shore suggests he dragged himself from the water."

Bourbon removed his heavy backpack and slid the two straps over a broken hemlock limb, leaving his gear hanging from the dead tree. The fifty-three-year-old man stretched his neck and shoulders, happy to be free of the backpack's weight. "He has bruises on his wrists—rope marks. He was tied up while being mutilated." Bourbon's hands balled into fists, thinking about Annabel's similar experience in Jesse Lewis's barn.

"But how'd he get here?" The question came from Deputy Simpson. He approached from behind and set the forensic kit at Hassett's feet. She went right for the digital SLR camera, removed the lens, and began capturing the crime scene digitally.

"Good question," Bourbon said.

Hassett viewed the body through the camera lens and began to snap pictures. *Click. Click, click, click.*

"I'm guessing the two letters carved in his abdomen are similar to your Sin-eater cases?"

"You read my reports?" Bourbon asked.

Click, click.

"Of course. And the articles in The Stoneville View. Pretty interesting stuff. I'd like to know more about this guy if I'm going to catch him. I want to get in his head."

No. No, you don't want to be in this fucker's head. Bourbon was silent for a moment, accessing whether Hassett's presence was a positive or negative occurrence. He wanted Jesse Lewis to himself, to find him and watch the life fade from his eyes, but he didn't want to give the Sin-eater more time to prey on hapless victims.

Click. Click.

"What else can you tell me, Mr. Bourbon?"

"Jeff. Just call me Jeff." The name sounded strange when he spoke it out loud. He'd been called Sheriff, Sheriff Bourbon, or just Bourbon for so many years that his first name seemed unfitting. But now, with his badge pinned to the ambitious young woman standing before him, he had to accept that he was just Jeff. A demotion from the world of political and community leaders to this dirty, unshaven shell of man scouring the shores of Cain Lake in a vague attempt to find a serial killer.

"There's nothing else I can tell you. Jesse Lewis probably left town by now—I'm sure. He's a man on the run, so he's probably running. Maybe he has family out of town or returned to where he came from."

Click.

"Body's not that old. What? Two days maybe? I think he's still in the area. But why stay? I agree—in theory—with what you are saying, Jeff. He should be running, but this body is almost a message. Like he's saying, 'Screw you, I'm not going to run. Come and find me.'"

"You won't," Bourbon responded. "You won't find him if he's out here. He's smart and desperate. That makes him dangerous."

Click, click, click.

"Oh, I'm going to find him," Hassett sternly glared at Bourbon. "Tell me something, Jeff. Why are you out here? You're looking for him, aren't you?"

Bourbon slapped another deer fly on his forearm. The dead fly stuck to his skin until he flicked it to the ground with his finger. "No, I'm just enjoying my retirement. Great fishing here. Hiking around Cain Lake is something I've wanted to do since I was a teenager, and now I have time to do it."

Hassett was staring through the camera lens. "Uh-huh, sure. Well, I know what he did to Ms. Thompson—your girlfriend. I understand you have a personal vendetta against this maniac, but I'm ordering you to step aside. Don't get in my way, please, or hinder my investigation, or you'll be the one incarcerated." She looked from her camera to the older man with an empathetic smile that meant she understood, but was serious.

"Don't worry, Sheriff; I won't be any trouble."

"Got a phone?"

Bourbon shrugged, "Battery's dead. But if I find anything else, I'll get in touch."

"Okay, I'd appreciate that."

They exchanged phone numbers.

Bourbon turned toward the two vultures sitting in a tree. They refused to leave the area and watched with frustration as the Sheriff and her deputy transferred their meal to a black body bag. Bourbon wanted to join them on the tree's limb and watch from afar. But he was, once again, a part of this. He helped the Sheriff and Deputy Simpson load the body into the boat so they could take it to Shari Kapoor, the county coroner.

Hassett moved to the boat's bow and looked down at Bourbon standing in knee-deep water.

"Shari's meeting us at the boat ramp," Hassett confirmed. "She wants to know how you're doing—seems concerned. What should I tell her?"

"I'm fine. Tell her I'm fine." Bourbon waited for her to sit and then pushed the boat into deeper water. Once Deputy Simpson knew the outboard motor was clear of the sandy bottom, he started the engine and gently backed away from shore. They drifted in reverse past the weeds and old tree stumps until the water was as deep as a man. He threw the boat into the forward gear and they zoomed away.

Bourbon watched them leave. Once they rounded a short peninsula and were out of sight, he returned to the scene. The two vultures were investigating where the body had laid, hopeful of finding any scraps left behind. Bourbon shooed them away. They jumped skyward and took flight. Thick wings beat the air, thumping, and whooshing. The hungry raptors ascended and flew away from the lake. They required dead meat to satiate their bodies. so they instinctively followed their innate nature to scavenge inland. They pointed their hooked beaks toward the highway, where they would likely find fresh roadkill. They flew higher, putting themselves above the forest, and vanished behind the tall pine and maple trees.

Bourbon watched them disappear like he had watched Sheriff Hassett and her deputy. Once alone, he removed his backpack from the tree limb and set it on the ground. The scaled bark of the tree was reddish brown with vertical fissures that began to split with age. The tree towered well over sixty feet, with twenty percent of its bark and needles missing at the top. The old tree was suffering a slow death.

Bourbon's backpack hid a carving in the rough bark from Jo Hassett's view. She hadn't seen it, and if she analyzed her photos, even with a keen eye, she would see nothing other than the pack hanging on the tree. It was a snap decision to hide the carving that even surprised Bourbon.

He traced the carving with his index finger, memorizing the shape. The carving, only a few millimeters deep, was strange but familiar. He'd seen the symbol before. There were no words or hints of its meaning, but he searched his memory to identify the source. The carved character was fresh—fresher than the corpse—evident from the wood shavings piled on the ground and clinging to the tree. Shavings not yet dried by the sun or carried away by the wind.

The shape of the carving made no sense to him—an inverted pyramid with three wavy lines on each side—but Bourbon remembered seeing the exact symbol on a necklace.

Flesti Thacd had been here after the victim had died, and she wanted Jeff Bourbon to know it.

Bourbon threw the gray backpack over his sunburned shoulders, intent on finding Flesti. What did she know? If he couldn't find Jesse Lewis, surely he could find the eccentric woman who knew more about Cain Lake than anyone else.

5

HOT SHOWER 

Cody slid the shower curtain across the chrome rod. He turned the water on and stepped inside before the heated water arrived. It was a cold shock to his skin, but the water warmed as the seconds passed. He turned in circles to wet every inch of his body and acclimated to the temperature. Once the hot water prevailed, he let it pour over his skin. He had no concerns about getting clean or rinsing Cain Lake's unique smell from his pores—no soap—no shampoo. This shower was only a catalyst for his clairvoyant ability.

He'd wrapped his bandaged arm with a small plastic bag and secured it with duct tape, just as the doctor had advised. The incisions on his back from his surgery three weeks prior had healed nicely. The surgeons had inserted two metal pins to support his broken back. The three ribs he'd broken when he crashed AJ's car were like new again. The accident at Cain Lake should have left him in a wheelchair for the rest of his life. Instead, he was giving Sammy piggyback rides.

The doctors were confounded by his recovery.

Cain Lake was giving Cody the ability to heal faster than expected. It was augmenting his psychic visions and changing him physically and mentally.

Cody wouldn't tell the doctors about Cain Lake's power. He never mentioned Flesti pulling him from the wreckage or how the microp-ods that swam in the lake must have affected him. He let the doctors believe that a higher power was watching over him and that he was a "miracle case," as they called him.

Soft water washed over his face, and Cody wondered if the little blue lights from the lake would ever make their way through the plumbing and into his bathtub. He turned, letting the water pressure massage his neck and shoulders, painting his skin pink with its heat. Tense shoulders relaxed, physically dropping a half-inch as Cody's head oscillated from side to side.

He was ready to give up and dry himself off when the room's light diminished. The walls disappeared, and the water quit flowing through the shower head. The smell of acrylic flooded his nostrils, and Cody knew his mental perception was turned on. He searched for the source of the odor, but his sight was limited to three yards.

Standing in the cool blackness of the room, abstract shapes transformed into representational images. Concrete floors, rough lumber, and open rafters formed the environment he occupied. A gray mouse skittered across the floor, keeping tight to the wall as it went. The furry creature stopped, looked around, and then stared at Cody for a moment as if the psychic had a tangible form, and then carried on his way and disappeared in the dark.

A whimper from behind, more prominent than a mouse, turned Cody on his heels. It was his reason for coming here—for taking a psychic journey to an unknown place where some lunatic tortured a man for no apparent reason.

The man in the chair was still there, beaten and broken, but still alive and slumped forward in defeat. Cody could see his shoulders rise and lower as he labored to breathe. There was an absence of clues that helped make sense of this scene. If he could figure out why this was happening, then maybe he could discern where this was happening.

Cody tried to study every nail, every board, and every detail, but there were few. Outside, the metallic clinging reoccurred—the same dinging noise he'd heard the first time he was here—like wind chimes with a solitary tube. He listened for other sounds, hoping to recognize something from outside, like a church bell, a train, or a fire station siren. The audible clues were as elusive as the man who set this all in motion, and the room's silence reminded him of the nights he spent at Uncle Bruce's hunting cabin deep in the Adirondack Mountains. The night air was so peaceful and tranquil at that cabin that it had an eeriness that even sleep feared. Cody would lie awake most of those nights, listening to mice scurry through the walls—their little feet scratching against the wood studs as they climbed up and down and then across the ceiling.

"How'd you sleep?" Uncle Bruce would always ask.

"Good," Cody would lie while nibbling on a piece of burnt toast.

It was always late summer—September maybe—and Cody would accompany his uncle for a weekend to help clear the hunting trails and reinforce the wooden tree stands where Uncle Bruce would sit on watch, hoping to harvest a trophy buck. Cody was too young to hunt then but looked forward to the year he turned sixteen and would acquire his hunting license.

The opportunity never came. Before his fifteenth birthday, Cody's parents died in his father's garage. That same year, Uncle Bruce became ill and never had the strength to return to the mountains. He sold the hunting cabin to help cover medical expenses and pay his mortgage, and while Cody bounced from foster home to foster home, no one ever really took him in. He wanted to stay with Uncle Bruce, but the courts weren't enthusiastic about a teenage boy living with a dying man who had a couple of prior arrests.

The memory disappeared as the victim in the chair began coughing and spitting blood on the floor. An open wound on his temple dripped blood that ran to the corner of his eye. Cody watched a fly investigate the cut, and the man in the chair did not react to the insect's intrusion. The fly followed the red streak downward, and when it finally reached the lashes, the man lifted his head and shook side-to-side to protest the insect's invasion.

The light in the room was dim, and Cody thought his vision might be distorted, but he could see clearly now. The man's facial features mirrored his own, as if he saw himself tied to the chair. No, this man was younger and smaller, and once he shook the fly loose again, Cody recognized the face that could only be his brother.

"Michael?"

There was no doubt in Cody's mind. If what he was observing were true, the man in front of him was the sibling he hadn't seen in a dozen years.

Cody's vision faded as acidic bile crept into the back of his throat. A cold sweat formed on his brow, and the floor spun. He reached out for something to stabilize himself, but the world was void of solid objects.

The water heater strained to keep producing. The spigot above his head spit a burst of cold liquid. And then the heat was gone completely. The cold shower snapped Cody back to reality, to the safety of his upstairs bathroom, where no one could attack him, and no flies were drinking blood. But darkness still held his senses, and vertigo overwhelmed him. He felt the shower again beating on his skin. His feet slipped out from under him. Before he could regain his balance, he fell backward, pinning the shower curtain against the ceramic bathtub with his calf muscles. His body weight pulled the shower curtain down, and it fell over his head and clung to his wet body.

Gravity forced him to the floor, but not before striking his head against the sink as his left elbow smashed into the toilet. Blackness retook him. But this time, there would be no vision of the man in distress. This time, he lay naked on the cold linoleum floor, a shower curtain draped over his head, in a dreamless sleep.

6

FINDING FLESTI 

Bourbon double-backed and trekked east. He passed the ashes from the small fire he'd cooked his perch that day. The thought of the fish and the smell of burnt wood made him hungry, so he stopped and retrieved an apple and a Slim Jim from his backpack. It was still too early in the summer to locate berries or fruit, so he had loaded his bag with dry goods from the small convenience store on the south side of the lake. Sometimes he'd stop at The Fuel Line, quench his thirst with a few cold Blue Moons from the tap, and then buy a stockpile of snacks.

He sat on an uprooted birch log and ate his insubstantial dinner. Red squirrels scuttled along the ground and trees, picking away at pine cones to access the nut within. They chattered at Bourbon's intrusion but kept busy anyway. Somewhere in the distance, a bald eagle called out for its mate, and a cricket, hidden under the dry leaves, softly chirped near Bourbon's feet even though the sun was still hanging in the sky.

Bourbon thought about the man who lay dead on the shore. His family would soon know his fate, and if the Sin-eater struck again, another family would be mourning the loss of a member. The discovery forced Bourbon to think about the tempo of his pursuit. Time was as much the enemy as the serial killer himself. Every minute Jesse Lewis was free was another minute he had the opportunity to murder another sinner.

How in the hell did Jesse choose the man Sheriff Hassett carried away in a body bag? How long had Jesse been stalking the victim? Or did the two encounter each other out here in the wild by coincidence?

Bourbon hoped Sheriff Jo Hassett would find the answers to all his

35

questions, even though she wasn't obliged to answer them.

The thought of Jo Hassett taking over as sheriff twisted his emotions like a pretzel knot. A month ago, Bourbon was frustrated with his occupation and ready to retire—especially during the week Darcy Poole disappeared, and he was forced to put a bullet into one of his deputies. The entire town depended on him to find the missing girl and stop a serial killer. The strain and pressure from the community were more than he could bear, yet he persevered until the girl was reunited with her family. It filled him with a sense of satisfaction—a job well done. The story hit too close to home, to his heart, to have a happy ending. The events that unfolded that week destroyed his relationship with Annabel.

Now, here he was, a disheveled man stalking the Sin-eater through the thick forest of Cain Lake. No one knew his location. He was lost in the woods and buried by the trees. Fewer than a handful of people would notice or care if he never returned. Stoneville had a new sheriff, and she was the big story in town. She'd come here to save them and find the Sin-eater.

Bourbon prayed she would. His knees hit the ground, and he bowed his head. Thick fingers interlocked in prayer that only he and the deer flies swarming his head would hear. He paused halfway through and considered it might be a waste of time. A mosquito bit his ankle. Bourbon smacked the pest, leaving an X-shaped blood splatter on his skin.

He bowed his head and finished the prayer.

After his impromptu plea to a higher power, Bourbon recommenced his hike along the water's shore, stepping lightly with controlled speed and balance, like a deer hunter stalking prey with far superior physical attributes. It was a snail's pace, but the former lawman had nowhere to be. He just needed to be aware—observant, invisible. This was not a race to beat Jesse Lewis to some imaginary finish line. This was a game of spot-the-serial killer that Bourbon could not afford to lose. He would never admit it to himself or anyone he knew, but there was some enjoyment to the game, and Bourbon was ashamed of himself for thinking so.

A scuffling sound to his left drew Bourbon's attention away from the lake. He could hear the walking—quiet steps with a slight shuffle.

The hammer in his chest thumped against his ribs. Sweat formed on his brow, and he held his breath to silence the huffing of his lungs. He heard the sound again, but no one was in sight. Had Jesse Lewis donned camouflage that would give him an advantage? Bourbon feared that he might be the prey, and Jesse Lewis was the hunter.

Bourbon sidestepped twice to hide behind a large pine tree. He squinted hard to make his eyes focus and find the source of the sound. He kept his right hand on the pistol's grip, which was still holstered on his left rib. He'd changed the holster from a hip design to a shoulder holster before beginning his journey. He hoped the shoulder holster would be less prone to snag when bushwacking through the thick bushes.

Anxious fingers tapped the leather ever so lightly in anticipation of an attack. He became conscious of the wound on his shoulder blade that still gave him pain when he moved just right. That wound came from a shot the Sin-eater had taken at him weeks ago from an upstairs window as Bourbon approached the barn where Annabel was held as a prisoner. Thanks to Cody Savage, Jesse never got off a second shot.

When the noise's source finally appeared, Bourbon drew his pistol angrily and lined the front sight with his target, an intrusive quail strutting along the leaves. He imagined squeezing the trigger softly and popping the bird in the head. The fowl's thick breasts would make for a great meal, and Bourbon would benefit from the protein. But the noise of the Smith & Wesson would give his location away, and he could not afford to alert Jesse Lewis of his presence.

The intimate feel of the engraved wood in his hand and the smell of gun oil reminded Bourbon of the last time he drew the pistol on a living target—the night he put an end to Charlie Archer, his former deputy sheriff.

"Go ahead. Blow his fucking head off, asshole." The voice was familiar. Bourbon spun 180 degrees on his toes. He turned back to the bird, which scurried through a crop of green ferns and darted out of sight. The woods fell silent again until the voice spoke once more.

"Well, you missed your shot. Now the little chicken shit is gone."

Bourbon recognized the voice this time. It was the same voice he'd heard complain about night shifts and no bonuses for years. The same voice that bugged him about his partner drinking all the fresh coffee. The same voice that called him on the radio every time the Bears beat the Bills.

"Fuck you, Archer."

The voice went silent, so Bourbon recommenced his pace as the quail took flight, thumping its wings with great power with a drum-like sound that faded as it flew through the trees. As Bourbon watched the bird disappear, a figure appeared in the shadows. It contrasted with the flora and straight trees that reached skyward, and Bourbon recognized the female figure standing in front of him.

Flesti waited for the former sheriff to reach her location before she spoke in a soft voice, "Hello, Jefferson. I've been looking forward to seeing you again."

"Dammit, woman, where the hell have you been? I've been scouring these woods for weeks looking for you."

"How do you think you'd ever find me or Jesse Lewis when you're stumbling around like a drunk in an antique shop?"

Bourbon wasn't sure what to think about Flesti's insult. He'd thought he'd been quiet and careful all along but realized she was much stealthier than he and was only exposed when she chose to be.

"Where's Jesse Lewis? I know he must be somewhere near Cain Lake."

She nodded, "You're correct. The Pastor is on the southeast side, past the boat launch, near the sandy pines."

"You've seen him?"

"I see everything that lives or happens around this lake."

A crow swooped down and landed on a limb above Flesti. The black bird cawed and bounced through the trees until it blended with the dark shadows of the evergreens.

Bourbon approached Flesti. He immediately noticed that she looked younger since the last time they'd met. He looked younger after losing weight—maybe three or four years had come off his appearance—but she looked like she'd dropped decades. Her skin was tighter and brighter; her hair seemed thick and full, although the color was still gray; she had a tight belly centered on curvy hips; and where the hell were those perky breasts the last time they met?

The two wanderers stood four feet apart, locked in a stare that Bourbon broke once he realized he was blushing. They looked the same age—early fifties—and both were in excellent condition, despite needing a hot shower.

Flesti dressed lighter than she had during their first encounter, donning a lightweight jacket meant more for repelling rain than keeping warm. Her hair was pulled into a messy ponytail that rested on her shoulder, and her shorts were chosen for their pocket space rather than their fashionable style. She stood on sandals with thick nylon straps that hugged her ankles and feet. A colorful Native American pattern of triangles and squares was embroidered in the nylon straps, and she wore a matching bracelet on her left wrist.

It was her necklace that really interested Bourbon. He pointed to the jewelry hanging from her neck, "I got your message—back at the body. Do you have any idea what happened to that poor guy? Or will I have to beat it out of Jesse Lewis?"

Flesti gently grasped the pendant and rubbed it between her left thumb and index finger. A sad look took the place of her gentle smile.

"Too much death," She said. "This lake has seen too much death, my friend."

Bourbon cleared his throat. "Can't argue with that. My concern is why. All this death you're referring to seems to be centered around the lake, like it's cursed or something."

Flesti peered out over the gentle waves as she searched her thoughts, as if they'd wash up on shore with the driftwood. She started to speak, but the words lost their buoyancy and drowned in her throat.

"Take me to him," Bourbon said. "I want that sonovabitch's head."

She could feel Bourbon's rage emanating like fire and hear the hate in his voice. She knew the hunter would never stop until he or his prey were dead. She nodded to acknowledge her cooperation and then finally spoke again.

"Come. Let's get some real food in our bellies first, and I'll take you to him in the morning."

"I want to go now. We can eat after we find Jesse."

She ignored him and turned toward the dense trees. She climbed uphill, navigating the foliage, ducking pine tree limbs and spider webs. Bourbon shuffled behind her, the backpack making him less graceful and heavy-footed. The forest floor was littered with pine needles from the Scotch and red pine trees that formed the forest. Squirrels, sleek with red fur, scattered to hide as the two interlopers passed.

Bourbon kept his eyes on the crow that seemed to lead them to their destination and then realized that a black dog—medium in size—had joined the duo. The mutt heeled at Flesti's side but peeked back at Bourbon every ten seconds. Bourbon wondered if the canine was checking his pace or following his innate instincts to protect its owner. Caution favored the latter, so he kept a safe distance from the animal until he gained its trust.

"What's his name?" Bourbon called ahead to Flesti.

"Hetzen. His name is Hetzen."

"Really? That's exactly the name I would have chosen," Bourbon said sarcastically. "Don't suppose you've got a name for the bird, do you?"

Flesti lifted her arm and made a clicking sound with her tongue. The feathered creature swooped through the branches and perched on her extended elbow. "This is Poe. He's been with me for nine years."

Poe sprung from her arm and traversed through the trees, fluttering and flapping from limb to limb. He seemed to stay just ahead of Flesti, as if he knew the course she was taking.

Once they were through the evergreens, a small clearing sprawled before them with knee-high grass. In a few weeks, the grass would be waist-high, growing like the suspense of a good book. The clearing was roughly the size of two houses. Wild apple trees, with white blossoms and bright green leaves, grew along the clearing's edge. Bourbon spotted a hunting stand on the eastern side. The wooden platform was dilapidated from years of neglect. The deer must have appreciated the tree-stand's deteriorated state and spent hours hiding in the tall grass while they slept. Bourbon counted nine deer beds—freshly packed grass in oblong ovals—before they entered the woods again on the other side.

Flesti's tent was nestled under a large beech tree with spacious burly and gray limbs that reached outward like a bodybuilder flexing on stage. A dark green hammock stretched from the tree's trunk to a small straight red maple.

Flesti motioned for Bourbon to sit on a makeshift bench made of a log with no bark to identify its species. Bourbon tested his weight on the wood and decided it would hold. Little holes made from carpenter ants and beetles perforated the seat.

Flesti was working on a small fire, bent over hot coals, blowing gently to bring the flames back to life. A flicker, smoke, and another hot breath, and the heat began to build. Bourbon realized he'd been staring at Flesti but not her face, and then he shook his head to erase his impure thoughts and focus on why he was here.

"Why do you stay out here?" Bourbon asked.

Flesti broke three small eggs into a frying pan. She lifted the pan and set it on the hot coals. She spoke as she leveled the pan over the heat. "Why wouldn't I stay out here? Clean air, fresh water, plenty of plants and berries to eat from spring to fall."

"And in the winter? No one can survive a New York winter outside."

"I have a cabin. And a house in Arizona."

"No shit," Bourbon smiled. "I thought you hibernated like all the other forest animals."

She scowled, then smiled as she sat beside him, "I grew up here, at Cain Lake. My father taught me how to hunt, trap, and fish. My mother showed me which berries were edible and how to preserve them. And I used to help them tend to their garden. Everything a person needs can be found right here." She leaned backward with a small knife, cut eight tender fiddleheads from the ground, and put them in the pan with the eggs.

Bourbon's stomach growled in anticipation as the scent of the cooking food filled his nostrils. He picked a tall piece of grass and chewed on the broken end, tricking his brain into thinking his meal was ready. It stimulated his salivary glands, and he swallowed hard.

"Are you really going to kill him?" Flesti asked as she scratched Hetzen's ear.

"Jesse Lewis? Hell yeah."

"I don't think you will. You're not a cold-blooded killer, Bourbon.

You're a lawman, who believes in trials and lawyers, and all that other due-process bullshit that goes with it."

"You're right. I'm not a killer. But I'm no longer a lawman; he deserves to die for his crimes. I'm here to represent all his victims; Connor Bayley, Darin Cloudwater, Peter Felton, Brody Sherwood, and Annabel Thomspon. I think about those people every day. Sinners or not, they deserve justice, too. Jesse Lewis will keep killing as long as this lake keeps compelling him. The body I found this morning is just the beginning—I'm sure of it."

Flesti took a small spatula and checked the eggs. They were fully cooked.

"You're right, Bourbon; this is just the beginning. But there's something you should know." She set the hot pan on a flat stone and spoke seriously, "I've been watching Jesse Lewis for weeks. He's killed no one."

Bourbon threw the piece of grass he'd been chewing into the fire and watched it slowly curl and burn. *Shit.*

"That means we have another killer terrorizing Cain Lake."

7

PHANTOM PAIN

Cody opened his eyes, but his world was still dark. The smell of plastic and soap and the running shower made him realize he wasn't in his vision world any longer. He peeled the wet shower curtain off his head, revealing the afternoon sun burning through the window, which stung his eyes. How long was he unconscious? A few hours, he guessed.

His left arm throbbed like hell—even more than his head. He remembered feeling the toilet seat break under his weight and the echo in his head as it struck the sink.

Stupid. Should have taken a bath.

He climbed to his feet, wondering if his left arm was broken, and turned the shower knob to cut the water. His mother always asked him if he could move his fingers any time he hurt his wrist or arm—apparently, not being able to wiggle the digits indicated a fracture. He tried opening his hand and moving his fingers as if he were playing the piano, and then he remembered he didn't have a hand or fingers. But he could still feel them. There was a compressed ache every time he tried to make a fist. A slight pain would flicker when he wanted to open it, like a faulty light bulb.

The doctors told him he would have this sensation. What'd the doctors call it? "Phantom pain?"

He ran his fingers over the back of his head and then checked them for blood—nothing. Just a lump that would need an ice pack and a beer.

He toweled himself off, redressed, and made his way downstairs. In the kitchen, he realized he didn't have any ice, but the beer was no problem. He popped the top off the cold Busch and tipped the bottle until it was half empty.

The thought of Michael tied up and beaten was like a hot spoon through the heart. His heart swelled with childhood memories of the twosome building forts in the woods, racing bikes, and catching fireflies in the summer. He didn't know his brother anymore—he'd gotten used to a life without him—but now he wanted to find him. He needed to find him. He needed someone good at research. He needed Daisy. If anyone could dig through public and private records and get the info he needed, it was her.

And if he discovered Michael was in another state, he'd need money. His personal bank, AJ Timmons, would gladly help with any costs. Cody never asked AJ for money, but he may have to this time.

And a gun. As much as he hated them and as much trouble as he'd be in if caught possessing one, he needed to go into this fight fully prepared. Whoever was holding Michael was dangerous. Cody was going to have to be well-prepared for a fight.

He took out his phone and began dialing numbers. Daisy freaked when she heard what had happened to him in the shower. She said she'd be back over after she fed Sammy. Her mother was staying with her and could watch him for the night.

AJ didn't answer, and Cody didn't leave a message. He figured AJ would see the missed call and call back or come by later. It was Saturday night, and they had plans to hit The Mineshaft for a few drinks and chicken wings.

Cody wasn't in the mood to go out, but he needed to inform AJ of what he saw and formulate a plan. He'd start searching first thing tomorrow, when it was daylight.

After he packed a backpack with supplies, he paced the floor for an hour. He went into the yard to escape the clocks and hopefully lose track of time. He fed the birds, watered the dead flowers, and began mowing his small yard with a Toro push mower. Waiting was a bitch.

A blue truck finally rumbled down the street with music playing so loud Cody could hear it a block away. The volume slowly died as the Ram TRX approached. The signal light flashed at the last moment, and the vehicle turned into Cody's driveway. The driver didn't exit immediately, and Cody could see him talking on the phone.

When he finished his call, AJ Timmons stood in the driveway. Cody turned off the engine of the Toro push lawnmower.

"Maybe you should get a riding lawnmower," AJ said, studying the crooked tracks across the lawn.

"Have you ever tried to push a lawnmower with one hand?"

"Nope. And if it looks this bad, I hope I never do."

The two best friends took their conversation to the garage, where Cody parked the mower, leaving the rest of the job unfinished. Under normal circumstances, he'd never leave a job unfinished, but these weren't normal circumstances.

"I saw you called. Sorry, man, I was in the shower. Are you going to shower before we go? We are going to The 'Shaft, right?"

"Not tonight, pal. I need to ask a favor."

"Sure," AJ said. "Anything. What is it?"

"I need help. I had another vision today—at the lake and then again in the shower." Cody told AJ the horror of his vision and how the man was beaten with a wrench.

"And you want to find him, right? Be a hero again?"

"It's not like that, AJ. The guy taking the beating—I'm pretty sure it was Michael."

AJ gave him a confused glare. "Who?"

"Michael—my younger brother."

"No way, man. I'm sure you're just seeing what you want to see. Or, maybe you're not getting enough sleep."

"It was him."

"Bro, you don't even know what he looks like. What's it been, like fifteen years?"

Cody gave AJ the details about his vision and how he fell and hurt himself afterward. He left the part about the shower curtain falling on his head to save himself the embarrassment. Before he finished, Daisy pulled into the driveway, and he had to repeat the whole story while AJ retrieved a couple of beers from inside.

"Didn't I tell you to avoid showering? I'm pretty sure that was my suggestion. My exact words were 'stay out of the shower.' Jesus, you can be stubborn.""I had to know, Daisy. I had to see more. And I'm glad I did. Now, I know who's being tortured. I need to find the man doing it. I need your help."

AJ returned with three beers, stepping between the two lovers. Daisy refused the beverage with a palm gesture, so AJ placed the bottle on an old workbench.

She watched Cody drink for a moment before she spoke again. "Why would this be happening? I have a feeling that whoever is doing this wants you to see. He wants you to come looking for your brother."

"The Sin-eater," AJ said. "He's the only one who hates you."

"No," Cody said. "If Jesse Lewis wanted me dead, he'd have killed me in the barn when he had the chance. He may be a sadistic sonovabitch, but he only kills those who sin—evil killing evil. This is something different."

AJ set his beer on the workbench. "I gotta agree with Daisy on this one, pal. I think you should just leave it alone before you get yourself killed."

"I can't. I won't."

Daisy had heard enough. There were tears in her eyes now. "Do what you need to do. I can't watch you do this to yourself again." She gave him a peck on the cheek, like a sister kissing a brother, and walked away. She climbed into her car and drove away. The Subaru sputtered down the road faster than usual, and Cody wondered if it would ever return.

"Always gotta be the hero, eh, pal?" AJ said.

Cody gave him a questioning look.

AJ elaborated, "You always swoop in and kick ass, right? That's what you do. You've never been a bully—just the guy who beats up bullies."

"Like the ones in high school who used to kick your ass?" Cody asked.

"Yeah, like the ones who used to kick my ass. Some people have to fight their own battles. For all you know, your brother might be involved in some messed up shit. Maybe he's a drug dealer and deserves what he's getting. Maybe he's hurt people, and someone like you is exacting their revenge."

"I won't know until I find him."

"If you find him."

The two stood in silence for a few sips. Cody couldn't ask AJ for money now. Not with his opposing view of the situation.

"So, what are you going to do?" AJ asked. He knew there was no talking Cody out of his search. "How are you going to find him?"

"I have an idea," Cody said. "But, you're not going to like it."

8

THE PLAN

"Two Cokes, please." AJ set a twenty-dollar bill on the bar. The bartender half-filled two highballs with ice cubes and then drowned them with the syrupy soda. She placed the cold drinks in front of AJ and traded them for cash. On a typical Saturday night, the two friends would visit The Mineshaft, where Alyse bartended. They'd put down a few cheap beers and a dozen wings each. But tonight, their destination was too far from home to risk mixing alcohol with the drive, so they stuck with the soda.

Full Throttle was one of two biker bars in Stoneville—home of the Road Barons—on the edge of town adjacent to the railroad tracks. The building stood alone so that no noise complaints could be filed with the local law. They could play music loud as hell, yell to the moon, and rev their bike engines all night without bother. The second floor had tables and an open balcony under the stars. Grayish blue sheet metal covered the exterior walls, and a row of beat-up hedges surrounded the building.

Inside, antiquated neon lights blinked on and off; their lifespans approaching their final hours. The neon that had already died was replaced with bright LED lights shining brightly and consistently. Their various colors illuminated the barn wood walls. The bar was a semicircle in the middle of the floor with a door leading to a small kitchen with an oven and a couple of deep fryers. The smell of grease, stale beer, and flavored cigars filled the air. AJ counted twenty-two people in the bar because that's what AJ does.

Many patrons drank soda, unwilling to risk a DWI or wrecking their overpriced motorcycles. Nobody knew if the new sheriff, Jo Hassett, would play nice or be a hard-ass on the group. Despite their image, the Road Barons were some of the county's friendliest and most generous people. They were moms and dads, members of the PTA, local business owners, and retired law enforcement. They held bike rallies, raised money for charities, and they hosted an annual ride for autism awareness.

And some of the Barons were less amiable and less charitable. Some were ex-cons, and some were just cons. Some were drug addicts, and some were drug dealers. But the good outweighed the bad, and they mostly policed themselves.

AJ Timmons stuck out like a giraffe in a pride of lions. He was tall and thin and wore a gray T-shirt with a skewed letter A in a circle printed on the front. The left sleeve had a silkscreen MARVEL logo. He spent much of his night at the bar explaining to fellow patrons that the A did not stand for asshole.

AJ made his way across the barroom without spilling the drinks or dropping two small bags of pretzels. He set everything on the high-top table where Cody was waiting.

"Think he'll show up?" AJ asked.

"I sure hope so," Cody replied. "I haven't seen him in a few weeks, but where else would he be tonight?"

"Are you sure about this?"

"No."

They drank their Cokes and lost a few games of billiards. Cody found shooting especially difficult because the cue stick stuck to the bandage on his regrowing left hand. They opted for a game of darts, hoping to change their luck, but realized they weren't much better at that. The games helped pass the time while they waited to meet their acquaintance.

Cody used the opportunity to use the restroom. He set his phone on the table and meandered through the tables to the men's room. He waited inside the bathroom for an empty urinal and returned to the table five minutes later.

AJ was still sitting by himself.

At 9:26, the man they'd been waiting for finally walked through the door. He was instantly surrounded by other Barons, offering to buy him drinks—shots of chilled blackberry schnapps—which he mostly declined. After getting a beer at the bar, Levi Thompson noticed the giraffe and the company he kept. He strutted over to Cody's table, only pausing once to shake his hips with a couple of pretty girls standing by a vending machine. They joined him momentarily, and then they all laughed in unison. The leader of the Road Barons kept making his way across the building, greeting everyone with a crushing handshake and a smile.

AJ recounted the crowd—thirty-three.

"What the hell are you two doing out here," Levi asked when he reached the table. "The Mineshaft closed tonight?" He extended his right hand to both men in a handshake. AJ was hesitant but gripped Levi's palm anyway.

"No," Cody answered, "Just needed a change of scenery, and I was looking for you."

Levi removed his leather jacket and wrapped it on the back of the tall chair. Muscles, grown on the family farm, tortured the tee shirt he was wearing. His left arm was covered in a full-sleeve tattoo of a biker with a flaming skull riding a motorcycle with airplane wings. The rider, reminiscent of the Red Baron of World War I notoriety, wore a leather jacket and goggles. The image was bursting through a cloud that formed cumulus eagle wings. A banner circled the motorcycle with calligraphic letters that read "Road Barons." The tattoo wrapped around Levi's arm, stopping halfway down his forearm.

AJ was intimidated by Levi's physique, suddenly aware of his wiry frame. Even Cody looked smaller as the big man took a seat.

Cody seemed less impressed with Levi and certainly was not intimidated. He knew that despite his size and strength, Levi was the most benevolent person he'd ever known. He couldn't recall a single time the man had ever been in a physical altercation—perhaps because no one in Stoneville was brave enough to challenge the beast.

"How's the hand?" Levi asked Cody, nodding to the mess of bandages bulging at the end of his forearm. "I thought you cut the fucking thing completely off. It looks like you still have it."

Cody stuffed the ugly appendage under the table, hoping to change the subject. "It's fine. I'm getting used to doing everything with one hand now."

"Except mowing the lawn," AJ jabbed.

They all reminisced, talking about the biker gang, changes to Stoneville, and Willa—Levi's sister and Cody's deceased wife. Cody and Levi fought tears, knowing she was gone, until AJ changed the subject of their conversation.

"Tell him about your vision, Cody."

Levi shot a questioning look at Cody, "I heard some shit about that—you having some sort of psychic ability. What's that all about?"

"It's true," AJ said, nodding at his friend.

"It's—" Cody began. "It's complicated. I don't know what you'd call it, but yeah. When I get near water—especially Cain Lake—I see people in danger."

Levi gulped his beer while Cody explained, then set his emptymug down. A pretty waitress appearedbehind the big man and put a fresh pitcher of beer on the table with two mugs for Levi's company. She walked away without saying a word.

Levi filled his glass, "No shit. So, that's how you saved my mom. You saw her in your vision. I still owe you for that, buddy."

"No, actually, I never saw your mom in danger. It was just pure luck that I came along when I did."

"Pure luck or Karma," Levi said. "Either way, she might be dead if it wasn't for you picking her up and getting her to the hospital."

"How is she?"

"Good, I guess," Levi poured the amber brew into his glass mug. "She doesn't leave the house, though. Keeps to herself these days. I'm not sure what hurt her more—Jesse Lewis carving her stomach up or the sheriff leaving her."

"He went looking for Jesse Lewis—."

"Yeah, well, he sure is taking his fucking time catching him, isn't he."

Cody poured a beer for himself and AJ. "Well, that's why I'm here, Levi. I need a gun—a pistol. Something untraceable and clean."

"Something easy to shoot with one hand," AJ said.

"You fixing to find the Sin-eater yourself? I'll get you all the guns you want."

"Yes, but it's not what you think. I had a...vision. I saw somebody torturing a man, beating him almost to death."

"Gotta be Lewis," Levi said. His hand curled into a tight fist. "Did you get a look at his face?"

"No. And I don't think it was Jesse Lewis. I think it's someone else."

"So? What are you going to do, shoot the guy you saw?"

Cody turned in his chair, squarely facing Levi. "I think the man being beaten was my brother."

"Shit, man, I didn't even know you had a brother. I'd shoot the bastard, too, if he beat up one of my brothers." Levi scanned the room as if looking at all the brothers he had. Then his eyes turned back to Cody. Cody was his ex-brother-in-law, and the two were close before Willa died. Levi always felt Cody was a good match for his sister and would care for her better than her previous male relationships.

"I need to find this guy fast, but I'm afraid I'll be too late. I need help," Cody said.

"I said I'd give you the gun. I'll even go with you, bro."

"No, I can't ask you to do that. I mean—" Cody looked down, worried about Levi's reaction to his following statement. "I need Jesse Lewis's help. He can sense sinners—corruption—people with secrets."

"Like my mom?" Levi said. His tone was bitter, and his voice raised enough to get the attention of a few people around them.

"No, no, not like your mom. You know I think the world of Annabel. I mean, Jesse Lewis's psychic power is much more powerful than mine. He may be my only hope, but I've got to get to him before Bourbon."

AJ backed up his friend's claim. "You know how angry Bourbon was—for what Lewis did to your mom. Once he finds him, he won't hesitate for a second to put a bullet between his eyes."

"Good! That fucking asshole deserves to die," Levi said. "I don't know, guys. I want to help you, but not if Jesse Lewis gets away or comes out on top."

"He won't," Cody assured him. "Once he finds my brother, I'll put a bullet in him myself."

AJ hid behind his beer glass. If there was one thing he knew for sure about Cody Savage, it was that he was incapable of taking another human's life. There was no way Cody was capable of keeping that promise.

Levi thought momentarily, swallowed hard, "I'll give you a gun, but there's a condition. Once you find your brother, you hand Jesse Lewis over to me."

Chills crept up Cody's neck, and he felt his face get flush. He couldn't imagine the pain Jesse Lewis would have to endure if Levi and the rest of the Barons imprisoned him. The Barons were known for their generosity, not their forgiveness. Would they kill him instantly, or keep him alive for months, torturing him repeatedly? Still, Jesse Lewis was a monster, even if he thought he was doing some good by killing the town's sinners.

Cody finished his beer and stood. He looked around the room at all the good people he'd come to know over the last decade. He would hate for them to get involved in such a scheme. He looked at AJ, who gave him a shrug and thought about what it would be like to lose him to someone like the Sin-eater. He finally spoke:

"It's a deal."

9

FIRESIDE

Bourbon sat opposite the fire from Flesti. He stared in awe at the infinite number of stars spanning the night sky. He tracked a satellite with his naked eyes, traveling faster than anything else in view until it disappeared behind a cloud. The lack of light pollution at Cain Lake provided the majestic vista, and Bourbon felt he could stay there forever. Maybe he would.

"Rain's coming," Flesti said.

"I doubt it. Look at all those stars. Not a cloud in the sky."

Flesti was sharpening a fresh-cut stick from a little beech tree. She tested the chiseled end with her index finger, gave it another stroke with her Buck knife. Satisfied with the sticks tip, she placed the newly chiseled point into the flames to harden. Bourbon watched her work, anticipating a few soft marshmallows would be impaled and roasted.

Satisfied with the little spear's strength, she reached into a small canvas bag, peeked inside like a kid trying to find the cheesiest Dorito. When her hand re-emerged, she was holding a reddish brown crayfish not much larger than a credit card. As the little creature squirmed and tried his best to pinch her, she took the improvised skewer and stuck it through the crevices in its body armor, pushing until it was six inches down the shaft. She then repeated the act with three more crayfish she'd caught earlier in the day. She returned the spear and the unfortunate crustaceans to the fire for a primitive meal and threw a few mushrooms and cattail roots in a frying pan to simmer while the crayfish cooked.

She murmered something to the crayfish that was barely audible to

Bourbon. Something about appreciating their sacrifice and nourishing her body. Bourbon began to see just how much Flesti appreciated the bounty Cain Lake provided.

They had just eaten the eggs and fiddleheads a few hours prior. They could have waited until morning to eat their next meal, but cooking kept them occupied while they stargazed and conversed about their predicament.

"Have you seen anyone else lurking around the lake," Bourbon asked his host.

"No one of distinct character," Flesti answered. "I've seen a few fishermen, some state troopers looking for Lewis, and some teenage kids partying on the peninsula." She pointed the stick northwest, but all Bourbon could see was darkness.

"I wondered if the troopers are still here searching. I spoke to one a week ago. They were sure Lewis had left the area. He's figured out how to beat them and their dogs."

"He has," Flesti agreed. "But he hasn't fooled me—not yet."

"I don't think he could fool you."

Flesti laughed for a moment. "Was that a compliment, Mr. Bourbon?"

"Please, just call me Bourbon. And yes, that was a compliment. Don't get used to them."

"Why didn't you tell the state boys where Jesse was camping?"

She waved her hand in front of her face as if a fly was pestering her, "Ah, to hell with them. They'd go trampling through the woods, guns blazing, dogs barking. This isn't their territory." She seemed upset by the thought of a manhunt. "This is my home. I've been keeping an eye on Jesse and things have been quiet and peaceful. Only you can take him in quietly."

It won't be quiet. You're going to hear this pistol shake the trees.

Flesti turned the skewered crayfish that hung over the fire and gave the frying pan a little swirl with her wrist, mixing the cattail roots and mushrooms so they would cook evenly. Bourbon was enjoying the smell much more than he predicted he would enjoy the taste. He was ravenous, even after the eggs and fiddleheads, and envisioned fresh-cut venison and onions in the pan Flesti was holding.

"How much longer?"

Flesti just shrugged, "Gotta be patient. Things aren't done until they're done."

Bourbon opened his water bottle and guzzled, hoping to fool his stomach into thinking it was sustenance. A gurgle boiled in his stomach as it protested the attempt. Bourbon decided to deepen the conversation to occupy time.

"How long have you been coming here, Flesti?"

She looked at the approaching clouds swallowing stars as if they were bringing her an answer. She spoke toward the fire, watching the flames turn the wood to ash, "A long, long time. I was born here—on the edge of the lake—close to the church. My family died when I was young, and I pretty much raised myself. I left in the eighties, traveled a little, lived in Germany, and then returned to stay. This lake will always be my home. Cain Lake water doesn't just fill this valley—it fills my veins, my soul."

"You're searching for something," Bourbon said. It was a statement and a question. Bourbon felt a cold nose under his forearm as Hetzen finally warmed up to the unfamiliar human. Bourbon scratched behind a chamois cloth ear awaiting Flesti's reply.

"I'm searching for peace—inner peace. I don't give a shit what happens outside of this lake, but everything that this water touches is mine to protect. These trees," she gestured with her hands, looking left to right, "These trees, the land, the animals, the whole ecosystem."

In silence, Bourbon stared at her momentarily, the firelight highlighting her features. He saw Flesti in a new light as if they were meeting for the first time. This was not the woman he'd met before—the crazy woman who emerged naked from the lake in total darkness weeks prior. This was not the woman who spoke in riddles and broken sentences.

Still, something about her was dark, scary, and intriguing.

They ate their second meal in silence, chewing slowly to appreciate every bite. It was the first time Bourbon had eaten crayfish or cattail root and decided it was quite delicious. Even the mushrooms tasted better in the wild.

The fire hissed as a drop of water hit the hot coals. Another drop fell from the sky, and Bourbon could hear the rain thump against the canopy of leaves above his head.

Flesti stood, gathered her backpack, and entered the small tent under a plastic tarp. Bourbon stayed outside the tent but under the tarp, until Flesti stuck her head through the open zipper door.

"Well, you can't sleep out here. Come on, get inside."

Hetzen beat Bourbon inside, and for a moment, Bourbon thought she might have been talking to the dog, but she did not protest his entrance. His eyes adjusted to the lack of light, and he could see her wiggling into a sleeping bag on the ground. Bourbon reached back through the door, pulled his sleeping bag from his pack, and claimed the vacant side of the small tent.

Hetzen curled up at Flesti's feet as the sound of the precipitation grew slightly louder. Exhausted from the day's events, they were all asleep within minutes.

10

THE PROMISE

AJ Timmons wasn't ready to go home after leaving Full Throttle. He convinced Cody to stop at The Mineshaft to cap off the night. They drove across town while AJ talked to his new girlfriend on the phone.

"You're going to love her," AJ said. "She's pretty cool. She's also super hot."

"Where'd you meet her? And why haven't you mentioned her before this, man? Trying to keep it a secret?"

"No, it's not like that. I just wanted to be sure things would work out with us. You know my luck with women?"

Cody laughed. "Remember Roberta?"

"Dude, you promised we'd never bring her up again."

They both laughed at the memory.

"River might be the best thing that's ever happened to me. You'll see. You'll recognize her when you meet her again."

"Again?"

AJ couldn't hide his smirk. But before he could explain, they reached their destination. Cody could sense his excitement, and he was happy for his friend. AJ's history with women was like watching a train wreck in slow motion, each boxcar crashing one behind the other.

AJ steered the Dodge Ram into The Mineshaft's parking lot. Rain drizzled over the windshield, and puddles began to form in the gravel. They jumped from the truck and jogged toward the front door, dodging the little pools. Once inside, they pushed through a group of college students and approached the bar.

Cody expected Alyse Burns to be working behind the bar, serving drinks to local patrons. Instead, a college kid with shoulders like a Roman statue was learning the difference between top-shelf and rack whiskey. The manager, Nicole Brigham, seemed annoyed by his lack of understanding, but that didn't stop her from touching his arm repeatedly.

AJ beat Cody to the bar and slid a twenty across the hardwood top. A few minutes later, two beers appeared in front of them, backed by a shot of chilled blackberry schnapps.

The schnapps was a cool burn inside his throat—failing to wash away the fire that had been building in Cody's stomach all day. He felt he was wasting time bar-hopping when he should have been out looking for Michael. But what could he do? Where would he even begin to look?

Maybe there was no saving his brother. He should forget about Michael and focus on reality. Was there anything he could do to save him?

The beer tasted like shit after the smooth berry flavor of the two-ounce shot, but he drank it anyway.

He felt a set of eyes bearing down on him, searched the room, and finally locked eyes with the prettiest girl in Stoneville. Alyse was perched on a stool, peeking around the shoulder of a burly construction worker.

She gave him a tainted smile as their eyes locked.

The construction worker politely excused himself when he saw Alyse's attention turn to Cody, knowing that the two had some connection.

"It was nice talking to you, Debbie," the construction worker said. He curled his beer and stepped between a couple of his friends to join an argument involving professional hockey.

Cody slid his beer along the bar and claimed the vacant seat beside the brunette.

"'Debbie,' is it? Hi, Debbie; it's nice to meet you."

Alyse punched his shoulder playfully, "Stop it. I don't want him to know my real name. Jesus, he's been sitting here for twenty minutes talking about his truck. Wanted me to go for a ride."

"Guess he really loves his truck," Cody said.

"Yeah, probably more than his mother, I think."

Cody faked a laugh, not because Alyse wasn't funny, but because he wasn't in the mood to laugh.

"Where's your girl tonight?" Alyse asked. Her short, non-manicured fingernail cut through the wet label wrapped around her beer bottle.

"Good question. But I don't have an answer. She's upset about something."

"You know I love her, but boy, she gets emotional easily."

Cody nodded in agreement. "She's got every right this time. I had another vision—"

"Of someone in trouble? Who is this time?"

"My brother." He gave her the details as she bit the fingernail that had been peeling the beer label. When he finished recounting his story, she leaned over and hugged him.

"And you're going to run off and be a hero again? I don't blame her for being upset. Look what happened the last time you acted on your stupid premonition." She nodded toward the bulging mess of bandages. "And you're lucky to be walking after breaking your back."

Cody held his left forearm up, made a fist in his mind, and flexed fingers that no longer existed.

Phantom pain.

He swallowed the last drop of his beer, placed the empty bottle on the bar, and waited for another to appear. It didn't. He looked around, scanning groups of people, and stared down the length of the bar.

"He's at the pool table with River," Alyse said.

"You knew?"

"That he's got a girlfriend now? Hell yeah, I knew. Who do you think convinced him to ask her out?"

Cody almost fell off his bar stool when he recognized the redhead standing with AJ at the pool table. To AJ's right, an attractive and fit redhead stood with a pool stick in her hands. She held the cue stick with both hands and leaned against AJ as she discussed her next shot.

"Holly shit. Is that the woman from the dive team? The one that pulled me out of the lake?" Cody asked Alyse.

Alyse snickered, "Of course, you'd remember her—she's beautiful."

"Good for AJ. It's been too long since he's been in a relationship."

"Remember Roberta?" Alyse giggled.

"Oh, we're sworn to never talk about that again," Cody answered. "But, yeah, of course, I remember."

Cody watched the woman for a moment. Her red hair, thick and wavy, flowed over her shoulders, and her serious expression indicated that she was listening to AJ intently. He popped off his barstool and told Alyse he'd be back. He cut through the crowd, focused like a lion on the hunt, keeping track of AJ and River. He finally reached his destination.

"Cody," AJ yelled. "Cody, you remember River, don't you?"

"Yes, of course; hard to forget a person when they save your life."

River Kelly stepped closer to Cody, but her beauty was front and center. Brown eyes stared as if Di Vinci himself had painted them. She wore minimal makeup and a yellow tee shirt with a Jeep logo across her breasts. She put her right hand forward, and Cody gave it a gentle shake. Her skin was as soft as kitten fur. She looked at the wad of bandages on Cody's other hand, "Nice to see you again, Cody. How's the hand?"

"Feel's fine. Makes me suck at pool, though."

"You sucked when you had both hands," AJ laughed.

Cody couldn't argue. He turned back to River, "So you're still in Stoneville? Are you here diving?"

"No," River said. "I'm here on vacation—summer vacation. I'm a physical education teacher in Albany, but I love to spend my summers here. I'm staying in my dad's Air B&B for a month."

"Your dad lives here?"

River moved into a shooting position at the billiard's table and lined up to put the three-ball in a side pocket, "Dale Kelly is my father—the District Attorney." The three-ball dropped into the intended hole.

"Dale Kelly is your father? I know him," Cody said. "Not in a good way."

River moved to the end of the table and sunk the five-ball with a bank shot. "My dad's not too thrilled with me staying here this summer—with the recent murders and all. But this is the only time of year we get to see each other, so—" Nine-ball in the corner pocket.

"Well, it's great that you're here. There's a lot to do in Stoneville during the summer," Cody said. "I'm sure AJ will find ways to keep you occupied."

River blushed, "He already has."

Cody felt a cold sensation against his arm and turned to see Alyse holding five fresh beers. She passed the round of beers out and pulled Cody to the side.

"So," Alyse started, "Did AJ tell you why he wanted you to come here tonight?"

"No, but I assume it was to meet River. Why? Was there another reason?"

Alyse took a long swig of her drink. "No, he wanted you to try to talk me out of leaving."

"Leaving?" Cody said. "Your leaving town? Or your job?"

"Both."

"Why? I thought you were happy here?"

"I was—at one time."

"What's changed? You have friends here," He nodded to the construction workers standing by the bar. "You have fans here, a job, and people that care about you."

"I just feel empty right now. If I don't get away from this job, I'll become the next Veronica." She subtly pointed her thumb to a sixty-seven-year-old woman at the bar with a potbelly and skinny legs. She could barely hold her head up but still poured more alcohol into her mouth.

Cody cringed. "She seems fine."

As if on cue, Veronica's front false teeth fell into her tall glass of Bud Light.

Alyse patted Cody's shoulder, "I'm not ending up like that. I feel one-dimensional lately. There's got to be more to Alyse Burns than barmaid at The 'Shaft. Jesus, it sounds even worse when I say it out loud."

They watched Veronica fish her teeth out of the beer mug and snap them back into her mouth.

Cody realized what Alyse meant. He empathized with how she felt and wished he could do more with his life. He was an ex-con with no job, mooching off his filthy rich friend and dating a woman for whom he couldn't even buy flowers. He realized Alyse was brave for wanting to go and correct her pathway. She was also right about becoming Veronica if she didn't.

"Look—tomorrow's my last shift. I'll be working the lunch shift, and then I'm heading south. Stop by and see me if you're not out on your witch hunt. It'd be nice to see your face before I go."

"I'll be here."

"Promise?"

"Promise."

She gave him a hug and left—her perfume still hugging him as she made her way to the door. Cody wasn't sure he could keep his promise. He was going to the sheriff's office in the morning to file a report. And then he'd set out on the impossible mission to find his brother.

11
KNUCKLE BUSTERS

Sheriff Jo Hassett leaned back in her office chair, rocking gently, the springs squeaking softly in protest. She hugged a thermal travel mug to her chest with her left hand, inhaling the steam from the fresh coffee inside, while her right hand flicked her phone's screen, scrolling to the next page of her social media account. She paused on a picture of her sister, an embarrassing shot in a yellow bikini, an inflatable pool unicorn wrapped around her waist, and an icy drink in a margarita glass while she stood in thigh-deep water.

According to the clock on her computer, her work shift had just begun. She'd been sitting in her office since six, finalizing a report, reading applications, and scrolling through her phone.

Hassett smiled at the image of her baby sister.

The door to her office was closed in an attempt to drown out the annoying sound of the vending machine in the hallway. She thought about removing the ugly box since no one used it, but upon further inspection, she realized it was hiding a large hole in the Sheetrock that allowed a draft to enter the building. The removal of the machine would have to wait until she could line up a contractor to patch the hole and paint the wall.

Deputy Simpson gave a two-knuckle knock for intruding on her thoughts, even though they shared the same office. Hassett smiled, but Dave didn't notice, too busy closing the door behind him while balancing a stack of papers, a coffee cup, and a cinnamon donut.

"Good morning, sheriff," Dave said in his low voice. He was short with thick forearms and broad shoulders. There was a strength about him, but it was apparent the man had never visited a gym and had no concerns about eating well. Yet, somehow he stayed fit enough to perform the duties bestowed upon a Stoneville Sheriff's Deputy.

His teeth tore away a quarter of the donut and chewed while as he pulled his chair from his desk with two free fingers.

"Any word from Shari about the body we hauled in yesterday?" Dave asked as he sat. He wasn't much for small talk unless that talk included muscle cars or country music, which Hassett knew very little about.

Hassett sipped her coffee and checked her email, "Nothing, yet. I'd give her until the end of the day, at least. But some of the lab results may take weeks."

"Just an identity would be a good start," Dave said.

Hassett spun in her chair, stood, and crossed the room toward her deputy sheriff. She laid a job application on his calendar as she sat on the corner of his desk. She held her nearly empty mug with one hand. "Give this a look. What do you think about this guy?"

Simpson turned the application around and read through the document, a neatly typed resume stapled to the fill-in form. The handwriting was crisp and neat. He ran his right index finger along the baseline of each sentence, reading the candidate's responses to the formal questions.

Hassett noticed the deputy's knuckles almost immediately—light bruising blushed the skin, accented with a couple of bloody abrasions freshly scabbed over. Simpson took notice of the keen-eyed sheriff's interest in his hands.

"What happened to your knuckles?" Hassett asked. "They look like you went a couple of rounds with some of the meat-heads down at The Mineshaft."

"Oh, uh—it's nothing," he responded. "I've been restoring a '74 Mach I in my free time. Lot of knuckle-busters on that thing."

"'Knuckle-busters?'" Hassett replied. "I'm not sure what that means."

"You know, when you bust your knuckles trying to loosen a nut or bolt in a tight space. It's easy to bust your knuckles open—especially if your wrench slips."

Hassett's face cringed, thinking about the pain of bare knuckles scraping against steel. She washed away the thought with a sip of coffee. "Got it. Knuckle-buster. Busting knuckles working on an engine." She was nodding her head like a bobblehead in slow motion. She reclaimed the application and returned to her desk.

She was about to discreetly open her search browser when a gentle knock sounded from the office door. It was the new front desk clerk, Marissa Taft. She was twenty-seven, with light brown hair in a tight ponytail and just enough freckles on her face to count if you engaged her in a thirty-second conversation. Round rim glasses complimented her pretty face.

The man standing behind her was handsome, maybe thirty, with chiseled muscles and a four-day beard. Hassett thought the two would make beautiful babies if they were a couple, but the Sheriff knew Marissa had no interest in anyone of the opposite sex.

"Um, Sheriff, this is—what'd you say your name was again?"

The man stepped from behind her, "Cody. Cody Savage."

Marissa stared at him momentarily, lost in his gray eyes even though he was a he. "Cody—"

"Yes, Marissa," Hassett interrupted. "I heard. How may I help you, Mr. Savage?"

Marissa faded back into the lobby as Cody thanked her. He then turned his attention to the new sheriff. When she stood to greet him, she seemed to keep standing until Cody had to look up at her smiling face. Her handshake was vice-like, and Cody had to refrain from matching her grip.

"So, what brings you in, Mr. Savage?"

"I want to report a crime in progress."

Hassett looked around the room and then glanced at her deputy. "'In progress?' Okay, and what crime would that be?"

He swallowed hard, looking for a way to begin, then gently bit his lip to stimulate his mouth to start talking. He recounted the premonition he'd been having; the beating, the empty room, the victim, all intangible clues that were mere constructs of his mind—perhaps fictional for all he knew. He omitted the incident about falling out of the shower.

Hassett listened to Cody's vivid description of his vision, hanging on every word, but mostly to be polite. When he finished, his hands shook but not enough for her to notice. His face was red with fury.

Hassett leaned back, the springs of her chair protesting out loud. She gently bit the tip of her thumbnail without cracking the polish, then wheeled the chair close to her desk, propped on her elbows, and gave Cody a stern glare. "Mr. Savage, I'm sorry that you are experiencing these hallucinations—"

"I assure you, they're not hallucinations. I've had this ability—"

"I'm sorry. I don't mean to make light of the situation, but surely you can't believe this department has the time or resources to investigate anyone's gut feelings. This is just too flimsy. Why don't you come back when you have concrete proof that your brother, or whomever this victim might be, is truly in danger? I promise, we'll delve into this deeper and do a thorough investigation."

"Sheriff, I don't think you understand."

"I do understand. I understand that we have a body in the morgue. I understand that we need to identify this victim so his family can have closure. I understand that someone may have murdered this individual. Would your psychic ability happen to know anything about that, Mr. Savage?"

"Of course not. I never saw what happened to that man. I only see what's happening in the present." Cody said.

"Sorry, but you seem to be right in the middle of everything around here lately."

"Find Jesse Lewis, and most of your problems will be solved."

Hassett nodded at a stack of papers on her desk, "I've got a lot of work to do, Mr. Savage. You bring me some concrete proof that your brother is being tortured, and I'll put your case at the top of that stack."

"It might be too late by then. We need to move now. Start a search party, patrol the vacant buildings, and call the damn FBI if you have to. I don't know, but we need to do something."

Hassett's bobblehead nods had turned into side-to-side shakes in protest. "Listen, bring me proof, and I'll call in the state investigators. But until then, my hands are tied." She immediately regretted her choice of words.

Before he could forget his manners, Cody stood abruptly and took a few breaths. "I knew it was a long shot. Had to try. Thanks for your time, anyway." He retreated to the office door.

"Mr. Savage," Hassett called after him. "What are you planning to do?"

Cody didn't turn around. He softly spoke over his left shoulder, avoiding eye contact, "I'm going to find my brother, and no one better stand in my way."

*****

Hassett watched Cody from her office window. He crossed the street with his head down, temper up, and never looked back. When he was out of sight, Stoneville's dutiful sheriff retook her chair and pulled the application she'd been reviewing within reading distance. The words seemed jumbled, and her focus was lost. The vicious story Cody painted gelled her gray matter.

She pushed the application away and spun toward Deputy Simpson, who was as stoic as usual. "Well? What do you think about his absurd story? Any merit to it?"

Simpson peered over a pair of reading glasses at his new boss, "Guy's a little nuts, but some people in town say he found the Poole girl because he had a vision. Some people say the ghost of his wife is haunting him, and others think he must've been doing drugs in prison."

Hassett went back to the window to observe downtown Stoneville. She pulled the window blinds up, letting the sun shine directly into the office while she looked at the town in a new light. Had she moved her career to a town full of crazies? Or was there something else at play here? Could there really be something dark and twisted infecting the people with supernatural powers and hysteria?

The intrusive sunlight burned Dave's pupils as it reflected off the smooth surface of his metal desk. He stood and joined Hassett at the window, waiting for his eyes to adjust to the morning light. He lifted his coffee to his lips and sipped quietly, unsure what to say.

Hassett studied the few cars that drove by, a small group of people walking to Sunday brunch, two joggers, and a woman walking three

69

small dogs. She came to Stoneville because it was a quiet town of about 30,000 people—a tenth of the population compared to her hometown in Indiana. She hoped this would be an easy transition from Mafia types, drug lords, and repeat felons, but there was more to Stoneville than meets the eye. There was some faceless creature clawing from the depths to show its teeth, turning the town into a murderous zoo. Hassett wanted to know what was truly happening here. She wished she could believe Cody Savage, but she couldn't. She was a realist. She believed in the facts and figures and the evidence, the way the academy had taught her.

There was so much she didn't know, but her curiosity arose like the water in Cain Lake after a heavy storm.

"Simpson?"

"Yeah, Boss?"

"What's a Mach I?"

12

BUCK NAKED 

It took Bourbon a moment to remember where he was. He hadn't slept with a proper shelter over his head since the last rain had fallen on Cain Lake. That was nearly a week ago. He slipped a warm flannel shirt over his shoulders and fastened the buttons. The flannel warmed his skin, staving off the cool morning air and smothering his goosebumps.

He exited Flesti's tent, still working on a couple of the buttons, and slipped into his hiking boots. Flesti was nowhere to be found, but her pack still hung from a tree, and she had refreshed the fire. There were no flames—just hot coals steaming several pieces of wood stacked in a crisscross pattern that allowed air to flow to the interior.

Bourbon could see a light trail leading to the lake where Flesti had walked, knocking fresh dew from the bushes and the grass. She'd gone to the lake, and Bourbon hoped she'd return with a fresh catch of perch or frog legs. He squatted adjacent to the smoldering fire, absorbing the warmth with the palms of his hands—heating the engine oil, hoping it would make his muscles less stiff.

Flesti's backpack was unzipped for easy access—hers, not his. He stood tall, trying to see down the trail, and then scoped his surroundings 360 degrees. She was nowhere to be found. He didn't think there was anything in the pack she'd be trying to hide. Still, as a former officer, he wondered if she might have identification—a driver's license, passport, or even a damn voter registration card. Anything that would shed light on her true identity.

He pulled the side of the pack and peeked inside. It was hard to discern anything in the jumbled mess, like picking out a sock from a laundry basket. He moved a couple of articles of clothing and a light blanket to one side.

Nothing of interest.

A stick snapped behind him, a sound only capable of being made by one's body weight stepping down. Bourbon's heart jumped, and he hoped she wouldn't be angry about his intrusion. He turned around, already thinking of excuses for his trespass, but it was not Flesti that faced him.

An eight-point whitetail deer stood with his back to the sun. His antlers, lit by the beams of light filtering through the tree canopy above, were branches covered in soft velvet—thick at the base but grew smaller as they reached outward. It was early in the year, and his crown still had ten weeks to grow in height and harden to bone. By early fall, his neck would be swollen with muscle, and his proud headdress would be put to task, becoming a weapon to spar with the younger bucks for dominance.

Bourbon and the buck blinked at one another, neither wanting to move first. They stood eye to eye, equals in the woods—brothers of the forest.

Bourbon enjoyed the moment. He'd seen many whitetail deer over the last two weeks, but they were always running away from him, their namesake waving goodbye as they sprinted through the dense forest. This was the first time he'd come nose to nose with the noble creature.

He thought back to days when he was just a deputy—to the days he hunted not far from here. It was easy then—to shoot a buck, to take a life. It was easy not to feel guilty and to justify the kill as 'putting food on the table.' But the truth was—

He'd forgotten what the truth was. He'd forgotten that he only hunted because it was expected of a man in this county, as if dealing death was a manly thing. No, respecting life—the simplest form or the most ferocious beast—was what a real man did. For his friends, hunting had become an excuse to shoot and kill, firing high-powered rifles at deer feeding in planted fields. He thought of the irony—a man spending hours, week after week, clearing fields, and planting alfalfa or winter rye just to attract an animal to shoot. The sport was gone. The chase had ended. Now, hunting was no different than going to the local butcher shop and picking your choice of meat cuts.

Bourbon held his breath and tried not to flinch. The buck appeared to be holding his too.

"Why don't you shoot it," Archer's voice asked. *"Go ahead. Plenty of meat on the fucker's bones to feed you and that bitch for a month."*

Shut up. Shut the hell up. It would be a waste.

"Shoot him in the neck, just like you did to me. That'll do the job."

You deserved it, you sick bastard. That deer didn't kidnap a child. Get out of my head.

"Never."

The deer finally made the first move, so swift and graceful that Bourbon could only watch him flee. His white tail waved goodbye, bounding over logs, dodging trees, and was gone as quickly as he had appeared. Their encounter was brief, but Bourbon was glad for the chance meeting that may never happen again.

"You blew it," Archer's voice taunted. *"You blew it because you're such a damn pacifist."*

A pacifist? Maybe so. I can live with that.

There was still no sign of Flesti. Bourbon scanned the forest hard, looking for any movement. The woods were still. Even the intrusive crow was nowhere to be seen.

He checked a side pocket of the backpack, which revealed a Swiss Army knife, a toothbrush in a case, a man's wallet with nine ten-dollar bills, and a rolled piece of leather.

Bourbon looked over his shoulder. Then the other.

He slowly unrolled the leather, opening it until it was the size of a sheet of paper. A map, crude and lacking detail, was burned into the surface by a hot knife or carving tool. Bourbon studied the marks, recognizing the general shape of Cain Lake. There were landmarks that he recognized and some he did not. A cross marked the white church's location on the north shore. To the west, crosshatching symbolized the bridge over the creek, built just thirty years ago. A house occupied the northeast corner, but a large X had been drawn through the structure, surely indicating that it was no longer there.

But more curiously, the cartographer had marked the lake with nearly one hundred small Xs.

What are you looking for, Flesti?

He rolled the map tight and returned it to the backpack pocket.

His stomach gave a hungry growl, warning the fifty-three-year-old that his body didn't run on revenge. He hoped to find Jesse Lewis before the sun set but needed to face him with a full belly. His backpack was low on supplies, maybe half day's worth of fresh water, and depleted food storage. He rummaged through his clothes and gear and thanked the Heavens when he came up with a granola bar he'd forgotten about.

He crunched on the maple and brown sugar flavor, imagining his encounter with the Sin-eater. He hoped to catch the murderer by surprise and reminded himself not to underestimate the former pastor of the now empty church. He was ready to put this all behind him. Killing Jesse Lewis would appease the sour taste of revenge that coated his tongue. Killing Jesse Lewis would allow himself, Cody, and Annabel to sleep peacefully at night. Killing Jesse Lewis would be the last violent act he'd ever commit.

Once Jesse Lewis was six feet in the ground and the Sin-eater no more, life in Stoneville would return to normal. He could find a way to forgive Annabel for her crime, for running away the day she hit poor Charlotte Archer with her car. He'd find a way to be with her, keep loving her, and move past all the shit they'd been through. They'd been together for so long, shared so many memories, that she'd become a part of him. Now she was gone from his life, and it hurt. He closed his eyes briefly and could still feel her, like a missing limb.

Phantom pain.

He rose from the cold rock that supported his weight and watched a woman duck a tree limb as she approached him. She stood upright and pushed a lock of blond hair away from her face. Bourbon would have bet his former salary that her hair was gray when they first met. She was shaped like a cheerleader, fit, with just enough fat and muscle to give her body the curves that men can't resist. The ends of her hair were wet, and when she stepped from the shadows of the thick leaf canopy, Bourbon realized she was carrying her clothes, dressed only in her fair skin and confidence.

Bourbon admitted to himself that she was attractive, but his stomach was more interested in the walleye pike she was carrying at the end of a crude wooden spear. Poe shot over her shoulder like a shadowy spirit and perched upon the tent's peak. Hetzen trudged up the trail behind his companions with his nose to the ground. He seemed to be following the scent of the fish rather than his master.

Flesti held the spear straight, pointing at Bourbon's belly, "Gotta spear 'em early in the morning, while it's still dark. That's when they're in the shallows."

He couldn't help but smile and took the spear with his left hand. He pulled the big fish free with his right.

"I caught it; you clean and cook it," Flesti said.

"Sounds like a fair deal to me."

Bourbon went to work on the fish with a six-inch knife sheathed to his hip. Hetzen sat by his side and watched him butcher the walleye. He slit the fishes belly and extracted the internal organs. Hetzen gulped the entrails down in two swallows. Once the organs were removed, Bourbon began peeling the scaly skin from the tender white meat. He then skewered the fish over the two prongs of a Y-shaped stick.

After redressing, Flesti worked to bring life back to the fire and added a few cedar bows to give their meal a smokey flavor. She would have preferred to smoke the fish over low heat for hours, but Bourbon's patience would never agree.

When the fish was cooked and their bellies were full, they packed up some of their gear. Bourbon insisted they travel light, so they left the tent, cot, and tarps behind. They could return in a day or two to retrieve the rest.

As they made their way through the deciduous forest, Bourbon kept his pistol, a Smith & Wesson 686, ready to draw from his shoulder holster in case Jesse Lewis got the jump on them. His pace was quick, but his steps were light as Flesti called out the directions from behind.

She directed them away from the lake to avoid the thick marshes of sticky mud and tall grass. They increased their elevation as they hiked southeast, and Bourbon could feel the arduous climb torching his thigh muscles. The gentle wind relieved his sun burnt skin as it cooled his body. His panting increased—lungs pushing and pulling oxygen from his chest to fuel exhausted muscles.

Proof her body was capable of the steep climb, Flesti's skin was still dry. Her breathing was normal and controlled, as if she were out for an evening walk with her dog. Leaning on her tall walking stick for support, she stopped and watched Bourbon lumber up the hill, clumsy from his haste and determination. She hoped he'd slow down before he became a danger to himself. She was beginning to like her hiking partner and admired his determination, but she'd known men like this before. They usually ended up getting themselves hurt or killed.

13
THE KEY

Cody crossed the street, walked down South Main street, and turned toward his home. His steps were quick, but last night's drinks made him feel a little sluggish.

He stopped walking, only to try calling AJ. No answer. Cody cursed, knowing full well that AJ was blowing him off to spend time with River. Then he realized he'd done the same thing over the years and cut AJ some slack.

The rain had accumulated along the edge of the road, failing to drain properly due to a plastic bag and water bottles covering a sewer grate. Cody stared into the water, past the surface. Downtown Stoneville reflected in the still water of the puddle. The buildings and trees were inverted and dark, and Cody felt upside down, the only person not grounded. The water rippled when a young teenager passed through riding a bike, creating little waves that distorted the buildings and trees, and for a moment, it looked as though the tranquil town was crumbling—drowning in the water.

Cody's phone rang. The caller identification showed Daisy's name, but Cody knew he needed to forge ahead without distractions. He ended the call before it began, hoping she would understand but knowing she wouldn't. He couldn't afford to be talked down. Michael deserved his full attention.

He knelt beside the pool of water, cupped his hand, and stirred it gently.

"Come on," he whispered. "Show me something." With both eyes closed, he focused on what he'd seen before, the beating, the blood, the walls. But the vision refused to appear.

The boy on the bike turned around and peddled for another pass through the liquid. When he saw Cody, he swerved around the water and peddled away, cautious not to disturb the grown man stirring the puddle with his right hand.

The water produced no vision and only diluted Cody's patience. He tried to stimulate his insight for two minutes before finally giving up. He stood, wiped his hand dry on his pants, and continued his march home.

The walk was exhausting, and he didn't remember feeling this way on his way to the sheriff's office. He was angry now, each step feeding his temper, but he hoped his mood would change when he got home. He was supposed to meet Levi in eight minutes and still had a ten-minute walk. His steps quickened.

*****

Levi was sitting on his motorcycle waiting for Cody. He was early and wasn't alone, which was no surprise to Cody. He had a tight circle of friends that followed him almost everywhere he went. The three men joined Levi and the Road Barons for all the wrong reasons. Unlike most members of the Barons, these three weren't the type to participate in charity rides, fundraisers, or community events. They had their own agendas.

One of the men stayed behind the steering wheel of the red truck, scrolling through his phone and singing a country song Cody didn't recognize.

The second man was Duke Bristol, but Cody had only ever met his cousin Aaron. The two cousins looked almost identical. Duke was leaning on the back of the truck with his elbows and staring at Cody blankly.

The third man with Levi was a young biker named Jeremy Morrison—better known as Cricket. He was sitting on the tailgate of a red truck, holding an energy drink to his lips while he scrolled his phone's screen. The last time Cody saw Cricket, the kid was studying for his general diploma. Cody always liked the impressionable kid, but here he was now all grown up and running with the wrong crowd.

"About time," Levi said to Cody.

"We agreed to meet at ten—you're early. Do you have it?"

Levi answered the question by reaching around his back, withdrawing a pistol, and handing it to Cody. "Taurus 1911, 9 mm Luger with a five-inch stainless steel barrel. Nine-round capacity and semi-automatic action."

"Does it shoot bullets? 'Cause that's all I friggin care about." Cody racked the slide back, which would have pushed a bullet into the chamber, but the pistol lacked its magazine.

Levi presented the loaded magazine, "Six rounds in the mag, so use them wisely."

The gun's weight was heavier on Cody's soul than his hand. He disliked the idea of carrying the 1911, but he had to be prepared for his confrontation with Jesse Lewis. He had no idea what he was up against. For all he knew, Jesse could be armed. There were reports of several hunting camps being broken into, and he might have found a rifle at some point. Cody pointed the gun to the ground and peeked through the sites, getting accustomed to the view.

Cricket sprung from the Chevy's tailgate and fist-bumped Cody. "Been a long time Cody. It's good to see you. You'll like that piece—I shoot it down at the range sometimes. Fits my hand like a cold beer bottle." He opened his hand wide, stared at his palm, then turned his attention to the gun.

"I don't intend to use it. I'm just being overly cautious. Jesse Lewis is more dangerous than he looks, and I need him alive."

Cricket's red eyes widened like he just remembered why the interest in the former pastor. "Oh, yeah, that's right. They say Pastor Lewis has psychic powers and can lift shit with his mind."

Cody scowled, "I don't think that second part is true—at least, I hope not."

Levi interrupted, "Don't forget our deal, Savage. You find Jesse Lewis and get what you need. Then, his ass is mine. You bring him to me." He thumped his chest with a heavy fist.

"I haven't forgotten, Levi," Cody said, but he was thinking, *no way in hell I'm going to hand Jesse to you to murder.*

"Need anything else?" Levi asked.

Cody checked the caller ID on his phone. AJ still hadn't returned his call. "Yeah," he said, looking at the second truck parked in his driveway. "I could really use that for a couple of days." He pointed to a Suzuki 500 ATV in the back of the Chevy.

"Sure," Levi said, "But Amos won't be too happy. That's his four-wheeler."

Before Cody could ask who Amos was, Levi whistled and called his name. The truck door opened, and a man larger than Levi stepped out. Amos McGrath was four inches taller than a six-foot man. His beard, eyes, and hair were all dark, with a crimson face that was most likely from something other than sunburn—perhaps a medical condition. His size intimidated the rest of the Barons but not Levi. A tattoo of a Scottish flag and a lion adorned his left forearm, and Cody was sure there were more beneath his clothes. Although the temperature outside was creeping toward eighty-three, Amos wore worn out denim pants and a long sleeve shirt rolled up to his elbows. The shirt was burgundy, with no graphics displayed.

"Amos, this is Cody. He's going to borrow your four-wheeler for a couple of days."

"Like hell he is," Amos barked at Levi. "You know I was planning to take Tish's nephew fishing later at Sutter's Pond. We're going to need my four-wheeler to ride out there."

"Why don't you just hike?" Levi advised.

"Three miles in; three miles out? Screw that, Levi. I ain't walkin' no six miles to catch trout."

"I wasn't asking for your permission, Amos," Levi barked back.

Amos shook his head, "Not happening. He wants it; he'll have to go through me."

Cody stepped closer to Amos, and the two men stood only four feet apart. "Look, Amos, I can't cover enough ground without a vehicle." He held up his bandaged hand, which swelled and throbbed under his bandages. "I can't operate a clutch. I need something I can drive with one hand, so I'd appreciate it if you just let me borrow it for a day or two.

I'll take good care of it."

Amos took a step toward Cody. He stood five inches taller and forty pounds heavier. He took the key for the four-wheeler out of his pocket and dangled it in front of Cody. "You want it; come take it."

Cody took a half-step back, "Fine. It's okay; I'll find another way to get around." He scanned his property, knowing there was no other option.

"That's what I thought—chicken shit."

Cody took a half-step forward.

"Amos, just give him the key before someone gets hurt," Levi said.

"Are you worried about this piece of shit after he killed your sister, Levi?" Amos said.

Cody's skin burned from within.

Levi leaned back and took a sideways seat on his parked motorcycle, waiting for the the two men to settle their dispute, "Actually, Amos, I'm worried you might get hurt."

"By this one-armed ass-hat?" Amos chuckled. "Cricket scares me more than this asshole."

Cricket flipped his middle finger skyward, "Screw you, Amos."

Cody forgot about the key. He forgot about his brother, and he forgot about his missing hand. But he remembered his wife and how her life was taken by a man that wanted to possess her like a trophy. A man who was sick and confused because she reminded him of his dead wife. He didn't want a fight right now, but Amos was pushing buttons for no reason other than he believed Cody had killed Willa. If nothing else, Cody needed to shut the big man up—shove his ego in the mud.

Amos made the first move, reaching for Cody's shirt collar. He didn't care that Cody was missing a hand, and Cody read the man as a true bully. Cody hated bullies.

Amos' big hand never reached the T-shirt Cody was wearing. Cody stepped forward and threw his left arm in a circular motion, wrapping it around Amos' attacking right arm. The arm lock only stopped Amos for a moment. The bully pulled hard to release Cody's grip.

Amos felt something sharp strike the bridge of his nose, followed by a painful tingle that spread across both cheekbones. It wasn't until he tasted blood running down his throat that he realized Cody's knuckles had struck the blow. The big man reacted with rage, lunging for Cody's neck with both hands.

Cody threw both of his arms up, elbows forward, in defense. He knocked both Amos' arms outward, followed by thrusting his bony elbows into Amos' chest. The force knocked Amos backward, which was Cody's intent. He planned to keep the aggressor at a safe distance so that he could throw kicks or punches. He knew there was no way he'd be able to defend himself in a ground fight with only one hand.

As Amos stumbled backward, Cody followed with a kick to Amos' midsection, which knocked the wind out of his opponent. Amos hit the truck behind him with his back and fell to his knees. He was breathless, gasping for air like a fish on the beach. Once he finally stood, the air returned to his lungs, and he breathed the sweet sensation. He had more fight left in him but decided to save himself from further embarrassment.

As Cody stepped backward to put some space between them, Amos came up like a wobbling boxer after a tenth-round knockdown, using the side of the truck to haul himself to his feet. He was holding the four-wheeler key in his left hand, pissed off that he'd underestimated Cody's fighting skills.

"I warned you, Amos," Levi said. "Now get your damn four-wheeler off the truck. We've got other shit to do."

Amos followed the orders with assistance from the third man, then Cody climbed onto the four-wheeler and started the 500 cc engine. The machine growled a little, then settled down and purred like a satisfied lion.

"Be careful, brother," Levi said. "I don't want to hear the next corpse they find is yours."

Cody thanked Levi, threw his lightly packed bag on his shoulders, and sped down the road.

Levi watched the machine, and its driver disappear in a cloud of dust until Amos slammed the tailgate shut on the rusty Ford. Amos wiped his bloody nose with his hand, "Think you can trust him?"

Levi threw a pair of Rayban sunglasses over his eyes, "No. No, I think he'll take that sonovabitch straight to the sheriff. So we need to make sure he doesn't. No matter what, Jesse Lewis can't go to prison."

14

FEATHERS & BLOOD

Bourbon, Flesti, and Hetzen hiked for three hours, utilizing the energy from the walleye they had at breakfast. The calories from consuming the fish were wearing off, but Bourbon was only focused on his goal. Jesse Lewis could be packed up and on the move again, creating more distance between them. Flesti knew where the serial killer was camping, and Bourbon wanted to make sure they got to him before he pulled stakes and ran.

Or maybe he couldn't run any longer. Perhaps the injury he suffered three weeks ago had taken its toll. The night Jesse and Cody fell through a second-story window onto the porch's roof and then dropped to the lawn, Jesse landed on a garden rake. The injury should have crippled him, but the ground, soft from the rain, absorbed the impact.

Bourbon rubbed his back, thinking about how that must have hurt like hell.

He stopped for a drink of water, but his thermal bottle only offered a few sips. He leaned against a high rock, not quite in a sitting position, and waited for Flesti to catch up to him. She shared her water, then poured a small amount in her cupped hand for the dog. Hetzen lapped up the water in seconds.

"You're not sweating," she said to Bourbon.

"No. Not really. Guess I'm getting used to the heat." His speech was slow, and he had to spit the dry words out to make a sentence.

"You're not getting used to anything; you're overheated. Follow me. We need to cool you down before you have a damn heatstroke."

"No, we gotta keep moving...toward Jesse's camp."

"You stubborn fool. You'll die out here if you don't stop and rest. You'll never catch Jesse Lewis if you're dead. Now, follow with me."

Bourbon couldn't stop her. Flesti turned and started down a steep bank, following a deer trail through a patch of shrubs that would be thick with blackberries in a month. They moved with caution as the thorny brambles reached out and stung their skin. Bourbon felt a needle dig into the thin skin of his right elbow. With the opposite hand, he pulled the branch away, releasing the woody talons and letting the blood flow from the punctures in his skin.

A cedar waxwing with earthy brown feathers, a black mask, and a touch of yellow on his tail flickered through the shrub, branch by branch, as if it had memorized the whole maze of thorny wires.

For a moment, Bourbon watched the bird flutter through the branches and stems and wondered if the bird ever got stuck or bloody. It occurred to him that the bird didn't mind the danger of the brambles but relied on it for safety. Here, no predator could catch the flying creature. As dangerous as this environment was for his predators, the blackberry thorns were a sanctuary for the waxwing.

He also wondered if Jesse Lewis would take sanctuary in a similar place. He knew he was being hunted. What lengths would he go to hide from those who wanted his head upon a spike?

Flesti gave a little whistle and motioned with her hand to keep moving. Bourbon obeyed, sliding sideways along the narrow trail for another twelve feet until he cleared the treacherous thorns. Two streaks of blood from his elbow ran down his forearm and merged, stopping just above his wrist.

They walked downhill until the trees grew more spacious, and the couple entered a small clearing of tall grass and open sky. The scent of Cain Lake—just a wisp in the wind—teased Bourbon's nose, and he knew they were close to the sandy shore. Trace scents of seaweed, clay, fish, and a hint of pine, beckoned him to the clear water. They stopped near the rocky beach in the shadow of a large cedar tree and put their backpacks down. Bourbon's shoulders felt light. He stretched the tense muscles in his neck, realizing how much tension they were under.

Flesti stripped her clothes off while she watched Hetzen wade into the cool dark water. He swam in a small circle while watching a pair of Canada geese with six goslings. While the dog held Flesti's gaze, she held Bourbon's. He stood at the edge of the cool lake, removing his clothes with a bit more reluctance.

Flesti plunged beneath the surface with the grace of an otter, so Bourbon shyly finished stripping and waded in behind her. He stood waist-deep, waiting for her to surface. She finally appeared.

"Come on, it will cool you down," She said.

"Give me a minute," He said. "It's cold. I need to acclimate." He looked into the water around him, spinning back and forth as if the water was infested with piranha.

Flesti understood his phobia, splashed the water a little, and giggled at him. "They don't bite. They're perfectly safe."

"Yeah, well, they still creep me out."

Hetzen swam back to shore, stopped behind Bourbon, and shook the excess water from his fur coat. The frigid water sprayed Bourbon's back, shocking his body, and he jumped forward in a half fall, half dive, into deeper water. His feet left the lake bottom, and he treaded water toward Flesti.

She laughed and took a few strokes toward him, "See, doesn't this feel wonderful?"

They swam for ten minutes while Hetzen lay in the sun's warm rays. He kept his keen senses focused on his master.

Bourbon watched his companion dive to the bottom repeatedly, her ass rising from the surface every time she submerged. For ten minutes, he'd forgotten about Jesse Lewis. He'd forgotten about Annabel Thompson. He'd forgotten about the body he'd found the day before.

Images flooded his mind of his teenage years, swimming in the lake with Monica Pearson, fishing the shores with Carl Tice and Larry Hix, and driving the little fishing boat his father had restored. So many happy memories were linked to Cain Lake, and now Cain Lake seemed to be linked to everything wicked happening in Stoneville.

He'd been enjoying his swim so much that he failed to recognize the micropods that swarmed around him. When he finally noticed them, they were running a pattern around his body, swimming around his chest and hips, flowing between his legs and ankles. He began to feel some comfort regarding this phenomenon. The little micropods felt like a life jacket, ensuring the man stayed afloat.

When he finally had enough, he backstroked toward shore, leaving Flesti soaking in the lake. He exited with more confidence than he had entered. His muscles felt invigorated. He was strong and eager to recommence their hike to find Jesse Lewis, although he could have been convinced to stay here all day. He redressed himself while watching her swim. He even threw a stick into the water for Hetzen to fetch, but the dog was uninterested in the game.

Flesti finally walked out of the lake to join him. The two stood face-to-face as she dressed in the hot summer sun.

"Feel better?" Flesti asked.

"Amazing, actually. Thank you, Flesti. I didn't realize how hot I was."

"No one does, until it's too late. Try to be more careful and slow down. Okay? Sometimes you can get where you're going faster by taking it slow."

They both picked up their gear, and started the climb up the steep hill that led to the footpath they'd been following all morning. The sun was at its peak now, but they stayed cool under the forest canopy, making their way south. Flesti led the way this time, and Bourbon decided it was okay to slow their pace. They still had plenty of daylight left to continue their hike.

They'd only traveled 300 yards when Bourbon recognized a familiar sight; two turkey vultures perched on the ground ahead. Their red heads bobbed up and down, feeding on a meal out of Bourbon's view. He stopped momentarily and prayed the raptorial birds were devouring a deer or raccoon. He pointed the grisly scene out to Flesti. She studied the activity for a moment with a stoic pose.

Bourbon approached. His heart knocked against his sternum, and he visibly shook. He hesitated while Flesti passed him to examine the scene. The corpse he had found yesterday was still fresh in his mind, and he hoped not to add to the horror.

Flesti took her tall walking stick and pushed aside a short pine tree so she had a clearer view. Hetzen shot past her with a low bark and growl, and the two birds spread their wings and took flight. The mutt circled the area and returned to Flesti's side purely instinctually.

Flesti turned to Bourbon, "It's not good. Not good at all. Look's like we have another victim. "

"Fuck!" Bourbon cursed. Anger doused his fear, and the big man trudged forward until he was staring down at the face of another murder victim. Flesti circled and approached the body from the other side, giving Bourbon space to deal with his emotions.

Flesti expected the former Sheriff to act professionally, stay back, and not contaminate the scene. But Bourbon fell to his knees, put his right hand over the dead man's heart, and began to sob.

"You knew him?"

It took Bourbon a moment to compose himself, "Yes. Yes, it's Andrew Mills. His father and I were friends—went into the Army together." He stood, shaking his head in disbelief. "This kid didn't deserve this."

"Was he a sinner?"

"No. He was a good kid. Tried to rob Tabitha's Diner last month because he was hungry, not greedy. He was only guilty of being stupid. He was out on bail, waiting for his trial."

A turkey vulture boldly returned to the scene and perched on a tree limb just ten feet off the ground. It stared with hungry eyes down at the deceased young man at Bourbon's feet.

Bourbon reacted with anger and guilt. A volcano erupted inside him as he drew his pistol, "Fuck off!" The bird exploded in a puff of feathers and blood. Flesti watched in horror as the body dropped twenty feet from where it had been sitting. Hetzen darted away, stopping twenty yards behind Flesti, and hid behind a large tree. Poe disappeared in the tree boughs, squawking in protest.

Feathers fell in unison to Bourbon's tears. The outburst cooled the magma flowing through his veins, and Bourbon composed himself. He holstered the Smith & Wesson, hoping the second buzzard would heed the warning.

Bourbon checked his phone, but he had no service this far south, "I need to let Sheriff Hassett know. And his mom. I need to let Andrew's mom know."

"Well, you can turn back, but it will make more sense to keep going around the lake. There are more houses and vehicles on the other side. You can catch a ride back to town."

Bourbon agreed with her suggestion. He took a shirt from his backpack and covered Andrew's body, hoping the human scent would keep coyotes and other scavengers away. He said a little prayer, loud enough for Flesti to hear, but he wasn't sure anyone else was listening.

They regained their elevation as they marched up the trail that led the way. When they arrived at a rocky pinnacle, Flesti pointed over the lake with her walking stick.

Bourbon squeezed the wood handle of his holstered pistol. "Good. Let's keep moving."

The fire in his eyes made Flesti a little nervous. She wondered if Jesse Lewis would suffer the same fate as the vulture or if Bourbon would cool down as they hiked the next mile. She was certain Bourbon wanted the killer dead, but it would take pure hate to pull the trigger on another human. She didn't think Bourbon had that in him. He was a good person—the last good man she knew. But men change, even if they don't mean to.

"Let's go," He said. "I've got a bullet with that murdering bastard's name on it."

15
WILD GOOSE CHASE

Sheriff Hassett drove her Jeep Gladiator over the south bridge of Cain Lake. The bridge had been resurfaced with concrete within the last year and received a fresh coat of green paint last week to protect the metal railings running along the entire length. The truck crawled down the bridge and stopped at the midpoint. It was a good view from here. There were no trees to block her vista of the calm lake, and she could see all the way across, although much of the ragged shoreline was hidden in deep bays.

Hassett pushed the Jeep door open and stepped to the side of the bridge. She pressed her eyes to a pair of Leupold binoculars and scanned the shore.

Deputy Dave Simpson left Hassett at the midpoint of the bridge while he walked the length. He peered over the rail at the slow-moving water below. This was the southernmost point of Cain Lake, where every bit of water eventually flowed. If something floated away during a storm or fell off a boat, this was the place to find it. Simpson studied the little eddies created by the bridge's pillars, watching for anything unusual. He walked the entire length of the bridge—407 feet—and back and rejoined Hassett in the same spot he'd left her.

"Anything?" Simpson asked.

"Maybe," she said, handing the binoculars to her deputy. "Take a look at those pines on the east shore."

Simpson turned to his right with the optics to his eyes. The shoreline was rocky, with various size boulders protecting the land from erosion. The granite fence, irregular in size and shape, was covered with moss and shadows from the mature pines that grew adjacent to the water. Simpson studied the thick evergreens, looking for anything out of place.

A thick hemlock tree caught his attention three hundred yards up the shoreline. One side of the tree appeared to have many limbs cut to the trunk. The pruning had stopped about six feet off the ground—the height of a man.

"Looks like someone's been doing a little trimming," Simpson said.

"Could be nothing—or anyone—a fisherman, hiker, or backcountry camper."

"Probably worth a look, though."

"Agreed."

The duo picked out a tall dead tamarack tree that defied gravity, despite its poor health. The tree was just fifty feet from the area they wanted to search, and its bare trunk and limbs were easy to spot from a distance. They'd use the tamarack as a landmark to guide them to their destination.

They climbed back into the patrol vehicle and drove a quarter of a mile from the bridge, keeping track of the dead tree. Hassett pulled the truck over when they were close. As they parked, the Jeep's wheels straddled a shallow ditch beside the road. They closed their doors quietly, keeping the noise minimal and their voices a whisper.

Simpson opened the vehicle's back door and retrieved a twelve-gage shotgun and a box of buckshot. Hassett opted for the same. They would be in thick foliage that hindered the distance of visibility. Any encounter with Jesse Lewis would be close, intimate, and possibly deadly. The shotguns would respond quickly to any threat, allowing the two officers to take less time to aim. The buckshot ammunition would scatter but would be heavy enough to penetrate the evergreen limbs with less deflection than a small-pellet shell.

Simpson circled the truck and held out his hand with three extra shotgun shells for the sheriff. She cupped her hand over the yellow shells and grasped all three. She observed dark green paint on Simpson's hand.

"Is that from the bridge?" She checked her own hands for a similar transfer of paint.

Simpson looked at his hand, "That? No. No, it's paint from my garage. I was cleaning up this morning. Must have gotten it off a bucket."

"Oh, thank goodness. I was leaning on the railing and was afraid I had it all over me."

They gently closed the truck doors and stepped off the road into the thick woods. Simpson led the way, meandering through the bushy evergreens that grew on the hillside. The road exceeded the lake's altitude, so they moved downhill toward the water.

When they lost their sense of direction, the tall tamarack realigned them with their destination. Simpson kept his eyes on the dead tree and the sun to his left. After walking seventy-five yards, they could see the glassy water below.

A squirrel, upside down on the trunk of a Scotch pine, chattered in protest to Hassett and Simpson's presence. Twenty yards away, another squirrel joined in—their furry red tails flicking up and down in synchronicity to their vocal chirps.

Hassett stepped lightly and felt like an intruder in this beautiful scene. She wasn't accustomed to the rigors of hiking through the Adirondack woods. In the past, she went for long walks with her sister but always sensed they were being watched. It didn't matter where she went or what time of day—she felt this way every time she stepped into the rugged landscape. It made her feel so small and insignificant.

Simpson stopped twenty feet before the water's edge, holding his green-stained palm toward Hassett. She stopped. She didn't realize it at first, but she caught herself holding her breath to hear better.

It was silent.

Simpson continued as Hassett followed his lead. She admired his keen sense of the woods. His experience in this environment was evident, with quiet steps, perfect balance, and the ability to navigate without a trail. She wished she had spent more time in the woods as a child rather than riding her scooter down the sidewalks of Chicago.

Simpson had his shotgun to his shoulder with the barrel pointing the way. Hassett hadn't seen him do it, so she followed his lead and shouldered her own weapon, carefully keeping the muzzle pointed at the ground.

The smell of smoke mixed with the scent of pine, and Hassett was taken back to the times she camped with her family. They would always go to Lake Shelbyville—fire burning, marshmallows toasting, pine pitch stuck to her bare feet. It's where they'd go every Independence Day weekend and a place she'd hoped to take her kids someday—but she never had any.

"Psst, boss. Boss," Simpson's voice pulled her from the memory. His voice was a whisper, but in the silent forest, it was loud in her ear.

"Right behind you, Simpson."

They stepped into a small opening where the terrain was more level than the hillside they had descended. A small fire pit, no larger than a car tire, was centered in the middle. A makeshift tent, formed from a camouflaged tarp, draped over a rope. Some litter was scattered as though the camp's occupant was scavenging from local cottages. The occupant, however, was nowhere to be found.

Hassett explored a narrow path, no wider than a deer trail, that led her to the lake shore. She brushed the trimmed pine with her hand and looked south to the bridge where she had parked just forty-five minutes ago.

The lake was calm, with just a few boats floating free on a windless day. It was too hot to be fishing, but a handful of anglers would be on the water around dinner time. A lone jet skier passed two hundred yards from where Hassett stood. She was annoyed by the whining engine as it cut through the tranquility like a chainsaw outside the window of a yoga studio.

Two geese swam offshore. They were fifty, maybe sixty, yards away. The pair were nearly motionless, keeping together so close that they sometimes looked like one. Hassett watched them momentarily, lost in their grace and envious of their contentment to float upon Cain Lake's pristine surface.

"Well," Simpson interrupted her peace. "He's definitely been here." He held up a bible and a necklace ornamented with a silver cross. "Fire pit still has a little heat, and there's a wet towel hanging on that branch." He pointed east to a ragged cloth in a tree.

Hassett turned toward the camp and inspected the evidence Simpson was presenting. She noticed medical supplies and two bloody bandages. "Then he can't be far. Let's get back to the Jeep. Call in for some help. We create a grid of this area—ten acres—and close in on this sonovabitch."

"Think we should call Bourbon?"

"Call anyone who can help. Call Bourbon, that former deputy—what's his name? Birchtree?"

"Birchcraft. Eli Birchcraft."

"Call him. Call his friends," Her chest heaved. "Fuck, call your mother if you have to. We need all the help we can get. And dogs. We're going to need dogs. This little prick is close. Let's not let him get any farther away."

They made haste to climb back up the hill to the truck but maintained their silence. They didn't want to alert Jesse Lewis to their presence, even though it was probably too late. Simpson tried to call Marissa back at the office but his phone had no signal.

"No service here," Simpson said. "We'll have to get out past the bridge to get service."

Hassett scanned the hillside one more time. They needed gear, food, water, and short-wave radios. Their trip out here had been an impromptu decision based on an anonymous call about the possible sighting of Jesse Lewis near the bridge. Now, it turned into their best opportunity to catch the killer, but they weren't prepared for a night or two in the woods.

Hassett occupied the driver's seat of the off-road truck and made a three-point turn to head back to town. Time was of the essence now, so she drove the vehicle as if her life depended on it. They meandered down the narrow road until the vehicle was seventy yards from the South Bridge. Hassett hit the brakes as a red Suzuki four-wheeler shot across the bridge toward them and veered off the road. It made its way up a dusty trail, spinning rocks and dirt. The driver, too intent on his destination, never looked their way. Hassett watched the powerful machine climb the rugged terrain of Bobcat Trail and disappear among the trees.

"Was that...? Was that Cody Savage?" Hassett asked Simpson.

"Sure was, boss."

"Where the hell is he going?"

"Maybe he used his psychic powers and knows where Jesse Lewis is."

Hassett gave Simpson a 'don't start that shit' look. She took her foot off the brake, and resumed motion. "If Savage finds Jesse Lewis first, we're going to have a big problem. So we better not let that happen."

16

DUST & DOUBT 

With the four-wheeler unloaded from the truck and a pistol in his pocket, Cody was eager to begin searching for his brother. He didn't stick around long enough to watch Levi and his three friends drive away.

He knew once he journeyed deep into the woods, cell phone service would be hit-or-miss. Cain Lake had a way of choking cell phone service, which could leave him vulnerable in an emergency. So he stopped a half-mile down the road and tried Daisy's phone number. She didn't answer. She was mad, he knew, but he could smooth things over when he got back.

The Suzuki's engine restarted immediately with a twist of the ignition key. Cody drove away, spinning loose gravel on the side of the road. He headed south, turned left on Cherry Street, and ignored the speed limits. He wanted to get to the woods as fast as possible, so he drove like hell, punching the throttle as he exited the corners. No one looked twice at the off-road vehicle tearing down the pavement. They were used to ATVs circling Cain Lake to access camps and hunting land. The motley assortment of transportation usually passed through here in late summer and peaked in early fall. It was early summer, which meant the trails would be empty today. He'd be the only person navigating the area.

Cherry Street and Grandview Road formed an intersection near the lake, but crossing over Grandview put him at the local Methodist church. The church stood tall, empty, looking over the lake like a sentry post. Cody parked at the intersection, knowing that driving any further would only be a distraction. He killed the engine of the machine he was riding and sat in silence for a moment. There was an overwhelming sense of guilt scratching him from the inside.

This is where it all began; he and Willa's wedding, Jesse Lewis becoming pastor, the Sin-eater hungry to take lives. This is where good people came to confess their sins, hoping to be forgiven. But Pastor Jesse exploited that knowledge and passed his own judgment, killing the guilty and stealing their sins. And then, by some evil force of nature, fed the sins to the lake. Cody still didn't understand why or how the lake devoured sins, but he didn't care.

He thought about burning the church down for a moment until a movie clip of Willa popped into his brain like a TV commercial. She was walking down the narrow aisle of the crowded church with a smile that rivaled Daisy's. She carried a bouquet of her favorite flowers, but they were pale compared to her beauty. That's the memory he decided to associate with the church.

He thought about the cemetery on the hill, behind the church, and the little headstone with his wife's name engraved on both sides. He wanted to climb the hill, say hello, and visit for a while. But there was someone who needed him more right now. Time wasn't a luxury.

Once again, he restarted the four-wheeler and continued his course. He never looked back, but he knew Willa would understand.

He didn't traverse more than a quarter-mile of asphalt when he felt his phone vibrate in his pocket. The engine overpowered the sound of the ringer. He pulled over, jumped off the ATV, and answered the call.

"Hello," Cody answered.

"I knew you wouldn't come." The voice on the line said.

"Alyse? I'm sorry. I'm so, so, sorry."

"It's okay, Cody. I understand—"

"No, it's not. I mean...well....this is my brother's life on the line. I need to find him."

She was silent for a moment; when she did speak, her voice was melancholy, "You won't see me again. I'm catching the next bus to Watertown and flying out from there. I just wanted to say goodbye."

"I know, Alyse. I'm sorry we couldn't say goodbye in person. I don't suppose there's any chance you'll change your mind?"

"No. I can't. I'm not sure why I came here years ago. I should have stayed in Louisiana. Something just drew me here...I think it was you."

Cody laughed at her remark, but she was being serious.

They said their goodbyes, knowing the fire between them burned too hot to control. They were in love, but that didn't mean they were good together. Cody knew Daisy, not Alyse, would keep his life in check—keep him out of prison and alive. Daisy was like a highway, keeping him straight and safe for the long journey ahead.

Alyse was like a drag strip.

Alyse disconnected the call and their friendship.

Cody pocketed the phone. The trees were his only company now. AJ was in the wind; no contact since last night at The Mineshaft. Alyse was leaving town, probably never to be seen again. Daisy was pissed and worried he was going to get himself killed. Bourbon had been gone for weeks; hopefully, he was still alive.

He'd never felt so alone.

The tears were impossible to stop, so he let them fall for a few breaths.

But only a few.

As much as he hated it, the gun felt good in his hand. He prayed Jesse Lewis wouldn't make him use it. He returned the pistol to his belt line, climbed back on the four-wheeled horse, and headed for the south bridge. The engine was hot on his legs, exacerbating the summer heat and making his blue jeans stick to his legs. He kept the RPMs and speed low, scouring Cain Lake as he drove. He assumed Jesse Lewis would stay far enough from the lake to be obscure but close enough to access the water.

Cody stopped temporarily on the bridge. He sat on the four-wheeler—engine idling like his thoughts—scanning the shore's wood line and his destination.

"Here I come, asshole."

He thumbed the throttle and was instantly propelled to the end of the bridge. He spotted a vehicle racing down the road toward him. It was Sheriff Hassett and her deputy in their Jeep truck. Cody put downward pressure on the brakes, then decided against stopping. He gave the Suzuki the gas it craved and once again he was racing.

He veered right, onto a trail that connected to a network of old logging roads. He intended to stay close to the lake but off the main road. He was sure the sheriff didn't recognize him, or she probably would have tried to stop him with her lights and siren—no way was he stopping now.

He left a cloud of dust and doubt behind, focused on the rough terrain and his objective—find the Sin-eater.

17

WOUNDED KNEE

Bourbon was silent for the next thirty minutes. The discovery of Andrew Mill's body was one of the worst things he'd ever witnessed in his entire career. Of course, he'd been around dead bodies before, but it never hit home like this. He remembered seeing the college kid a few weeks ago at Tabitha's Diner. Andrew had hit rock bottom, and this is where it led him.

The killer had carved those infamous six letters in his abdomen, impossible to erase from skin or mind. He checked the heigth of the sun over the horizon to guess the time. Noon was probably an hour away.

He wasn't hungry. For the first time in weeks, the thought of eating made him sick, guilty. He wanted to sit down and relieve the burning in his thighs, but his temper pushed him forward, disregarding all pain and suffering like a great wave from the lake bearing down on him. He just kept going; no water, no food, no rest, no more forgiveness in his heart.

Flesti had trouble keeping pace, but she wouldn't dare ask him to slow down now. She understood how he felt. She'd seen enough death in her lifetime to fill the valley they occupied. She kept a keen eye on Bourbon, and there was no need to call out directions anymore. They had a view of the lake from the cliff they were on. If they wandered toward the lake, they would encounter a forty-foot drop; walking too far uphill would bring them to Grandview Road. The road would be easier to trek, but it gradually veered away from the lake before meandering again. It would add miles to their journey. They made a straight line for the boat ramp. From there, they would stay close to shore until they reached

Jesse's campsite.

Hetzen's innate nature to lead kept him zig-zagging in front of Bourbon. The dog's desire to stay at the front of the pack was annoying the former Sheriff, and Flesti could sense his mood by his body language.

She gave a short whistle with her lips and clicked her tongue, signaling the black dog to her side, "Hetz'. Come here, boy."

The dog turned one hundred eighty degrees and plowed past Bourbon. Hetzen tried to squeeze between Bourbon and an ash tree, but the dog had no sense of his size. Bourbon felt his left knee buckle against Hetzen's weight. Losing his balance, Bourbon fell forward and tried to catch himself against a dead tree about as fat as a baseball bat. The rotten tree was no match for Bourbon's weight. It broke and Bourbon rolled to the right and tumbled, his backpack pulling him down a six-foot embankment.

His curse words were kept to himself. He was trying not to give their approach away in case Jesse Lewis was within earshot.

"Bourbon," Flesti whispered as loudly as she could. "Are you all right?"

"Yeah, I think so," Bourbon answered from under his pack. He rolled to his side and sat up. He was leaning on a small boulder that narrowly missed his head. He tried to stand. "Sonova...." He sat back down. "Maybe not."

Flesti removed her backpack and carefully descended the hill covered with slick wet leaves. "What's wrong?"

"It's my knee, dammit. I think I sprained it." *Fucking dog.*

She helped him stand and passed her hiking stick to him. Utilizing the crutch for support, he grasped some small trees and pulled himself back up the steep hill. Flesti followed with his heavy backpack in hand.

Above him, Poe watched with sharp eyes, cawing at the commotion below. Bourbon assumed the bird was entertained by his fall. *Laugh it up, feathered frigger, but remember what happened to the last bird that pissed me off.*

When they were back on the trail, Bourbon hoisted his pack to his shoulders, disregarding the anguish the weight brought to his injured knee. He commenced his hike at a slower pace, limping along with his body weight partially supported by Flesti's six-foot hiking stick.

"Are you sure you can keep going?"

"Hell couldn't stop me now—not when we're this close."

Hetzen stayed behind Flesti. The dog sensed Bourbon's frustration, and the intelligent canine hadn't forgotten the havoc the former lawman's pistol produced. Poe flew higher than usual after witnessing the feather explosion. He kept to the treetops now, vocalizing in short caws on occasion.

The foursome started to descend the high hills that hugged Cain Lake. Bourbon knew they were almost to the boat launch when they arrived at Shiner's Brook, a cool mountain stream that fed clear water into Cain Lake. The babbling water was a tremendous relief from the high-noon sun. Bourbon stripped his pack and splashed water over his face.

They were all glad to arrive at the freshwater creek.

Flesti filled her canteen, saving the water to boil and drink later. Hetzen seemed unconcerned with the brook's sanity and lapped it with his long pink tongue. He was upstream of Bourbon, and the ex-sheriff watched in disgust as drool floated by, so he struggled to get around the dog and to the fresh flowing water above.

"You should rest a bit," Flesti said.

"For a moment...no more." He rubbed the sore knee.

"We need to follow the brook down to the lake, let you soak that knee for a bit. We can make our way along the shallows from there. Walking along the beaches should be easier. And less hazardous."

Bourbon nodded in agreement, conceding to her wishes as the swelling in his knee began to throb. He sat on a rock, splashed some cool liquid on his knee, and rubbed it vigorously. His actions gave the knee some relief. Then he stood abruptly, listening to the sound that stirred behind them on the crest of the hill.

"You hear that?" Bourbon asked.

"Been hearing it for the last three minutes."

A dull roar of a four-wheeler engine revved behind them up the hill. The sound of the cascading water had hidden the sound until the machine was close enough to overpower the white noise of Shiner's Brook.

"Probably just someone out for a joyride," Bourbon said.

Flesti just shrugged, "I hear them all the time, ripping and tearing up through that trail. They tear the hill apart and create ruts that let the rainwater wash away the sand."

"They mean no harm."

Flesti didn't seem convinced, "They're a plague on the ecosystem. Them and those damn motorcycles that tour the roads around the lake. Every one of them should be parked—permanently."

Bourbon could sense that it was a sore subject with Flesti. He chose not to provoke her any further. Her voice was getting louder as she verbalized her opinion, and stealth was their greatest ally if they were going to find Jesse Lewis.

Satisfied with the short rest, Bourbon stood, gripped the hardwood walking stick, and hoisted his gear to his back. Flesti knew this was the last time they would stop until they reached their destination. She hoped Bourbon would heed her advice about walking the shoreline. She felt exhaustion creep into her muscles and knew Cain Lake would rejuvenate her body and spirit.

They didn't traverse more than fifty yards from the brook, and Bourbon stopped again. Hetzen regained his spot at the front of the pack, but the dog had stopped dead, smelling the air and staring downhill to a thick row of tag alders. The shrubby trees were a sign they were close to the lake's marshy shore.

"What is it, boy?" Bourbon whispered to the dog. Hetzen let out a long growl that was barely audible.

Flesti caught up to Bourbon, putting her hand on his shoulder. For the first time in a month, Bourbon was feeling the touch of another human being—a female's touch. He felt his body relax and a cool chill climb the nape of his neck. It wasn't the chill one feels from an eerie encounter or a cool night, but rather the sensation of calm drowning the heat of stress.

Bourbon pointed down the hill toward a row of tangled tag alders. Tree branches moved slightly, but the wind speed wasn't more than two miles-per-hour. The branches bent and swayed from the weight of an obscure force.

Bourbon hoped to see a wild animal, like the magnificent white-tail buck that presented itself that morning. Still, his sheriff instincts kicked in, and he took a grip on his holstered Smith & Wesson without drawing the weapon.

Flesti leaned into him, trying share his field of view.

Bourbon leaned into Flesti ever so slightly and whispered into her ear, "Someone's coming."

18
THE VOICES

Bourbon was staring down the sights of his favorite pistol. His hand was moist with sweat, which paled in comparison to the water running down his brow, but his grip was tight, his hand steady. He didn't realize he was smiling, but he couldn't help himself. The target made his way up the hill, pulling himself with the small trees well anchored by their roots. His grip slipped, and the target fell, a clumsy faceplant into the soft leaves, then stood abruptly and recommenced his climb.

Bourbon watched the clumsy hiker ascend like a wounded buck trying to follow a doe—too tired to keep up, too stubborn to die.

Within minutes, Jesse Lewis finally looked up to see Jeff Bourbon's steely eyes staring back at him. Once he realized those eyes were behind the Smith & Wesson, his stubbornness slipped away, falling back to the foot of the hill he had so ardently climbed. Jesse fell to his knees, conceding, forfeiting, but not apologetic.

"Please," Bourbon pleaded. "Try to run. Give me just one more excuse to put this bullet through your skull 'cause I'm done chasing you, asshole."

Bourbon deferred to rid the world of Jesse Lewis because, until this moment, he wasn't absolutely sure the man approaching was the man he'd been hunting. The person before him was a hollow shell, thirty pounds lighter than the Sin-eater. This man was ragged with a sand-blasted face from the sun and wind. This man had ribs showing through his wet T-shirt. This man looked more like a marathon runner from a third-world country than the stout and athletic pastor who nearly put a bullet through Bourbon three weeks prior.

But it was his elusive quarry. It was Jesse Lewis. His life on the run had been grueling, consuming his body and spirit. It was apparent that Jesse Lewis had no natural ability to survive the wilds of Stoneville's forest. If Bourbon had given Jesse two more weeks on the run, the refugee would have died of starvation.

When he spoke his first words in weeks, it was apparent his vocal cords were suffering from atrophy. His flimsy voice projected through a tin can, "I'm...I'm done running, sheriff."

Bourbon stared at his enemy as rage percolated in his head like someone was pouring it into his brain through a funnel. A whisper flowed through the funnel, floating on the anger like oil on water. The oil lit on fire, and the whispers turned into shouts. It was all the voices of Jesse Lewis's victims and more screaming for Bourbon to pull the trigger—to end the Sin-eater once and for all. Bourbon could hear Annabel Thompson, Brody Sherwood, Darin Cloudwater, Peter Felton, and Andrew Mills. He could hear them all, see them all, and as their voices faded, he could hear Flesti Thaed. But they were all screaming, "Pull the trigger. Shoot the murderer. Jesse must die. Kill the Sin-eater, now!"

His eyes took on a faint blue glow as if fueled by propane.

Bourbon applied pressure to the trigger, but not enough to trip the revolver's hammer. The trees blurred, and his vision narrowed like he was driving through a long tunnel. Jesse Lewis was kneeling at the end of the tunnel. He thought he'd come here to kill him, to avenge Annabel. She had suffered, and now he wanted Jesse Lewis to suffer too—not die.

He pushed the voices away, refocused his attention, and forced himself to lower the gun.

"You get to live," Bourbon said. "But I'm not sure for how long."

Flesti had backed away, anticipating the loud explosion Bourbon's pistol was supposed to conjure. Hetzen and Poe retreated, out of sight and out of range. Flesti took four steps forward and rejoined Bourbon.

"What are you doing?" She asked. "He doesn't deserve to live. Finish this."

Bourbon raised the pistol again. His world seemed to swim before him, silent and muffled, surreal in every way.

"This is what you came for," she said. She stepped behind him and whispered in his opposite ear. "The Sin-eater can exist no more."

Another voice poked at him, this one clear and alone, recognizable. *"Wouldn't be the first time you shot a man, Sheriff."*

"No," Bourbon cried.

The sound of his former deputy's voice spoke again, *"Go for the throat, boss. Worked on me."*

"Archer...Archer, you got what you deserved," Bourbon yelled.

Jesse Lewis kneeled with his hands exposed in surrender, trembling from Bourbon's moment of rage and confusion. He didn't dare speak.

"His fate is in your hands—same as mine," Archer said. "Now, do the goddam job you came out here to do."

Bourbon shook his head. *What the hell has gotten into me?*

He lowered the Smith & Wesson and placed it back in the shoulder holster. The voices faded away, even Charlie Archer's. Jesse Lewis was still on his knees but forced his tired feet under himself to stand. A small ash tree kept him steady.

"You look like shit," Bourbon said. "Why the hell were you in the water?"

"Evading the new sheriff," Jesse replied. "Pretty much all I've been doing for weeks."

"That, and finding a few new victims," Bourbon accused.

Jesse looked genuinely surprised, "What? No. No, I haven't hurt anyone since—"

"Since you carved up Annabel," Bourbon retook aim.

Jesse collapsed back to his knees; his head dropped like an anchor. Bourbon could hear him begin to weep. When the anchor was hoisted, tears streamed down his face, absorbed by the new beard covering his face. Bourbon wanted to believe him, but the evidence was carved in the flesh of the two bodies they'd found along Cain Lake's shore. Bourbon was at a loss for words, refusing Jesse the opportunity to convince him otherwise.

"Let's go, Pastor," He waved the pistol like a traffic flag. "Start walking, and don't make me change my mind about sparing your life."

Flesti interjected, "You're not going to kill him?"

"What good would it do? Death would be too easy. He's going to rot in a prison cell."

Jesse stumbled to his feet, "She's playing you, sheriff," Jesse said.

"I'm not the sheriff anymore."

"Bourbon, can't you see it? She is manipulating you," He pointed toward Flesti with a nod. "She manipulated both of us."

"Quiet, you pathetic liar," Flesti said in self-defense. "You're as insane as you are wretched."

"Both of you shut the hell up," Bourbon barked. "Nobody's manipulating or killing anybody. Turn your ass around, and start marching toward the boat launch."

Jesse did as he was commanded, stepping lightly in bare feet through the leafy forest. Bourbon followed behind, his right hand mounted on the mahogany handle of the Smith & Wesson, his left hand holding the walking stick with a stout grip. His pack felt less heavy, like he was carrying a lighter load.

Flesti trailed behind with her two animal companions. Bourbon could hear her steps, heavy on her boot's soles, while her toes dragged the leaves—like a spoiled child.

They made their way downhill to the water's edge. Cain Lake's surface looked like an epoxied tabletop.

Along the beach, two plastic geese lay on their sides. Bourbon walked over and turned one upright with his walking stick—decoys. They were still wet, as if they'd been carried to the beach by the waves. But there were no waves today.

"What the hell?" Bourbon looked at Jesse.

Jesse shrugged, "Been using them to evade the law. I can swim out into the lake and keep my head between the two decoys. No one gives a couple of geese a second look around here."

Bourbon shook his head in disbelief. *I can't believe that shit worked.*

"Someone on your heels now?" Bourbon asked Jesse. "That why you were running?"

"Some woman in uniform—a sheriff's department uniform. Her and another officer. I guess they're new. I didn't recognize them."

Hassett and Simpson.

Bourbon intended to take Jesse to town and relinquish custody of him to Sheriff Hassett. But his knee was throbbing, and his body was running on fumes. His blood sugar was declining, and the ground wobbled when he walked. He needed food.

"We'll rest for a bit," he said. The two hiking companions seemed surprised, but neither protested his suggestion. He relaxed a little, but kept the refugee in view. He took the fishing line from his pack, untangled it, and threw it adjacent to a row of lake grass growing in four-foot-deep water.

Flesti began collecting some small tinder and dead sticks that littered the beach. She arranged her collection in a neat pile on the wet sand and topped it with dry driftwood.

Bourbon was standing in two feet of water casting his makeshift fishing line. He watched Flesti build the pyramid of sticks to burn as he reeled the lure back. He hoped he'd have something to cook by the time the fire turned hot. His attention was divided between the firemaker and the former pastor. He wasn't concerned that the Pastor would run. Hell, he didn't think he could run. The man looked half dead, and Bourbon wondered when he had eaten last. It appeared that it may have been almost a week ago.

Jesse watched the older man cast his line by hand, then work the monofilament back toward him, winding it around a stick resembling a homemade slingshot. He was so malnourished that he wasn't even hungry anymore. His body was cannibalizing itself by consuming his fat and muscles for energy. Still, he watched wide-eyed in anticipation while Bourbon pitched the line over and over to no avail.

The pastor stood and approached the fisherman. Bourbon instinctively placed his hand on the pistol grip. His attention diverted, he let the fishing lure drop to the bottom of the lake like a dead fish.

"May I?" Jesse asked, putting his hand on the makeshift fishing rod. He bowed his head and began to whisper with a sandpaper voice. Bourbon could barely hear the words but knew they weren't meant for him. While he waited for Jesse to finish his prayer, he noticed the micropods begin to circle. They zig-zagged, swirled, raced, and bounced, but only around Bourbon. Jesse stood next to the former sheriff, but the little organisms had no interest in the former serial killer. Bourbon was beginning to believe Jesse had lost his connection to Cain Lake. Perhaps, they no longer needed each other.

"...Amen." Jesse stepped back to the beach and resumed his position on the flat granite boulder.

Bourbon felt the line jerk, then bounce, and then a little game of tug-of-war commenced with a small-mouth bass. He pulled the bass ashore and smiled in victory, "Hot damn. We're gonna eat good now."

After he unhooked the little bass, he caught three perch before the fire was lit.

*****

Their energy was partially restored from Bourbon's fish and a few handfuls of shad berries Flesti had picked. Bourbon kept his eyes on Jesse, and the scrutiny didn't go unnoticed.

"You still think I'm a threat, Bourbon?" Jesse asked.

Bourbon patted his pistol, "Not to me."

"You don't need to worry. I'm not the man you knew three weeks ago, sheriff."

"You tell that to Andrew Mills before you gutted him?" He took a sip of water.

"I have no idea who that is. My condolences, but I swear, as God as my witness," He raised his right hand and looked skyward, "I haven't hurt anyone since I saw you in the barn."

Bourbon popped a few berries in his mouth. The taste was sweet and tart simultaneously. He tossed the last two berries to Poe, and the crow took to the trees to savor the snack.

"Why didn't you kill me?" Bourbon asked. "That night when the barn burned...you could have left me to die. You could have bludgeoned me with that maniacal ax you built."

"Is that what you've come to find out?" Jesse asked.

Bourbon almost nodded, "But you didn't kill me. Why, Jesse?"

Jesse swallowed the last of his perch. He was slightly insulted by the question but answered honestly, "Because I was not—am not—a senseless murderer. My crimes had intent—intent to rid Stoneville of

112

the sinners. The innocent get to live."

"And the sins haunted you if you didn't," Flesti interjected.

"Yes," Jesse continued. "They did. And honestly, Bourbon, you may be the one truly good person left in this town. I sensed nothing from you but genuine care for others. I guess that's why you were such a good sheriff. I guess that's why I know you won't kill me now."

Bourbon stood abruptly and pulled his pistol free from the holster.

Jesse nearly pissed himself, "Or maybe I was wrong—"

"Quiet," Bourbon said, pressing his index finger to his lips. He pointed with his pistol down the shoreline, "We've got company."

19

THE POND

Cody leaned forward on the ATV as he traversed the steep winding trail. Four knobby tires dug into the sandy gravel, kicking up rocks along the way. The Bobcat Trail was a tight fit for the ATV this time of year. The path was choked by blackberry briars and weedy grass that would eventually die off by autumn. Cody slowed down several times to navigate over fallen logs produced by the spring winds. Winter was the busiest time of year for the Bobcat Trail. Snowmobilers traversed the route from Stoneville to Higley, stopping at a little tavern halfway to dine with a mountain view.

Last night's rain had been light on the south side of Cain Lake. Evident by the dust kicking up behind the ATV. The area received less than a quarter-inch of precipitation, which created scattered puddles on the trail. The puddles were starting to shrink as the temperature climbed. This made them perfect places to stop and look for tracks. Cody could see that some of the forest's local residents had already visited the water holes: deer, raccoons, coyotes, and bobcats—but no human tracks.

He drove along the top ridge, looking for signs that Jesse Lewis was still in the vicinity of Cain Lake. If he couldn't find Jesse, maybe he could locate Jeff Bourbon. Bourbon might have some insight into Jesse's general location, and the two men could search together.

He searched the sky for smoke. He looked for garbage on the ground, toilet paper, candy wrappers, animal carcasses—anything that might indicate Jesse was out here hunting and scavaging to survive.

The woods kept Jesse's secret quiet, ingrained in the fibers of every tree and plant. The flowers were close-lipped. The bushes stayed hushed. The ground was silent.

He slowed the machine to a crawl and jumped off every few minutes to search the path and listen to the wind. When he crested the top ridge of Bobcat Trail, he was surprised to fine the route flooded by a newly formed beaver pond. He turned the key to the off position to kill the engine. The motor ticked and hissed from the heat.

A swarm of deer flies had been following Cody for the last half-mile, bombinghisheadkamikaze-styleeverytimeheslowed,tryingtolandinhis dirty-blond hair. Now, they attacked the stationary target, and Cody swung with an open hand to defend himself. He caught one and gave it a gentle squeeze, hoping to exterminate the pest without a mess. When his fingers opened, the fly took flight, escaping Cody's grip.

He couldn't even catch a fly.

At the edge of the serene new pond, Cody stood and studied the depth of the clear water. The water was just knee-high, and he could success-fully drive through—if the bottom was solid. But fresh-formed ponds didn't usually have the aggregate lining along the bottom to hold a five hundred pound four-wheeler. If he tried to cross, the murky bottom would most likely swallow their weight, and he'd have to explain the messy situation to Amos McGrath. He decided to avoid the potential disaster altogether and continue on foot.

The water was as clear as glass, a window to the dark mud at the bottom. The pond was home to an entire ecosystem of animals that benefited from its creation. Cody could see countless frogs, some turtles, a muskrat nest, weasel tracks, and a porcupine sitting in an evergreen tree overseeing it all. At the back of the pond, the massive home of its creator ascended from the water. The stick built hut was like a domed castle, protected by its enormous moat. It was a simple design but impregnable by man or wild predators.

Cody knelt at the water's edge and submerged his right hand. The liquid was almost as warm as his skin, and he could see little insects swimming on the surface.

How nice would it be? To be able to run across the top of the water like that.

He closed his eyes and let his mind drift away. He thought about Willa. His former wife was always the first thing he saw when he closed his eyes. Then he thought about his parents, working nights in the garage, tinkering with small engines and tractors. The night they died, they'd fallen asleep in the garage, drunk and stupid. The engine they left running poisoned them with carbon dioxide, killing them in their drunken slumber.

A vision—no, a memory—his brother Michael riding a bicycle. He was wearing a terry towel cape, pretending to be a superhero, but the fabric jammed between the chain and sprocket, causing him to pitch over the handlebars. He tried to catch himself against the front of his father's 1955 Chevy, but the airplane hood ornament cut deep into his right forearm. The wound left an elongated L-shaped scar.

Cody opened his eyes and stared at his submerged hand. Pond skaters skimmed by his wrist across the water's surface in random directions. To his surprise, the bugs weren't the only creatures swimming in the water. A blue bug-like organism with the consistency of light—a micropod, as his group of esoteric friends called them—swam around his hand. One single, lonely micropod swirled around Cody's fingers like a lost kitten looking for a new friend. The micropods Cody had encountered in Cain Lake typically numbered in the millions, swirling and swarming with a hive mind rivaling large bee colonies. But this little micropod swam in a random motion—more like a bumble bee exploring a garden, drunk on pollen.

"How the hell did you get here?"

The little organism seemed to respond to Cody's voice, attaching itself to his skin.

A blue flash burned his retinas.

A memory—no, a vision; Michael wasn't a child this time. He he was standing, free from the confinement of the metal chair. The room was the same as in the previous vision. Michael's clothes were different. Did he change? There was little blood, but the bruises were proof of his torture. He was chained to a thick wooden beam that spanned the ceiling from wall to wall, forcing him to stand. The room was small, with no visible door. Concrete floor.

Michael's arms were stretched above his head, tethered by a rope. The shape of his face was nearly identical to Cody's, but Michael had brown eyes. His hair wasn't the same dirty blond that Cody displayed, but dark brown. He was thicker in build than his big brother, having more muscle and fat on his bones. A tribal tattoo spiraled around his left arm, but the right was clear skin—with an L-shaped scar on his forearm.

"Michael?" Cody asked, hoping his beaten brother could hear him, but there was no response.

Behind his brother, an old wooden garage door. Cody circled the room, wishing he was armed with Levi's 1911, but it was impossible to take a gun into his clairvoyant visions. There was nothing tangible here. Everything in the room was produced by the electric currents and chemical reactions in his mind. It made him feel like he was here. It looked like he was here. But he knew he was still on the ridge with his hand submerged in the pond.

As the vision progressed, the dimensions of the garage enlarged, and Cody started to see more details.

There was a plastic drop cloth spread out across the floor. An air compressor hose lay on the floor, coiled like a snake with no intent to strike. A wooden bench, newer in construction, spanned the far side wall with empty paint cans, and the fumes infiltrated Cody's nose—the smell of acrylic.

Someone's been busy. He checked the paint cans. A one-gallon can of gray primer with an acrylic base, a clear coat finish, and the last can half filled with dark green paint. He studied the drop cloth. Strokes of color created by the paint sprayer decorated the plastic floor cover. There were yellow strokes, black, and an abundant amount of green.

A void in the paint was created at the center of the dropcloth. The painter worked back and forth with a professional spray gun, creating a distinctive outline of the object he was painting.

Cody recognized the shape immediately.

The lack of windows made it impossible to ascertain his location. There seemed to be no other doors, and the small windows in the garage door were filled with black.

Outside, the dinging sound continued to play just as it had in his previous vision; wind chimes without notes.

He walked to the workbench and noticed the same wrench he'd seen before. He felt helpless, but now he knew he was looking for a garage. If he could find Jesse Lewis, Jesse could pinpoint Michael's location.

He lifted the large wrench from the workbench and whispered to his brother, "I'm coming, Michael. I'll find you."

When Cody opened his eyes, his hand was still submerged in the pond water, and the little blue light was still clinging to his skin. It blinked off a couple of times, seemingly sad or tired. Cody hated to leave the tiny light. They were kindred spirits—alone in the forest.

And then the light blinked out permanently.

Cody rose and wiped his hand dry on his blue jeans. He decided to leave the four-wheeler and walk to Cain Lake. He retrieved his small backpack from the Suzuki, put his arms through the straps, and tightened them over his shoulders. He tucked Levi's pistol in his belt with the magazine inserted. There was no trail, but the higher elevation meant less dense foliage. It allowed him to see a little further to plot his course. To reach Cain Lake, he just needed to descend the hill while hiking west and keep the sun on his left shoulder.

He took five to ten steps at a time, then paused to look and listen. He used the same technique when hunting big game with his uncle Bruce, although the pauses were much longer—as was his patience. The hardwood canopy above provided enough shade to keep him cool, but an uncomfortable heat was building between the backpack and his skin.

He twisted and turned down the hill, switchbacking along the steep slopes and granite cliffs but always working his way downhill. He imagined the terrain drawn as contoured lines, like the maps Uncle Bruce used to show him. Where the hill was steep, the lines were close together. Where the slope was gradual, the lines were more spacious. He cut downhill through the spacious lines but followed the hill where they were tight. He moved through the map like a mouse in a maze.

When he was forty yards from Grandview Road, a noise from the north startled him. Something heavy—a dark shadow—walked toward him from the north. It took a moment to believe his eyes, but he finally convinced himself it was not another vision. The shadow morphed into the form of an adult bull moose. Cody and the beast stared at one another, neither giving up the right of way.

The bull's head swayed gently from side to side, presenting his antlers in a display of power. It was the first time Cody had ever seen a moose, and possibly the last. So, as much of a hurry as he was in, he relished the moment. The privilege was short-lived when the massive beast lifted his snout, tasted the air, and turned away as if it had smelled something ominous in the wind.

Cody smelled it too. Smoke.

He crossed the road, slid down a steep embankment, and nearly shattered his kneecap on a boulder of quartz and granite. The bottom side of the leaves was wet and slick, making them untrustworthy footing. He arrived at Shiner's Brook and paused to splash the cool water on his face and forearms. The cool stream was enticing, inviting Cody to stay and enjoy the ankle-deep water, but it couldn't chill his will to find Jesse Lewis.

His pace quickened.

He followed the babbling brook downstream around cobblestones and cascades from granite cliffs. He came across tracks in the soft sandy bottom of the stream as he came closer to Cain Lake. The tracks, indistinct but definitely human, headed in the same direction he was going. He looked for other clues as to whether it was Jesse Lewis, Bourbon, or just a trout fisherman searching the eddies along Shiner Brook. He didn't stop until he reached the lake.

Something caught his attention along the shoreline, but he couldn't discern the shape. He drew closer, cautious of what the huddled black mass might be. A corpse—animal or human—first crossed his mind, but the form took shape once he was close enough. Two geese lay on their sides, motionless heaps on the sand.

He closed in, waiting for the stench of death to infiltrate his nostrils, but all he could smell was the sweet aroma of Cain Lakes weeds and flowers.

There was no smell of decay because the two geese were decoys made of plastic and rubber.

He dismissed the decoys and followed the scent of the smokey fire. As he trekked along the beach, a light gray plume ascended to the clouds. The young evergreens along the shore provided excellent cover as he moved toward his destination. He didn't remember pulling the pistol from his belt line, yet there it was in his hand, magazine inserted, one in the chamber.

20

PSYCHIC INSIGHT

Holy shit," Cody said. His words were stretched as if the moment was in slow motion. He stepped from the evergreens and stared into the eyes of Jesse Lewis, who was standing fifteen feet away. It was difficult to identify the former pastor, but Jesse's dark eyes were easy to recognize. Cody whipped his pistol forward, aligning the front sight on the fugitive's chest. Now that he had him in his sights, there was no way he'd lose him again.

Jesse stood stoic, with nowhere to go, nowhere to hide, no more fight left in him.

"Whoa, son," Bourbon said. "Easy now. You can put that thing away."

"Bourbon...Jesus, it's good to see you," he kept the gun pointed toward Jesse. "How the hell did you find this asshole?"

"It's good to see you too, but you need to lower your gun before someone gets killed."

Cody ignored the request from his friend. "Sorry, Bourbon, but there's no way I'm trusting that bastard. He's too dangerous."

Jesse stood with his hands raised to shoulder height, palms facing out. He slowly lowered them, careful not to make any sudden moves. He was certain Cody wouldn't pull the trigger, but he was too exhausted not to be cautious.

"What are you doing out here, Savage?" Bourbon asked casually.

"Looking for him." Cody pushed the pistol forward to indicate his target.

Bourbon scratched his beard and took a seat on an old driftwood log. His knee was throbbing, and he was happy to rest it. He cocked his head toward Jesse Lewis, "Seems like the whole town is chasing you."

"He needs to come with me," Cody said.

"Why's that? If you're going to shoot him, you might as well do it here. If you're not going to shoot him, then he needs to stay in my custody."

Flesti stepped toward Cody cautiously, but not because she was scared of the gun.

Cody's eyes widened like a cat spotting a mouse in the grass. "Flesti? Holy shit, I didn't recognize you." He looked her up and down, uncertain how she appeared so different since their last encounter. Her hair had blonde roots pushing the gray away from her scalp. Her waist seemed smaller, hips wider, and she stood as straight as tamarack pine. The skin on her face was smooth and taut as if someone had erased the wrinkles.

Flesti knew she looked like a stranger to Cody, "The lake affects everyone differently. It's helped you heal," she nodded at his hand, "And It's been good to me too."

"The lake makes you look younger?"

"I don't look younger; I am younger." She gave him a wink, "My little secret."

Cody turned his attention to the serial killer standing on the beach. "I don't have time for explanations. I need Jesse to come with me."

Bourbon's knee throbbed. He shifted his weight on the driftwood log and relieved his shoulders of his backpack's weight, "Try to explain because this man needs to be in police custody and nowhere else."

"Sorry, Bourbon, but you're not the sheriff anymore."

Bourbon stared at the ground, stung by Cody's remark but knew he only spoke the truth. He wasn't the sheriff anymore, and he'd forgotten that the second he saw Jesse Lewis.

Up the hill, a four-wheeler engine revved and then idled down, dropping its RPMs to a slow cruising speed but never stopping. It was pacing up and down the road, out of sight. Bourbon cocked his head and listened intently to the machine. It reminded him of the vultures circling the dead body of Andrew Mills. He feared Cody may have led others to their location. Almost every soul in town wanted to see Jesse Lewis killed or behind bars for the murders he'd committed.

Flesti's backpack dropped to the sand. She stretched her shoulders and twisted her torso to work out the knots from the cumbersome load. She flipped the top of her water bottle open and lubricated her throat to speak, "You need his help." She could read Cody's intentions. "You need Jesse's ability to find someone?"

"That true?" Bourbon asked.

"Yes," Cody said. "I need his ability, his psychic ability."

Jesse's head dropped. This was it, his legacy, his reputation. At that moment, Jesse Lewis realized he was no longer a pastor—he would never be a pastor again. For the rest of his life, he would only be known as the Sin-eater. He would be remembered for his crimes and uncanny ability to see people's sins.

He was glad to have lost his extra senses and hoped to reinvent himself in a new image—even if he had to do it from inside a prison cell.

"I'm afraid I am of no use, Savage," Jesse said. "The community has ostracized me, and now the lake's rejected me, too. I haven't had a vision in over a week."

"What are you saying?" Cody asked.

"He's saying he no longer has his psychic power," Bourbon said. "But I don't think he ever had it to begin with. He's been playing everybody, blaming the lake for his sick behavior."

"No," Cody said. "He has visions, like me. But more powerful—more control."

Bourbon pulled himself to a standing position with the walking stick and remounted the heavy pack on his shoulders. Flesti and Jesse echoed his movements. Bourbon stretched his back in a big arch, giving in to Cody's determination.

"I think you're wasting your time," Bourbon said. "What exactly do you need his help for, anyway?"

Poe flew downward, gliding between the group, then ascended to the sky. Cody watched the crow, thinking about the disturbing images he'd been forced to view for the last two days.

"Someone has my brother. They're killing him—beating him to death. I can see it in my visions." Cody thought it sounded crazy, even to him. He struggled to produce the words. His voice was thin, "I don't know how else to find him before it's too late."

"Your brother?" Bourbon asked. "How do you know it's him? The kid was adopted when you were teens. What's it been? Fourteen years? Why would anyone want to hurt your brother?"

"It's him, Bourbon, and I'm running out of time." He gripped his pistol a little tighter, hoping he wouldn't have to threaten the former sheriff, but desperate enough to do so.

Bourbon pivoted on his walking stick and faced the younger man. He spoke with a calm, cool voice, "Okay, Savage. He's your responsibility now. If you really think this hocus-pocus bullshit of his will save your brother, then go ahead. Take him with you."

"Michael?" Jesse asked.

"What?" Cody answered. "How do you know his name?"

"I...I don't know. It just came to me somehow. Maybe I still have some of my psychic insight. Maybe I can help you, Cody."

"Then we need to go. We can't afford another minute," Cody said.

The entire group made their way along the shore, meandering through the evergreens and staying parallel to the gentle waves of Cain Lake.

They didn't go more than one hundred yards when Bourbon had to stop again. It was clear that his swollen knee was going to hinder their progress. He couldn't keep up with the rest of the group.

Cody's patience was wearing thin. If Bourbon stopped to rest every five minutes, they'd never save Michael in time. He checked the sun; two-thirty, he guessed.

Bourbon came to the same realization. He couldn't keep up with the younger man on a mission. He acknowledged his handicap and permitted Cody to leave him behind. Flesti chose to stay with Bourbon.

Cody didn't argue. He shook Bourbon's hand, and he and Jesse disappeared through a curtain of pines.

21
THE SINNER

Cody kept the pistol pointed at Jesse's back as they traveled south. Their pace was quick, and Jesse struggled to continue, but the Taurus 1911 9mm was a great motivator. They kept moving until they reached Remington Bay, an impressive body of water stretching a half-mile back to the east and nearly a quarter of a mile wide at the mouth. An aerial view of the bay resembled the head of a sawtooth shark, with ragged edges for teeth. Each tooth was an inlet for superficial tributaries that fed Cain Lake. The duo started their journey around the shark's head.

They could have swum across the bay to alleviate the rigorous two-hour hike, but Cody feared the pastor might be able to overtake him in the water. Even though Jesse was weak from his time in the woods, Cody would be swimming with one hand, putting himself at a disadvantage. Better to walk the extra mile through the rough country than risk an assault in the water.

"Let's go," Cody said, looking over the cool flat surface.

They pushed east, opposite the direction they wanted to go, forced by the shape of the lake that had been carved during the birth of the mountains and reformed over the centuries by the run-off from the spring rains and snow thaw. They sloshed through marshes, scurried over boulders and logs, and pulled themselves up cliffs.

The half-mile hike to the end of the bay took fifty minutes through the rough terrain. Both men were winded and fatigued, but Cody was determined to get around the bay before dusk.

When they reached the tip of the shark's snout, they stopped briefly to drink from an artesian well bubbling with cold fresh water from the ground. Cody cupped both hands together and tasted the mineralized liquid that had probably been trapped within the bedrock longer than he'd been alive. The taste was nothing he'd ever experienced, fresh and smooth, with a touch of earth. Cody couldn't believe the warm sand was capable of producing such cool salvation.

He let Jesse get his fill of spring water. He needed him healthy and sharp for the job ahead. This was a perfect place to rest.

They sat in silence on a dead tree that had fallen years ago.

Jesse spoke first, trying to understand what the ex-con had planned. "So, this brother of yours...Where has he been all this time? I don't recall anyone ever talking about him or seeing him in church. Is he local?"

Cody didn't answer. Instead, he searched his backpack for two beef jerky sticks and tossed one to Jesse.

"Come on. I know you're pissed at me, but I'm curious. Are you two close?"

"No. I'm not sure where he's been. We were separated when I was fourteen."

"What's it been then? Twelve years?"

"Fifteen."

"Wow," Jesse said. He paused before asking more questions, but many were on his mind. "How do two brothers get separated? I'm guessing something happened to your parents. Am I right?"

"My parents weren't exactly model citizens."

"So they were incarcerated? I guess that would explain it."

"No, they weren't arrested. They died." Cody picked up a dead stick about the length of his forearm and started poking at the wet sand beneath his feet. He seemed to dig up an old memory—a memory he had buried his whole life.

"I'm sorry," Jesse bit into the greasy meat like a bear. "That must have been rough."

"It was rough for Michael, being so young. We went to live with a foster family, but someone adopted him. I bounced from home to home until I was eighteen."

Jesse thought about how unusual that was, dividing two brothers with nothing left in the world but each other. There was more to the story, so he contemplated whether he should press his captor with more questions.

But Cody had questions of his own. "What did you see when you and I first met?"

"What do you mean?" Jesse asked.

"When we first met, you were targeting me. What was it you saw that made you come after me?"

"I saw nothing. I'd heard rumors you'd killed your wife, but there was no response when I tried to read your sins. You, Mr. Savage, are as innocent as the sheriff." Jesse was still referring to Bourbon as the sheriff.

"I thought you saw something else."

"No, I only desired to cleanse the town of the sinners. I never asked for this ability—never wanted it. I became a pastor to help people, not hurt them. But when people came in to confess their sins, I became overwhelmed. I came to the realization that this whole town is full of fucking criminals. Nearly every damn person is hiding something."

"That doesn't mean they deserve to die. Maybe they need to be exposed—given a second chance—atonement." He dug the stick deeper, twisting it like a washing machine agitator in slow motion.

"That's what I thought, at first. But Cain Lake made me see the truth, gave me the insight to dig into a person's persona—if you will—and see their true colors."

"What if you were wrong?" Cody asked. "What if the lake made you see things that weren't true? Or failed to show you what was true?"

Jesse didn't need psychic abilities to sense something stirring in Cody. "You know, I've been listening to confessions and hearing people's heartaches for a long time," The hungry pastor took another bite of meat.

"I've come to sense when there's something burdening people. Something you want to get off your chest, Mr. Savage?"

Cody started working a new hole with his deadwood drill. Groundwater seeped into the hole from the bottom and became cloudy. When the hole filled, the water was dark and murky.

"How'd your parents pass?"

"Carbon monoxide poisoning."

"Damn, that must have been tough," Jesse said. He instinctively raised his hand to pat Cody's shoulder but decided not to invade his personal space. He hoped Cody would elaborate.

Cody began to see that Jesse Lewis, the pastor, was caring despite his past. He never attended his church but knew the man must have been good at his occupation at one time. He felt the need to tell someone—anyone—his side of the story and the truth about that night in the garage. He continued:

"They weren't the best parents if I'm being honest. My mother used to beat me with the flyswatter; my dad just used his knuckles. If I didn't cry, the beating wasn't serious enough. If I did cry, then the beatings were to 'toughen me up.' By the time I was a teenager, I was impervious to their abuse, so disciplinary action turned to chores. I pretty much had to do everything so they could sit and get high or drunk.

"Then Michael became the target of their abuse. I tried to protect him—keep him out of sight and out of trouble—but he was just so clumsy."

"And you feel you need to protect him now?" Jesse asked.

Cody nodded. He started drilling his fifth hole in the sand, working the stick around as old memories stirred in his mind. "The night they died, Michael and I were in the house. Mom had finally gotten a new microwave and...." He looked to the treetops, recalling the night. "They never told him not to put anything metal in the microwave. He was just a kid—how was he supposed to know?"

"And he ruined your mom's new microwave?" Jesse said with a painful look on his face.

Another nod. Another hole. "Sparks were flying all around the inside. He was so scared about what Mom was going to do to him. It was an accident. He started packing clothes and stuff in a garbage bag, ready to run away." Water seeped into his eyes, similar to the way it crept into the sandy holes he was digging. He sniffled, embarrassed by his weakness.

Cody grabbed both ends of his wooden drill, "They were going to beat him so bad." The stick snapped in half, little slivers flying upward and landing at their feet. "So I went to the garage to tell them that I had ruined the new microwave. I was going to take the blame."

"And you found them dead in the garage?"

Cody's head shook side to side, then up and down. "I don't know. They were asleep in their lawn chairs, drunk and stoned. The generator my dad was working on was still running. They were probably fine. But..." Tears were streaming now from his eyes, dripping off his cheeks.

"What happened?"

"I closed the doors. I swear I heard someone tell me to do it. At first, I thought the voice was my mother's. I pulled the overhead door down. Then the voice told me not to forget the man door. I felt like a puppet, obeying her voice. But my mom's lips weren't moving. It wasn't her. She couldn't have been talking. And I killed them." He stood and threw the two sticks into the lake like broken boomerangs refusing to return.

Jesse felt good hearing Cody's story. Not because he liked to see him suffer, but because it was an opportunity to help. This was the first time in months that he felt like a pastor. It was a reminder of how fragile even the toughest people can be, and Cody Savage was one of the toughest men Jesse had ever met. His concern was genuine. His empathy was sincere. "I'm sorry, Cody. I truly am. I know what you did was unintentional...."

"Was it? I'm not so sure. I would have done anything to protect my little brother."

"I know. That's why I don't understand why Social Services didn't keep the two of you together. It's unusual to break up a family."

"Because they thought I was dangerous. You see...one of the neighbors came forward after learning about their deaths. They were driving by and witnessed me closing the garage doors. So social services and the police investigators suspected I killed my parents intentionally."

Jesse's voice was almost a whisper as if he were talking to himself out loud. "Holy shit. And you were too young to prosecute, so they just kept you in the system."

"Exactly," Cody said. He picked up another stick that resembled the first but was much larger. He leaned on it, taking some of the weight off his soles. "I've got to find Michael. I can't let him down again." Cody put one foot up on the log where Jesse was still sitting. "That's the sin I carry. That's the sin I've been hiding, and I thought it was the reason you were hunting me."

Jesse looked perplexed for a moment, "I never saw it. Maybe because it wasn't a sin." He stood and gazed out over the bay as if he'd witnessed an accident, "Maybe because you were just a kid when this happened. An innocent kid robbed of a fun and nurturing childhood. There are some people in this world not meant to be parents, and I'm certain your parents were among that demographic."

"I've never told anyone else that story—not even Willa. You're the only one who knows the truth about that night. I prefer to keep it that way." He rubbed the throbbing bandage on his left hand.

"Okay, Savage. I'll help you," Jesse turned his body and looked his captor in the eye. "I'll help you find your brother and even help you deal with his captor. It's the least I can do, but, we'll need to work fast before Sheriff Hassett finds us. She's forming a search party at this very moment to scour the woods."

Cody nodded. Having Jesse's aid was an enormous step in the right direction. He wouldn't have to force him to help; they could focus on what was important.

Jesse returned to the artesian well and filled his belly with the invigorating water. He was excited by the prospect of doing something good. He was eager to regain his strength and atone for his crimes. "There's just one thing I ask before we go any further."

"What's that?" Cody asked.

"That we pray. Let us pray for the Lord's protection and guidance. Let us pray that he gives me my full psychic insight back so we can find Michael as soon as possible."

"I guess...I mean, if you think it will help."

Jesse turned back, a smile on his weak face, and Cody knew there was a chance now. He wished he'd known Jesse Lewis before he turned into a psychopathic killer. He hoped he would be helpful and that when this was over, he'd perhaps live out his days in prison, helping others—a prison chaplain possibly.

Jesse froze as if he'd just stepped on a landmine. His eyes were wide with fear or disappointment. Maybe both.

"What is it?" Cody asked.

Jesse turned around, "I'm sorry. We're too late." He stared into the deep woods behind him. Cody looked past the pastor but couldn't see anything through the dense leaves.

"What do you mean, 'we're too late'?"

Cody heard the crack of the gun as Jesse flew off his feet and landed on the sandy beach. The sound echoed off the cliffs and carried across the lake.

"No!" Cody screamed. He dropped behind a granite boulder for cover, expecting a hail of bullets to rain down. He watched Jesse's shirt change color from the hole in his chest. His life was literally draining from his body. Jesse's eyes were fixed on Cody, like he had one more thing to say, then turned skyward, looking for the door he hoped to go through.

It never opened. He just lay on a beach, staining the sand with his blood. He was no more of a living thing than the boulder at Cody's back..

Atop the hill, from the direction the shot originated, the lone four-wheeler sped away, taking Cody's chance of saving his brother with it.

22

DELICATE MATTERS

He's dead," Bourbon said. He scoured the tree line, looking for silhouettes. "Looks like we got to him before the buzzards."

Bourbon was on his one good knee, studying the body of Jesse Lewis. There were no self-defense marks, so it didn't appear like Cody was forced to kill Jesse. It didn't make sense. There was no way in hell Cody would have eliminated the only person capable of helping him find his brother Michael.

Bourbon was sick of finding bodies. This was his third in two days, and he prayed it would be the last. But this was Cain Lake, and nothing seemed to surprise him anymore.

He refrained from touching the body, although he didn't think there would be much evidence. He used his tall walking stick to prop himself into a standing position.

Flesti stepped forward and knelt beside Jesse Lewis's corpse. She took his hand and padded the backside. "Thank you, Jesse. Your work here is done."

Bourbon's eyebrows bounced; *What the hell is that supposed to mean?*

As if she heard his thoughts, she stood and peered out beyond the glassy surface of the lake, "He served the lake. He served the people. His servitude has concluded." She made three different gestures with her hands for each sentence she spoke.

She decided to rest for a moment and keep Jesse company. She sat on the same dead log Cody and Jesse sat on thirty minutes prior. She studied the holes in the sand formed by Cody's mindless drilling.

But Bourbon was too restless to sit, even though his knee felt like a bad toothache. He certainly didn't care if Jesse needed company. He scanned for any boats present on the water—nothing in the bay. He studied the tree line with more scrutiny than before. Everything seemed normal, but on the ground, just twelve feet away, fresh green tree boughs—no larger than a head of lettuce—lay on the sand. "The shooter was on the hill."

"How do you figure?" Flesti asked.

"Those leaves," he pointed. "They were shot down; bullet cut through those limbs."

"Think Cody was shot too?"

"We only heard one gunshot, so, no. I think he's fine. He headed back to town. He was only out here to find Jesse and use him to help locate his brother. Now he's—"

"Dead. Useless."

Bourbon wasn't sure what to think of Jesse's death. Jesse lay motionless in the sand like roadkill. Revenge was his motive for coming out here, but the lawman in him wanted Jesse to go to trial. He was looking forward to calling Annabel to tell her she could stop taking those damn sleeping pills. He was going to reassure her she'd never need to worry about Jesse hurting her again. Tell her he was coming home and hopefully they could pick up where they left off, and end their pain.

Flesti unburdened herself from the weight of her pack. She watched Bourbon walk around the fallen tree and begin his ascent up the hill.

"Where are you going?"

"I'll be right back."

He disappeared through a curtain of green. He limped up the hill, pulling himself with the walking stick and small trees. He kept looking back, checking the view, getting an idea of the killer's view. He reached the Bobcat Trail, the lower side below Grandview Road before it crossed over. There were four-wheeler tracks—as he suspected. Two machines went into the woods, uphill, following the trail. Only the second one returned. He knew Cody had left the ATV he was driving at the top of the hill. Someone was following him.

He began his return to Flesti, swatting at black flies and trying not to fall on his ass. He stopped about seventy yards from the beach, intrigued by a large overhanging rock. The rock was shaped like one end of an anvil and protruded from the earth at a slight angle upward. It would have made a perfect spot to sit and hunt for big game. The layers of granite were worn smooth from eons of erosion, and moss had camouflaged the boulder in dark green.

He made his way to the boulder and stood on top. The rock was about the size of a delivery truck, and when Bourbon climbed on top, he had a perfect view of Flesti sitting on the beach. A few tree branches blocked his sight, but nothing a good hunting rifle couldn't cut through.

The top of the rock was flat, with thick soil hiding its existence from above. Ferns, shrubs, and small trees had taken root in the rich earth.

Bourbon searched the stage for evidence of the shooter's identity. There was only a carpet of dead leaves and a single pink lady slipper flower. He admired the plant momentarily and stepped lightly to avoid harming the delicate orchid. Six inches from the flower's short stem, a hint of brass shined in a clump of leaves formed from the shooter's knee or elbow nestling into the ground. The empty bullet stood out like a wedding band in a box of rusty nails.

He picked up the casing, still shiny without a spec of rust, proving it was recently dropped on the rock ledge. As he slid the rifle shell into his pocket, he knew he was violating the crime scene and that the brass cartridge could contain a fingerprint. Also, a ballistic investigator could test the shell and potentially identify the shooter.

But Bourbon already knew who fired the killing shot.

23

CODY & Hassett 

Forty-five minutes had passed since Cody left Jesse Lewis's body bleeding onto the sand. Forty-five minutes of his scrambled brain trying to forgive himself for wasting time while his brother suffered. Forty-five minutes of cursing Stoneville under his breath and wishing he'd listened to Mr. Thomas, the Uber driver, the day he advised Cody that Stoneville should be left in the past. Somehow, he knew that his return was the reason Michael was being punished.

Nothing good had come from his arrival except Daisy. But he wondered how long it would be before she became a victim of his presence.

The sun was warm on his shoulders, his fury hot on his lips. He didn't have the canopy of the forest leaves to serve as a natural UV filter and wished he'd brought sunglasses.

Remington Bay was behind him as he hiked through an acre of evergreens. Beyond the pines, he entered the deciduous forest and walked until he intersected Grandview Road. His steps were as heavy as his heart. He wasn't going to waste time trying to be stealthy and silent. The clock was ticking. Getting back to town was his only goal.

Four crows, none of them Poe, quarreled over a dead squirrel lying in the road. They scattered on Cody's approach but only went twenty feet to perch in a cherry tree. They complained about Cody's intrusion until he passed. They didn't wait long to fly back to their free meal and continue their squabble.

Cody crossed the road, contemplating his next move. How was he going to find Michael now? Where would he start looking? Who, if anyone, could help him save his brother?

It didn't take him long to be back on Bobcat Trail. He followed the path until he reached the Suzuki 500 he'd left at the pond. The tracks from the second four-wheeler—the shooter's ATV—covered most of his. He wondered if he could follow them back to where they had originated.

He dismissed the thought for two reasons: first, he'd probably lose the tracks once the rider got back on the pavement, and secondly, he just didn't care who shot Jesse at the moment, although he was sure he knew the killer's identity. The man was dead. There was no way to change that, and maybe Cody could track down the killer later, but first, he needed to find Michael.

He tied his backpack to the storage rack, and fired up the engine. He made a three-point turn and drove back down the trail toward the south bridge.

Cody was furious with Levi Thompson and his buddies. By killing Jesse Lewis, they had blown his opportunity to find Michael. But it seemed odd that Levi would pull such a stunt. As much as he wanted Jesse Lewis dead, he wouldn't settle for a shot through the chest from a considerable distance. Levi wanted to stick a knife in Jesse Lewis and watch the life fade from his cold eyes. Levi wanted to savor the kill.

Jesse Lewis had wronged a lot of people; destroyed a lot of families. Finding his killer wasn't going to be easy.

Let Sheriff Hassett clean up this mess.

The wind relieved the burn of his skin and reduced his body heat. It did little for temper. His shadow grew longer now, and the sun was more merciful since he'd walked the beaches of Remington Bay. He sped down the hill on the ATV, chased by a dozen deer flies that were attracted to the heat of the four-wheeler's engine and the movement of their prey.

He shifted the four-wheeler into low gear to descend the last steep hill of the trail. The low gear fought with the gravity that pulled the machine down the hill. The engine's RPMs approached the tachometer's redline, and the Suzuki growled with power. At the bottom of the hill, Cody stopped, put the four-wheeler back into high gear, and thumbed the throttle until he was back on Grandview Road.

When the front tires hit the pavement, Cody was forced to push hard to activate the foot brake. The machine stopped immediately—face to face with Sheriff Jo Hassett. Deputy Simpson stood fifteen feet behind her with a shotgun across his torso and a grin across his face.

Cody killed the engine by turning the key counterclockwise. "Sheriff," he greeted Hassett. He knew this was going to go badly.

"Mr. Savage," She said. "I don't suppose I have to ask what you're doing out here?" She didn't wait for a reply. "I'm going to ask that you leave the area at once. This is your only warning."

"That's what I was doing. Headed home." He looked beyond Hassett, past Simpson, and noticed a half-dozen vehicles. A group of people in civilian clothing formed a semicircle at the tailgate of a shiny Chevy Silverado. "Having a tailgate party?"

"Yeah, something like that. And you're not invited."

Boy, she really hates me.

Cody saw a cage in the back of the truck and could see the outline of a canine—maybe a hound—inside. He guessed it was a tracking dog. "Looking for Lewis? Or someone else?"

"I found Jesse's most recent camp and evidence he was there this morning. He's close—I can smell him." She lifted her head to the wind for effect.

"Well, I hate to break up your party, sheriff," Cody said, dismounting the four-wheeler. "But the odor you're smelling is probably Jesse's rotting corpse."

Hassett glimpsed over her shoulder to Simpson, who stepped closer to hear the conversation.

"He's dead," Cody said. "Shot in the chest less than an hour ago."

"What the hell did you do?" Hassett asked. She pulled her pistol and pointed it at his torso.

Cody threw his hands up in surrender, "Wasn't me, sheriff. Promise. Someone sniped his ass from the top of that hill." He motioned with his right hand, pointing to the high ground to the east. "Shooter took off on a four-wheeler. You folks didn't happen to see anyone ride by, did you?"

"No," Simpson said. "Ain't nobody been by here in the last hour. We've been waiting by the bridge for our search party to arrive." Simpson lowered the shotgun to his side, ready to raise it quickly if necessary, but he felt Cody was no threat.

"Turn around," Hassett ordered Cody.

"Aw, come on, Sheriff. I've done nothing wrong, and I need to find—"

"I said, turn around."

Cody slowly did as she asked, knowing she'd see the pistol tucked into his belt.

Hassett approached while Simpson pretended to cover her with the shotgun. She confiscated the 1911 from Cody and studied it for five seconds. She dumped the magazine—no round in the chamber.

"It's just a loaner," Cody said. "Just in case the pastor didn't want to comply."

"So, how do I know he didn't comply?"

"I guess you don't."

She asked for a detailed location, and Cody was glad to give it, "Head around Remington Bay until you reach the easternmost point. There's a freshwater spring and a large boulder by the beach. You'll find him there."

Hassett gave Simpson orders to check the location and report to her every twenty minutes. Remington Bay was full of stumps, boulders, and sandbars. Deputy Simpson had learned that the hard way years ago while fishing with his nephew. He opted to hike. The last thing he wanted was to be stranded in such a remote location at dusk. He donned a light-weight backpack with water and a first-aid kit and carried his shotgun cross-body. He gave the sheriff an old fashioned tip of his cap and started marching toward Jesse Lewis's location.

Once Simpson was on his way, Hassett checked the time on her phone. She expected his first contact to be at 5:25. She then led Cody to the bridge, put him in her patrol vehicle, and called off the search—tempo-rarily. She wanted Simpson to report back before sending anyone else into the woods. The body count at Cain Lake was escalating, and she wanted it to end.

*****

Cody rode in the back seat of Sheriff Hassett's Jeep Gladiator. They'd left the search party on standby and Deputy Simpson alone on a body hunt. Simpson had driven the county's Sheriff's Department boat to the bridge and moored it to a tree along the shore. If the search party had commenced and they located Jesse Lewis, the vessel would have been ready for speedy transport across the lake.

Cody stared out the front windshield from the backseat. "Sheriff, you have to believe me. I'm not the one who shot Jesse."

"Let's say I believe you," she said. "Then who else would have the balls to pull a stunt like that? Any guesses who'd so badly want Jesse Lewis dead that they'd follow you through the woods and wait for the opportunity to blow him away?"

"Sure, just open a Stoneville phone book and pick a name. There's not a soul in town that wouldn't like to see him dead. Except me."

"What makes you the exception?"

"I told you—he's worth more to me alive. He was going to help me find my brother."

"The one you saw in your vision, right? Because someone's holding him hostage and torturing him? I come from Chicago. I've heard every story out there. I'm not ready to believe that one."

Cody didn't respond. He knew his story sounded far-fetched. Hell, even he was having a hard time believing it. He watched the trees go by as fast as his mind was racing, reflecting on the day, wishing he'd been more cautious.

A phone call came across the Gladiator's U-connect system. Hassett answered, and the coroner's voice came across the speakers.

"Hello, sheriff. I'm sorry to bother you," Shari said. "I've got some news on our DB Bourbon found at the lake. I have his identity and was hoping you could contact his next of kin."

Cody spoke before Sheriff Hassett could reply, "You mean Andrew Mills? Didn't Bourbon already tell you his identity?"

"Oh, I'm sorry," Shari said. "I didn't realize you had someone with you."

"It's nobody, Shari. Just Cody Savage."

'Nobody?' Jesus, she really hates me.

Hassett pulled the truck off the road and turned on the vehicle's emergency lights. She turned around and faced Cody, "Who the hell is Andrew Mills? And how do you know about this?"

Cody recited the same details he had received from Bourbon. He wasn't sure where the body was located, so they were going to need Bourbon to help them retrieve it.

"Sonovabitch," Hassett cursed. "This asshole's been busy."

Shari was silent, unsure if she should divulge any information without the sheriff's consent. Hassett sensed her reluctance to speak, "Please, continue, Shari. Ignore the voice in the background."

Shari continued, "The DB we have here, at the morgue, has been identified as Warren Gilcrest."

Cody felt a sense of relief. He sat back in his seat and listened for the rest of the information with less concern.

Shari continued, "He lived in White Plains. Age twenty-five, no family. His parents passed away five years ago in a private plane crash, but he has a sister."

"Cause of death?" Hassett asked.

"Secondary drowning. Looks like he was beaten pretty badly and then thrown into Cain Lake. He was able to swim to shore—mud and bark under his fingernails suggest he climbed out of the water on his own volition."

Cody could see the sheriff's confusion in the rearview mirror. He asked the question she was thinking, "How does a drowned man climb out of the water?"

"Secondary drowning occurs when the person's lungs fill with fluid, become irritated, and cause suffocation. In this case, the victim's lungs were already partially filled with blood from the beating he suffered. Then he inhaled water. Even though he did expel some of the fluid, he eventually succumbed to the lack of oxygen."

"Damn," Hassett cursed. "Hell of a way to go. I've seen this before, though; usually children."

Cody imagined Warren Gilcrest in his mind. He wondered if this was the man he'd been seeing all along. Perhaps his brain tricked him into thinking it was his brother to augment the serious nature of the vision. Maybe, Warren Gilcrest and Michael looked very similar. "Sheriff, may I see the body."

She was reluctant, but with all the strange shit happening anyway, what could it hurt.

She gave her approval and advised Shari they were just a couple of minutes away.

24
THE MORGUE

Cody hadn't been formally arrested, so he followed Sheriff Hassett without the hindrance of handcuffs. They walked down a short ramp with a gentle decline and through a heavy steel door and a single vertical window. So far, all Hassett knew was that Cody was in possession of an illegal firearm. He had no pistol permit and carried the weapon in a concealed manner. But she intended to charge him at the station, hoping he wouldn't lawyer up.

Cody was exhausted from the day's hike, and his hunger made him want to chew his arm off. What good was an arm with no hand attached, anyway?

Shari Kapoor, the coroner, greeted them at the morgue's door. She wore a white lab coat over a burgundy blouse and black pants. The top of her black eyeglasses lined up perfectly with thick eyebrows of the same color. She kept her thick black hair pulled back, which formed a perfectly shaped bun on the crest of her head. A few gray streaks blended softly with the texture of her locks. She smiled slightly, but it was enough to reveal a deep dimple on her left cheek.

"Good afternoon, sheriff," Shari said. "Mr. Savage." She led the twosome down a hallway lined with bulletin boards and flickering fluorescent lights. The air conditioner hummed through the vents overhead, and Cody relished the cool, dry air it produced.

Shari pushed through the right side of a set of heavy doors, suitable to be forced open with a gurney. She held the door with her body, and Hassett and Cody slipped by. When she let the door go, it swung silent and free without slamming or making a sound.

The morgue was even cooler, with bright lights and large tiles covering the floor. An island counter with a stainless steel top took center stage. A large washing sink was built into the end of the island, with a flexible water hose. A large light, mounted to the ceiling on an adjustable arm, pointed to the table. The bulb was off. A fan was mounted on the ceiling at the opposite end of the table from the light.

Cody imagined himself lying on the cold hard table someday. He hoped he was old and gray by then. He could see himself with a Y-shaped scar from an autopsy that spanned his entire torso. He'd be naked, but no amount of embarassment would cause him to blush. Just a piece of meat, ready to discard in the cremation chamber or buried next to Willa in the cemetery.

The walls of the morgue were adorned with artwork, simple posters framed in metal, and anti-reflective glass. Cody's favorite was a kid on a tricycle, dressed in motorcycle gear, pulling a wagon full of puppies. Shari caught Cody smiling at the photo.

"Reminds me that there's more to life than death," she whispered as if the dead could hear her.

The opposite wall had a work counter with cupboards above and another sink for cleaning tools. Adjacent to the cupboard, the wall was covered with less charming anatomy posters with scientific names pointing to various parts of the human body.

Shari moved past the island table to a large cabinet from floor to ceiling. It was twelve feet wide and eight feet deep. Six heavy doors made up the face of the storage unit. Shari opened the bottom left door and pulled a long shelf toward the middle of the room. The rack slid outward—a naked male body along for the ride.

The deceased man was identified as Warren Gilcrest. But who was Warren Gilcrest? Why would a person who lived in the southern part of the state show up murdered in Cain Lake? And why would anyone want him dead?

Cody stepped closer. Hassett stood on the other side of the sliding shelf.

Cody turned his head and studied the facial features, "Shari, does this man have an L-shaped scar on his forearm?" He stepped to the side and let Shari move closer.

"Actually, yes." She folded back a thin white sheet to reveal the corpse's right arm. She gave the arm a gentle twist outward to reveal the L. "How did you know?"

Tears cooled Cody's eyes, and he swallowed the grief forming in his throat, "Because this isn't Warren Gilcrest. This is my brother Michael."

*****

"What makes you think this is your brother?" Hassett asked.

"I just know. He hasn't changed that much. Wouldn't you recognize your sibling if you hadn't seen them in twelve years?"

Bassett thought about her sister. She could never forget her sister. "It's him."

Shari was confused. "We made a positive ID for Mr. Gilcrest, Cody. I'm sorry, but I don't think this is Michael. We reached out to his sister in White Plains this morning. She informed us that he'd been missing for a week. She filed a missing persons report and everything."

"I'm not arguing with your findings, Shari," Cody said. "All I'm saying is that Warren Gilcrest used to be Michael. He was adopted after our parents died. His name was changed. So, his sister must be an adoptive relative. I was never able to find him on my own, and I couldn't afford to hire an investigator. So, I figured he was probably in a better home now, away from the abuse we used to endure."

"We'll need to look into the adoption," Hassett said. "I'll give Marissa a call and see if she can find out something. There's got to be a record of it."

"I'll call the sister," Shari said. "She would have been about nine years-old at that time. She can tell us if her family adopted a boy."

"But we'll still need the report to make sure it was Michael," Hassett said. "Just in case, maybe we should get Cody's DNA sample to see if it matches the victim's."

Cody consented to the DNA test, which was quick and painless. He let Shari rub the inside of his cheek with a long Q-tip looking swab and then seal it in a glass tube. She labeled the tube with a blue marker and placed it in a cabinet constructed of clear plastic.

"That was easy," Cody said.

"Follow me," Shari said. She turned, pushed through the double doors .

Cody, Sheriff Hassett, and Shari, retreated to the coroner's office they had passed in the hallway. The office's walls were also adorned with artwork, drawn in crayon, ink, and marker, but more beautiful and intriguing than anything any of the three adults could produce. The artist, Roshan Kapoor, sat at a small table in the corner, working on his next piece of art.

Roshan was Shari's autistic son who would celebrate his twelfth birthday soon. He barely acknowledged the incoming group, seemingly focused on his work. Hassett stood in the hallway, just outside Shari's small office, to give the grieving ex-con some space. He didn't need the sheriff hovering over his shoulder.

Hassett's phone dinged. A text message from Simpson confirming Cody's story; Jesse Lewis was dead from a single gunshot to the chest. He was returning to get the boat to pick up Jesse Lewis's body.

She sent her response, "Good work. Call off the search. I'm at the morgue. I'll meet you at the boat launch."

Cody gave Shari the details about his parents' death—but not how he had killed them by closing the garage doors. Shari apologized for his possible loss and gave Cody advice on the next steps.

Shari was trying to call the sister in White Plains, who most likely was already on her way. There was no answer and no option to leave a voicemail. She hung up and made a mental note to try again soon.

Sheriff Hassett pocketed her phone and began shuffling through Michael's autopsy file. She stopped at a picture of Michael's abdomen. The letters S and R were crudely cut into delicate skin. Shari circled the image with a red wax pencil and wrote a question mark on the side.

Hassett was hungry for answers. "Shari, is it safe to say this is the work of Jesse Lewis, the Sin-eater?"

"I don't believe so, sheriff," Shari answered. "There was writing carved in the abdomen, same as his previous victims, but whoever did this," she thumbed toward the morgue, "wrote in a different style."

"How so?" Hassett answered. Her brow shortened.

"Well, the killer, in this case, made smooth lines, as if they made each letter in one smooth motion. Jesse Lewis cut in a jagged and angular style. It's like two different fonts. Two different weapons were used to make the cuts, which could be what produced the different styles."

"Are there any similarities?"

"None," Shari said. She posted two photos side-by-side on her computer monitor. The photo on the left was a graphic picture of Jesse Lewis's first known victim, Brody Sherwood. The word SINNER was engraved on his skin. The image on the right was Michael's stomach, but the wild animals had torn much of his flesh.

Cody looked away. He walked across the room and studied Roshan's process for producing artwork. The young boy never looked up from his creation.

Shari zoomed in on the first letter in each photo. "Jesse Lewis's cuts are shallow, barely breaking the epidermal layer, as you can see on victim number one."

Hassett squinted and bent at the waist to get a closer look.

"Warren Gilcrest—victim two—has deeper lacerations. The cutting motion was smooth, like the fine point of a sharp knife. The wounds bled more, which is probably why he was in a weakened state when he was in the water. But the two styles of letters are completely different. Someone copied the Sin-eater's work, but not his style."

"Great, he's got a fucking fan, now," Hassett crossed her arms over her breasts.

"Possibly," Shari continued. "There was also paint transfer on the victim's clothes."

"So, maybe he's a painter?"

"No, that's what I thought at first. But the paint was under his arms, too. Someone dragged him to the river and transferred paint to the armpit area. I think the killer was painting."

Hassett gave this some thought. "What color paint?"

"Dark green. I've sent a sample to the lab in Albany for detailed analysis. Still, initial reports confirm that it's an acrylic-based paint—probably utilized for automotive purposes, like a body shop."

"Sonovabitch!" Hassett cursed. "I have to go. Savage, I'm releasing you on your own recognizances—for now. Don't leave town. Go straight home and stay the hell out of trouble."

"Where are you going, sheriff," Shari asked.

"To arrest a murderer."

She bolted out the door, and Cody and Shari heard the powerful truck speed away, growling under the hood in anger.

Shari stood, nervous with anticipation. There was little for her to do but wait for the outcome of the sheriff's manhunt. She studied Cody for a moment. He'd been through so much in the last four years. She didn't know what kept him going. She walked to a coffee pot, still warm with the morning's brew. She poured a small amount into a ceramic cup, "Coffee, Mr. Savage?"

"Yes, please," Cody answered. He took a thick paper cup from a stack, filled it full, and added sugar. He stirred the liquid slowly, then spoke without looking up, "Who do you think she's going after?"

Shari shrugged, "Your guess is better than mine."

"I wish I knew where she was going. I'd follow her if I could. I want the S-O-B that did this," Cody said, watching his language in front of the minor in the room.

"She'll get him. She's relentless. Chicago gave her high praise for the work she did there. For some reason, she passed on a promotion to come here."

"What kind of promotion?"

"I think she was offered a detective position within her department."

"Hmm. Why leave the big city for Stoneville?"

"Her sister lives near by," Shari answered. "That's all I know. She wanted Roshan to draw a picture of her sister for her." Shari smiled with pride.

Cody stepped to the corner of the office where Roshan was working on a new project. He colored red lines over an alligator-shaped creature lying on a beach with a large boulder and green trees. The red lines bled into the blue water. It was as if Cody was back at Remington Bay looking down at Jesse's body—if Jesse were an alligator.

Maybe Jesse was the alligator.

Cody searched the wall, scanning all the pictures Shari had hung with pride. Roshan watched him for a second and then pointed to one with an interesting subject—third one down, second from the left.

Cody gazed at the picture of a crude-looking building with a flag-pole and old gas pumps at the front. Two garage doors occupied nearly half of the building. One of the doors was pulled open, allowing the viewer to peer inside the garage.

Cody stepped closer. Inside the open garage door, a faceless man sat in a chair. It wasn't detailed enough to tell if he was restrained or not. Footprints led from the garage to dark water with white-edged waves.

Cody dropped to one knee beside Roshan's table, pointing to the fantastical picture. "Ro, do you know where this picture is?"

Roshan pointed to his head.

"It's from his mind," Shari said. "He only draws what he imagines. He's never been there."

"No," Cody continued. "Do you know where this is in the real world?"

Roshan slid his chair away from the table and shuffled over to a map of Stoneville that Cody hadn't noticed before. The map was neatly framed in oak, on the wall opposite his little desk. His thin index finger pointed to a bay on the west side of Cain Lake.

Shari nearly dropped her coffee. She set the cup on her desk and glided over to the map. She put both hands on Roshan's shoulders, star-ing over his head. "There's nothing there. I'm Sorry, Cody, but his draw-ings aren't real. He makes them up."

Cody smoldered, "Oh yes, there is. Parson's General Store used to be there. I haven't thought of that place since I was a kid. I used to ride my bike there to buy Mountain Dew and Charleston Chews. It's been aban-doned for years."

Cody thanked Shari and her son and began walking toward the door.

"What are you going to do?" Shari yelled down the hall.

Cody turned briefly, "I'm going after the real killer."

25

PARSON'S 

Cody left Shari's office, crossed the street, and walked two blocks. It was four miles to Parson's General Store—over a one-hour walk. A car would get him there much faster. He thought about calling Daisy but decided against it. She was safe—somewhere—and Cody preferred to keep her that way. Involving AJ Timmons wasn't an option either. Cody was headed to the location of his brother's captivity and torment. The situation could be dangerous—deadly even.

He wished Bourbon was there to back him. Bourbon's experience and courage were just what he needed, but the former sheriff wasn't answering his cell phone—probably because he was in the vicinity of Cain Lake.

Cody was alone on this.

He missed his friends and his lover. It hurt to think they'd abandoned him when he needed them most. The sensation was similar to the feeling of his missing hand.

Phantom Pain.

A small hatchback car with wide road tires and a rumbling radio turned the corner, almost clipping the curb and diverting Cody's attention from his self-pity. The driver parked the car at the little drug store across the street and stumbled out of the vehicle. His steps were clumsy as he made his way around the front of the Honda Civic, leaving the car's engine still running. Cody cursed himself for the notion, but the car's running engine beckoned him inside. He was desperate for transportation to Parson's General Store, and there was an unoccupied vehicle with the motor running—right in front of him.

Serendipity.

He ambled casually across the street, popped open the door, and climbed behind the steering wheel like he owned the car. The seat was adjusted too close to the dashboard and reclined too far. Cody didn't have time to adjust the seat's position. He pulled the gear shift lever down, engaged the automatic transmission, and sputtered away.

Once he cleared the three-story buildings, he stopped at an intersection and changed the seat's position. The front tires spun as he peeled away, and he took the corners like a firefighter on his way to a three-alarm.

He liked how the little black car handled; it was fast and light and stuck to the road like a rollercoaster on rails. It took him seven minutes to reach the abandoned road to Parson's Store. He hoped his suspicion about the location was correct and stealing the little Honda was worth it.

The road was more like a long narrow driveway, just one lane wide.Fifty years of sun and frost had expanded and cracked the blacktop surface like desert sand, allowing grass to grow through the little fissures. The blacktop had turned to gravel after years of neglect, with a few patches here and there that were the only evidence that it used to be solid blacktop.

A set of fresh tire tracks packed two parralel trails through the weeds and tall grass. A basswood tree had fallen thirty yards from the entrance, and someone had cut the middle out with a chainsaw to allow access.

Someone's been busy.

He parked the black Civic fifteen yards down the road and exited. The sun was disappearing behind the treetops, no longer capable of casting shadows upon the ground. Cody knew he'd lose all light within the next thirty minutes, so he searched the stolen car for a flashlight. He found his prize in the back, rattling loose with the spare tire. The batteries were sleepy, but they would get him out of the woods in the dark.

He started down the road, listening for any danger ahead, but the sound of the spring peepers would have drowned out a marching band. At least they'd cover his approach.

The noisy little frogs indicated water ahead. But were they residing at the edge of the lake or in a small pond of water somewhere? The cacophony of noise they produced made it difficult to pinpoint their location.

Maybe they were everywhere.

Tall blades of grass brushed his thighs even though he stayed in the packed tracks on each side of the road. He kept low, not sure if it would make a difference if anyone were watching.

Parson's General Store was constructed in the 1940s by Edward and Betty Parson. The little store occupied an acre of Cain Lake's shore, and there was a town beach just a soccer field away. Beachgoers kept the store booming, and loggers would gas up their trucks in the mornings. The little store had something for every season. In 1981, the town had to rebuild the hydroelectric damn, and the entire lake's depth was raised seven feet. The resulting increase in water volume flooded the beach and the lower part of the road that led to Parson's. The popular store was nearly left on an island.

The town opened a new beach at Allison Park, much further south, and Parson's General Store suffered the consequences. They closed the retail location immediately after the flood and sold the property a decade later.

Cody wasn't sure who had purchased the land. Now a trespasser, he moved ahead regardless of the second crime he was committing in the last fifteen minutes. He was motivated by vengeance, and that made him dangerous—careless.

After an intentionally slow hike into the property, Cody found himself at a clearing where the abandoned building stood. The brick structure had large windows that were completely blacked out, but a dim light emitted from the garage door windows.

The two forgotten gas pumps had been removed years ago when the gas storage tanks were dug up for disposal. The cement island where the pumps once stood was stained with rust and bird crap. Eight rusty bolts, once used to anchor the pumps, protruded from the cement. The building was about sixty feet wide by forty feet deep. One-half of the structure was a two-stall garage—just like Roshan's picture—where Mr. Parson repaired cars. Both overhead doors were pulled down in the closed position.

The old road went past the store, circled right, and came back to the parking lot. But thirty yards ahead, three feet of water flooded the road.

That didn't stop someone from accessing the building. The tracks Cody followed cut to the right through sparse bushes, staying on dry ground. Cody followed the tracks, approaching the building from the side. Thakfully, there were no windows on this end of the building.

As Cody had closed the gap between himself and the old store, the sound of the frogs began to diminish. He wasn't sure if he'd just walked far enough to get away or if his presence had alerted them and they were silent in fear. But another noise caught his attention—the sound he had heard in every one of his recent psychic insights. The out-of-tune wind chime dinged from the far side of the building. Cody moved to the front of the building to investigate the sound. Like Roshan's picture, an empty flagpole stood at attention at the far corner of the building. The sound was produced by two snap-hooks fastened to a rope and knocking against the metal pole.

Cody was positive this was the place he'd seen in his vision. This is where Michael was held and tortured for what must have seemed like an eternity.

The gravel road led to a crumbled blacktop parking lot that surrounded the old business. During the years of operation, patrons could drive up to the gas pumps, fill up, and continue around the building for easier egress.

He thought about checking behind the store but decided against it. He wanted to get to the interior of the building and look for the clues he'd seen during his most recent vision. He needed tangible evidence of the killer's identity.

Fireflies began to appear in the tall blades of grass. Their iridescent bodies glowed as they flew in streaks of light. They reminded Cody of the micropods, moving in a blur of light—one creature in the water, the other in the air. Compared the micropods, the fireflies moved in slow motion.

A pair of mourning doves watched the intruder from the building's roof, taking refuge high off the ground, safe from predators. In a panic, the two birds took flight, but they flew only forty feet and perched on a power line supported by a splintered wooden pole.

Cody's eyes followed the wire from the pole to the building.

Let's go see who's paying the electric bill.

He entered the front door, a wooden beast with a shiny Marks lock and handle installed. The door was unlocked, and the hinges were well greased. It swung open with zero noise or resistance.

Who puts an expensive new lock on an old door and doesn't lock it? Unless, they're here.

He stepped inside, hoping the floor wouldn't creak, but was immediately disappointed. The sound of two floorboards rubbing together under his weight was like a Jurassic insect attacking. It was nearly as loud as the frogs outside, which were gathering in numbers and strength for their second vocal chorus of the night.

Cody's second step was less obtrusive—quiet as a church aisle. He thought about Michael in this place. Was he forced here, or did he enter through the heavy door of his own volition? Was he blindfolded and gagged? Was he kicking and screaming as his captor dragged him inside?

A claw hammer lay on the store counter. Cody picked it up and shook it to determine the weight. It was the only defense he had now if he were attacked. He felt at a disadvantage.

What's that saying? Never bring a hammer to a gunfight?

He scanned the shelves that once held canned goods and fishing tackle. They were empty now except for the dust and mouse feces. The smell of acrylic paint invaded his nostrils—the same smell he'd experienced in his visions.

His stupid vision of the past, not the present. How could he have been so off? Until now, Cody's visions were always in the present tense, but the images of Michael had already happened.

Michael was dead when this all started. He'd been trying to save a ghost.

Cody didn't want this power any longer. He was determined to find a way to exorcize Cain Lake's gift when this was over—if he survived.

He moved deeper into the store. He left his dying flashlight off, saving what little life it still had. Across the room, a dim light glowed around the edges of a door that led to the garage. Cody stepped toward it, hammer loaded, and gave the door a gentle push.

He focused on a man squatting in the middle of the room. He was large, even in his squatting position, with his back to Cody. His hands were working a wrench on a motorcycle engine. Cody could tell the Harley-Davidson was recently painted green, as an overhead light displayed the vehicle like a showroom piece.

He recalled his last vision; green paint overspray on the drop cloth. The outline created the shape of a motorcycle gas tank—the very one he was looking at now. The benches inside the garage were exactly the way he'd seen them in his mind.

The big man adjusted his kneeling position, dug into a pocket, and came out with a red pack of cigarettes. He tapped the top of the box several times and then pulled a loose cigarette free. A lighter clicked; a flame was born, and Amos McGrath inhaled through the tube of tobacco.

Shit. Why couldn't it have been someone smaller? Like King Kong?

He knew his first round with Amos—when they fought over the four-wheeler key—was a little bit of luck. He wasn't sure if even the hammer would help him the second time. He raised the hammer slowly and needed to keep his cool. He needed to knock Amos unconscious, not kill him. He only took one step.

The movement from his left came swiftly. Before Cody could take evasive action, a bundle of knuckles smashed into the side of his head. Cody didn't have time to counter before another blow sent him reeling. He stumbled forward and away, the room spinning and the floor rising. The floor dealt the next blow to his cheek. A fire burned his eyes briefly, and a metallic taste filled his mouth. The frogs chirping outside seemed to sing in slow motion now, and a deep voice he could not discern faded into the distance.

Darkness came for Cody Savage.

Cody didn't need to see his attacker to identify him. When the second punch landed, it was evident who threw it. Nobody in Stoneville could hit as hard as Levi Thompson.

26
REMINGTON BAY

Jeff Bourbon was sitting on the dead log when Deputy Simpson arrived at the crime scene. Bourbon watched the deputy guide the fourteen-foot-long boat through Remington Bay with a small trolling motor. The electric trolling motor was designed for patrolling shallow water and was less of a risk from damage caused by rocks and stumps. The boat made a wide arch and approached the beach from the south. Simpson nosed the bow into the soft sand eight feet from Jesse Lewis's body.

"Hey, Simpson," Bourbon said. His voice was soft, as if he didn't want to disturb the corpse at his feet. Simpson greeted Bourbon in return from the bow of the boat.

Bourbon's thoughts drifted in and out with the waves created by the boat.

Hell of a place to die.

There would be no crosses left here in Jesse's memory. No memorial or tributes would adorn the beach for the once-respected pastor. Jesse Lewis would be forgotten as the town began the healing process. The wounds from his violence would begin to scab over, possibly taking years to heal, but for some victims the scars would last a generation.

Deputy Simpson had already snapped his photos the first time he was at the scene. It had taken him fifty minutes to go back to the bridge, call the sheriff, and return with the boat.

"Need a lift?" Simpson asked Bourbon.

"That would be great. I need to get the hell out of these clothes and find myself a beer."

"Can't blame you," Simpson said. "What about her?"

Flesti was standing in knee-deep water, splashing lake water on her face. She marched straight over to Bourbon, "You can't go home yet, Bourbon. There's more work to be done."

"What the hell are you talking about?" Bourbon said. "Jesse's been found. That's what I came out here to do. Now he's dead. I'm done, lady. This guy's going home to take an appropriate shower and drink himself into a coma."

She grabbed his arm with both hands and squeezed it tight, "No, listen to me, please. We need to get to the old store on the west side of the lake."

Bourbon huffed, "Where? You mean Parson's store?"

"Yes, that's the place."

"Why, exactly do we need to go to Parson's? That place has been shut down for over twenty years."

Flesti didn't answer him, "Get Jesse's body loaded, and I'll explain on the way."

"Dammit, Flesti...fine," Bourbon said. "And Andrew Mills too. I'm not leaving this lake without that boy's body."

Bourbon joined Deputy Simpson, who was standing over Jesse Lewis, preparing himself for the grim task at hand.

"Goddam," Simpson said. He rolled Jesse's body to the side and examined the exit wound in Jesse's back. "That weren't no pistol to make a hole that big."

Bourbon shook his head gently, "No, it wasn't."

"Had to be a rifle," Simpson said. "Too long a shot from that hill to be accurate with a pistol."

Bourbon froze, looked up the hill and back at Deputy Simpson, "How'd you know the shot came from the hill?"

Simpson pointed at the body, "Hole in his chest is dead center. The exit hole in his back is near his kidneys. The bullet entered on a downward trajectory. And look at his foot prints. He was standing in front of the boulder with both feet nearly together, but he never stepped back. He musta flew four feet and landed on his ass. The bullet had to clear the boulder to hit its target. The only way to do that is from up above. Up on that ridge. Ain't no pistol gonna make that shot, Mr. Bourbon."

Bourbon nodded this time, impressed by Deputy's astute observation. "Grab his feet, would ya?"

Simpson took hold of Jesse's feet, lifting the emaciated figure high enough to set him over the side of the beached boat. Jesse looked like a corpse before he was shot dead, and now he was the real deal.

The two powerful men made short work of the job while Flesti watched stoically from the water's edge. She turned back to the north, her eyes fixed on the horizon where the mouth of Remington Bay opened wide. A black ghostly shadow approached from the direction of her gaze, skimming across the mirror surface as if it were racing its reflection. Wings beat up and down but never broke the mirror's smooth surface.

Poe cawed several times to announce his approach, glided to the boat and perched himself on top of the windshield.

"Now, let's go get Andrew," Bourbon directed.

Simpson noticed Bourbon's eyes were a little glossy. He had no idea who Andrew Mills was, but obviously, Bourbon knew him well enough to make a positive ID and get emotional over his death. "We best hurry. We're losing light fast. Let's try to get off the water before it gets too dark."

Bourbon stopped him, "Simpson, may I use your phone before we go?"

"Sure, Mr. Bourbon, if I've got a signal." He pulled the phone from the safety of his pocket. "You're in luck. One bar. We'll definitely lose service once we're on the water, so you best make your call from here."

Deputy Simpson handed over the phone and went back to the boat, sensing that Bourbon might want privacy.

Bourbon quickly dialed a number. Shari Kapor answered the call.

"Hello, Simpson," Shari said.

"Shari? No, it's me."

"Jefferson? Bourbon, is that you?" Her voice rose a few octaves.

"Yes," Bourbon said. "I'm on Simpson's phone."

"Oh, good. Good. I mean, it's so good to hear your voice. Are you okay?"

"I'm doing much better than Jesse Lewis."

"I heard. Sheriff Hassett was here with Cody Savage. She told me all about it."

Bourbon spun away from the cawing bird on the boat and took a few steps toward the woods, so they could clearly hear each other. Bourbon asked if Cody had been arrested.

"No—not yet, anyway," Shari said. "Sheriff Hassett thinks Cody killed Jesse Lewis, but she's on her way to arrest a suspect for the death of Cody's brother."

Bourbon shook his head in confusion, "Cody's brother is dead? How the hell did that happen? Cody said he was having visions of 'Michael' being beaten."

"Ugh," Shari said, imagining the horror of seeing a sibling suffer like that. "The man you found yesterday morning is the same man Cody saw being beaten. His name is Warren Gilcrest, but Cody is certain its his long lost brother Michael. If that's true, then Cody's visions were the past, not the present. Michael was already deceased."

"Sonova..." he stopped the cuss word, not wanting to spit it into Shari's pretty ear. "I'll bet whoever killed Warren Gilcrest, also killed Andrew Mills."

"Yes, I'm sure of it, too."

"I should go. We've got to retrieve Andrew's body."

"Bourbon, wait! There's something you should know."

Bourbon said nothing. He waited for her to reveal what was so urgent.

Shari continued, "I called Hassett after Cody left my office. She believes Deputy Simpson committed the murders. She's coming to arrest him. She thinks he killed Michael and possibly Andrew. She's already called Judge Hathaway and the DA to get a search warrant for his garage."

"Motherfu..." Bourbon trailed off again. He casually rested his hand on his pistol. "Is she sure?" He peeked over his shoulder at the boat's captain.

"She is, but Cody thinks he knows the real killer. He's going after him."

Bourbon was in a mental game of tug of war; his brain was pulled in two directions. If Deputy Simpson was guilty of killing Andrew, Bourbon couldn't let him return to the crime scene. But Cody seemed to think another killer was on the loose, and the kid was beginning to have a pretty good track record. He had to make a gut decision.

"Ready?" Simpson called out from the bow of the boat. He was waiting for Bourbon to climb in before pushing off into deeper water.

Bourbon held one finger up, signaling that he just needed a moment.

"Shari, tell me what you got," Bourbon said to the phone.

She recapped what she had told Sheriff Hassett and Cody. The evidence painted a profile of a strong man with bruised knuckles who'd been working with green paint. A large wrench was used for some of the beatings, perhaps a 17 mm open-end wrench, someone with mechanical skills.

"Hassett told me Deputy Simspon was restoring an old car in his off-time," Shari said. "Now, she thinks he's using it to cover up the evidence of his crimes. I think she might be correct. She was almost a detective in Chicago, you know?"

It didn't make sense to Bourbon. Sure, that description could fit Deputy Simpson, but what was his motive? Why would Simpson kill Cody's brother and possibly Andrew Mills?

Shari continued, "Cody saw a drawing that Ro created. It was hanging in my office, and he felt it was relevant."

Bourbon knew of the pictures well. He'd been in that office too many times over the last year. Roshan drew images and scenes from his imagination. Could the kid have the same psychic insight that corrupted Jesse Lewis and afflicted Cody Savage? The 'hocus-pocus' he was skeptical about was beginning to seem like the only logical reason Stoneville's residents were starting to act insane. He hoped Roshan wouldn't end up on his list of crazies.

"What was in the drawing, Shari?"

"It looked like an old gas station, with a man sitting in a chair," She replied.

"Parson's," Bourbon said. "Cody's going to Parson's old store." *Flesti was right.* "Does Cody still have a pistol?"

"No. Hassett confiscated his weapon to run the serial number. It's also going to be tested by forensics."

"Sonovabitch," Bourbon said, letting the word fly this time. "He's going to get himself killed. Thanks, Shari. I need to get over there."

"Jefferson, be careful, please."

Bourbon didn't hear Shari's last sentence as he pushed the red circle on the phone's screen. He hobbled over to the boat and handed the phone back to Simpson. "We gotta go. Simpson, I need you to drop me off at the old Parson's General Store. Just nose up to the beach there, and I'll jump out. You can take Flesti straight to the north boat launch."

"The hell with that," Flesti said. "I'm going to Parson's with you. You're going to need my help."

They all climbed aboard the boat. Simpson's cell phone rang. It was Sheriff Hassett checking on his status. When he told her what he was doing, she interrupted.

"Negative," Hassett said. "I need you to come straight back. It's urgent. You can drop Bourbon and his girlfriend off, but do not go after the other body." She was adamant he stayed away from the crime scene because he was her lead suspect.

"10-4, boss," Simpson replied. "Sorry, Bourbon, looks like I'll be delayed picking up your boy."

"No, that's good. We'll get Andrew in the morning—first light. We need to get to Parson's fast."

Bourbon's heart broke a little for Andrew Mills—again. He wanted to get him home and ensure he got a proper burial. He didn't want to leave him out here rotting like forgotten fruit in a garden. But Cody's life might be on the line.

The boat backed away from the sandy beach under the power of the little electric trolling motor. Simpson stood at the boat's bow, steering with the long handle attached to the motor and watching for stumps and rocks. When they safely navigated to the deep mouth of the bay, he tilted the motor up and out of the water, locked it in place, and moved to the driving console in the middle. He started the large Evinrude engine at the stern of the boat and pushed the throttle forward, putting the forty-eight-horsepower engine to work.

27

RIGHT LEFT RIGHT

Cody awoke from Levi's violent punch. It had been three minutes since the lights had been knocked out of him. He sat on the concrete floor, propped against a metal support beam. His arms were pulled behind the post and tied together. He could hear Amos McGrath on the other side of the wall that divided the garage. He was still tinkering with the parked motorcycle. The garage was dim; the five square windows in the overhead garage door barely had any light left filtering through. A single light bulb hung from a retractable extension cord, ascending from the ceiling, just like the one above Amos working on the motorcycle in the adjacent stall.

The man-door to Cody's left was filled by a figure nearly as wide as the door's frame. Cody immediately recognized Levi.

"You fucking sonovabitch! You backstabbing, piece of shit, asshole," Cody fought against his restraints; two thick zip-ties wrapped around each wrist and and interlaced together. "When I get out of here—"

"Please," Levi mocked. "You're not going anywhere. I'm not sure how you found this place. Oh, wait," a laugh and patronizing tone followed, "That's right, you're a goddam psychic." He walked to an antique propane refrigerator and grabbed a long-neck beer bottle. "What's your psychic ability telling you now, asshole? What's going to happen to you?"

"What the hell is going through your crazy fucking mind right now, Levi? I saw what you did to my brother. Why'd you kill Michael?"

Levi held the 17 mm wrench he had used to bludgeon Michael Savage. It was the length of a man's forearm with a chrome finish. The tool had been wiped clean, and a glimmer of light bounced off its metal surface.

Levi reached the middle of the room and pulled the lone lightbulb hanging from the ceiling. He waved the light toward his captive. The flash of light burned Cody's eyes for a moment.

"You tell me; you're so smart, Cody. Why am I doing this?"

Cody swallowed hard. The taste of blood oozed down his throat and then disappeared. "Revenge; is that it? You still think I killed your sister, don't you?"

"I don't think you killed her. I know it," Levi said as if it were as true as a math equation.

"So, you found my brother, brought him to Stoneville just to torture him to death," Cody said as if he too could solve equations.

"Okay, first of all, I didn't find your brother. Michael came here, to Stoneville, looking for you. He gave me some shitty story about being adopted by a rich family downstate and having to change his name. But he vowed to find you someday, blah, blah, blah.

"He'd heard about the shit storm you were in and came to reconnect. It was just my luck that someone pointed him in my direction to help find you."

Cody struggled against the zip ties again. The bulky bandage, with the regrowing mass underneath, prevented him from slipping his bonds.

Levi continued, "Secondly; I didn't kill your brother. Well, not on purpose, anyway. He was alive when we put him in a rowboat and pushed him out into the lake. What happened after that—" He gestured with open arms and shrugging shoulders.

"I thought it was Jesse Lewis you wanted? He's the one who carved up your mother!"

"Oh, I do. You're both on my 'Dickheads I should kill' list. And I'm not the type of man who leaves a list unchecked."

"Shove your checklist, Levi. Because I swear, there's no way you're completing it."

Levi paced around the garage for a moment. He stopped and leaned against the bench as if he wanted to explain himself. "Do you know that some animals use mimicry to catch their prey?"

Cody gave him a confused look, "What the hell are you talking about?"

"Mimicry. They look or act like the animal they want to attract—sounds, camouflage, and even behavior. Once their prey is close, they strike. So how do you catch a killer like Jesse Lewis who preys on sinners? You become a sinner. Simple as that. If the Sin-eater could sense my sins—be attracted to my sins—then I could lure him close enough to strike." His face turned solemn, "But he never did."

"So you used my brother as bait?" Cody shrained again, but only the skin on his arms was giving way.

"Using your brother was just a bonus," he laughed a little. "If the psychic, Cody Savage, could see people in danger, then surely he must've been able to see what I was doing to his brother. Oh, that must have driven you crazy?"

It had driven Cody crazy. Levi's plan for revenge was simple but only half effective.

"But you never drew Jesse Lewis out of hiding, did you?"

"No!" Levi yelled and smashed Cody's knee with the wrench. Tears filled Cody's eyes, but he refused to scream in pain. That was a satisfaction Levi would never get from him. "No, he never came looking for me. He never saw my sins. But you saw what was happening. I still haven't gotten Jesse Lewis, but I have you. Maybe the Sin-eater will see me tearing your head off for killing my sister and come after me."

"I didn't kill Willa." Cody shouted. "I loved her more than anything," He was talking fast now, not because he was trying to convince Levi, but because he wanted his last thoughts to be about her. "She was everything to me. Charlie Archer killed her—everyone knows the truth—and he paid for it. Bourbon made him pay. Bourbon loved your mom, and he's been out there," he nodded toward the state forest with his chin, "Out there tracking Jesse Lewis down. We had him until you shot and killed him yourself."

Levi gave Cody a genuine look of surprise and confusion. "He's dead? Jesse Lewis is dead?"

"Yes! Don't play stupid. I know you—or your men—put a bullet in his chest."

The wrench struck again, but this time it was the opposite knee. Levi didn't swing hard enough to break the bone. He wanted Cody to suffer before he killed him.

"Amos," Levi called to his associate. "Did you shoot Jesse Lewis?"

Amos McGrath had been sitting on an upturned bucket, trying to focus on the motorcycle rather than the violence. He appeared uninterested in Levi's agenda. He stood, wiped the grease from a ratchet, "Hell no. But he might be telling the truth. We heard a single gunshot from the south ridge of Remington Bay." Amos stepped around Cody and looked him up and down. The man had no emotion on his face but spoke freely. "Cody, we didn't kill your brother. Levi's telling the truth. We put a hurtin' on him." He shot a remorseful look at Levi. "But we're not killers."

"Amos shut the hell up," Levi interrupted.

Amos barked back, "This has gone too far, Levi. We're going to go down for Michael Savage's murder. Isn't that bad enough? You want to add Cody's death to that, too?"

Levi swung the wrench again, although Cody was not his target this time. Amos's head jerked to the left from Levi's backhand. The big man stumbled, fell against the wall, then slumped to the floor unconscious.

Levi's breathing was raspy and heavy as he stared down at the big biker.

Cody felt some empathy for Amos. The wrench birthed treacherous pain in the legs, but Amos took the steel right to the cheek.

Levi paced the floor, considering what to do, when a motorcycle circled the old building and parked in the back. Jeremy "Cricket" Morrison entered the dim room carrying a six-pack of Bud Light and a bag of convenience store junk food. "Holy shit! You got him," he was pointing at Cody, and Cody felt the second betrayal of the night. He thought Cricket was a good person who would do good things and eventually leave Stoneville. He was wrong.

Cricket shed his warm leather jacket to let the evening air cool his skin. He was wearing a sleeveless shirt and his skinny arms were covered with tattoos—the Road Baron insignia and the name "Cassidy" in red ink. Cricket noticed Cody reading the name on his arm, "My girl. Cassidy and I are going to get married someday." He laughed at the memory it conjured. "You know, Willa used to babysit me when I was a kid. I loved that girl. Thought we were going to get married. Of course, she was an old lady by the time I turned eighteen." He laughed again.

"Guess she had to settle for me," Cody said, giving the kid a dirty look.

"So, what's the plan, Boss?" Cricket said to Levi. "Tear him up?"

Levi removed his jacket. His arms were smaller than in previous years but still twice the circumference of Cody's. Levi had worked less on the family farm since Willa's death, and it was showing in his form. Yet he was still a formidable opponent. The wrench was dropped on the workbench. Levi twisted the cap off a beer bottle and poured half of the amber brew down his throat.

Cricket hopped himself onto the bench and sat guzzling his beer. He pointed with a beer bottle toward the man slumped in the corner. "What happened to Ass-hat McGrath?"

Levi set the beer bottle down, "We had a disagreement."

Cricket laughed again. He seemed to laugh at everything. He had no love for Amos McGrath and wasn't concerned about his condition. For all he cared, McGrath could be dead.

Levi took a wide stance over Cody, and struck him three times with a right jab—no wrench this time—just bare knuckles doing the work.

Cricket popped off the pail, arms raised as if he'd won a boxing round. The skinny biker turned on a radio, blasting the garage with a heavy metal sound that would cover any screams Cody produced. He set his phone on the bench, swiped to the camera, and began recording the violence.

Cricket kicked Cody with a Wolverine work boot. The steel toe cut his cheek.

Cody refused to scream, yell, or even flinch as he took the beating. Instead, he closed his eyes and imagined the good things that had occurred during the twenty-nine years of his life. He thought about Michael, his Uncle Bruce, and Willa. They were gone now—taken too early—and he knew he was on his way to greet them.

A hard blow came from the left—Levi, "Admit you killed her, and I'll make your death quick and painless."

A softer blow from the right—Cricket, "Fess up, you piece-of-shit."

Two blows from the left, "You want me to beat your ass all night?"

A kick from the right, "Guess he likes it."

They kept coming from both sides, like coyotes snapping at a dying buck.

Right.

Left.

Right.

Levi stopped momentarily, his right fist cocked back like a firing pin. He could tell Cody was about to speak and wanted to hear and record the confession. He knew the recording wouldn't be admissible in court, but he didn't care. This recording was for his personal pleasure, so he could brag about the beating he dished out and remind himself that he was the one who served justice to his sister's killer.

Cody spoke through swollen, bloody lips, "I'm done trying to convince you, Levi. Kill me if you have to, but everyone knows Charlie Archer killed Willa."

"Archer was a scapegoat! You and I know the truth."

"No. No, Bourbon wouldn't kill an innocent man, and you know it. You know him better than that. And whatever you do to me, Bourbon will make you pay."

Levi walked to the bench and picked up the wrench. "Bourbon will be the next dickhead I cross off my list." He swung the wrench and shattered the beer bottle like a cheap pinata. Glass shards rained down on the captive with the remaining brew. Cricket howled in laughter and gave the camera a hand gesture—pinky, thumb, index finger pointed out, ring, and middle finger tucked into the palm.

Levi squeezed the wrench as if he were going to twist it into a knot. "Bourbon should have protected my mom. He should have been there for her after the attack, but he's been off playing happy hiker."

"Annabel killed Archer's wife, Levi. Jesus, she shouldn't have run. Willa might still be alive if your mom hadn't run over Archer's wife with her car."

The blow from the wrench was Levi's argument. He was done talking.

Cody's world swirled. His ears rang. Warm blood ran down his head, curled around his neck, and soaked his collar. Everything blurred like the ingredients in a blender.

Silhouetted from the dim light that came through the windows, Cody could see a woman. She was the only thing in focus as the blender spun the walls and ceiling. He could see his former wife with an outreached hand and a look of sorrow.

He tried to take her hand, but his wrists were still tied. He started to cry—not from the pain, but because he couldn't reach her. Because he couldn't hold her.

28
WAVE OF LIGHT 

We're dead in the water."

"What the hell, Simpson? What's wrong with it?"

"I don't know, Bourbon. Give me a minute to check it out." Deputy Simpson stepped to the back of the boat and lifted the cowl covering the Evinrude engine. Bourbon and Flesti watched from the bow of the craft. Flesti's eyes drifted like the boat they occupied. She fixed her gaze upon their destination. A half-mile of open water lay between them. She sensed Cody's pain and spoke with urgency in her voice.

"Bourbon, we can't wait. We have to go." She grasped his forearm.

"I know. How's it looking back there, Simpson?"

"Not good," Simpson said. "I think the diaphragm's cracked on the manual fuel pump."

"Is that bad?" Flesti whispered to Bourbon.

He shrugged, "Doesn't sound good to me."

"We don't have time to wait." The smooth hand gripped tighter. Flesti sat on the gunwale and removed her boots. Bourbon watched. He knew exactly what she was going to do. He looked back at the deputy/ mechanic, unsure if he could fix the engine promptly. He scoured the lake shore and could see the sign for Parson's General Store. The structure was unmistakable behind the trees—rusty and faded from years of neglect. It was only a slight silhouette of no notice to a person who didn't know where to look, but Bourbon knew where to look. He stripped his boots but kept his holstered Smith & Wesson on his ribs.

Flesti dove overboard. Her splash was barely audible, and she disappeared into Cain Lake. Bourbon jumped feet first with much less grace and sent water flying when he broke the surface.

When his head popped out of the water, he shook it violently to expel the excess water from his long hair. He pushed the matted mess back and began to swim toward Flesti. She only waited for a moment to be sure he was following.

"Stay close!" Flesti yelled.

Bourbon did his best to keep up but lacked the conditioning to stay in the race. Flesti grew stronger by the day, gaining vitality from Cain Lake or the blue micropods. Whatever it was, Bourbon was starting to feel it too. His joints were more fluid, and the arthritic pain that afflicted his back and shoulders was absent. His only real complaint now was the sprained knee. His knee throbbed when he kicked in the water, so he mostly used his arms for propulsion.

Flesti was getting further ahead. *Jesus, she's like a friggin mermaid.*

A glow of light illuminated the bottom of the lake just below them as if the pool lights had turned on minutes before dark. Bourbon felt a pull and a push, both forces working in the same direction simultaneously. And then, he could feel himself moving faster through the water. Micropods swirled around him, rushing around and beside him like dolphins surfing the wake of a great ship. He seemed more buoyant and floated easier as the water around him created a streamlined current that carried him toward Parson's Store. It was like riding a slow wave.

So this is how she gets around the lake so fast.

Bourbon felt amazing, other than his knee. His lungs were clear, his muscles tireless and energized, and his body tight and powerful.

He kept his eyes on Flesti and the store. The last of the sun's rays were creeping away, and the twilight was losing strength.

Behind them, sitting in the boat, Deputy Simpson watched the glowing blue water carry them away.

Deputy Simpson rubbed his eyes, but the illusion was still there. Two people were swimming through a blue ribbon of light toward an old store to save a man who might be captured by a biker who's looking for revenge because his sister was killed and his mother was attacked by the serial killer. Now, that very serial killer lay dead in his boat.

"How am I going to put this shit in a report?"

29
THE OPEN DOOR 

Cody was caught somewhere between awake, unconscious, and dead. His eyes stayed open as Levi and Cricket took turns beating him. The pain chewed at his bones and muscles. His nerves were on fire. His eyes fell on the only person in the room not trying to kill him.

Amos started to awake, stirring in the corner on the greasy garage floor. He picked himself up, barely, and rubbed his jaw. It was a miracle his mandible wasn't broken. Maybe the big guy was tougher than Cody thought, and Cody hoped for a moment that he might go after Levi in a fit of rage. But Amos had been put in his place by the wrench—which loosened the bolts in his brain. He was wobbly from a concussion and just stood there—spectating the mayhem occurring in Parson's small workspace.

Levi stopped swinging the wrench and took a moment to revel in his brutality. His breath was labored from the exertion. He wanted Cody's pain to last the night, but Cody wanted it over now. Only one man would get his wish.

Levi set the wrench down and pushed a button on the wall. Thanks to a newly installed opener, the large overhead door lifted from the floor, and the cooler night air entered in a rush, giving Levi the fresh oxygen he desired to rejuvenate tired muscles. The twilight had faded; the sky had been unplugged, except for a few stars and one planet that teased the dark. The single light bulb still glowed in the center of the garage.

Levi turned back to Cody and stood at his feet. "Still alive?"

Cody managed a one-finger gesture.

"Good." Levi and Cricket had been careful not to land their blows on any of Cody's vital areas. They confined most of the beating to his legs and arms, only lightly striking his head and ribs. But a light hit with a wrench was like a slight burn with a flame thrower.

"Piss off," Cody said, spitting blood as he spoke. His regrowing hand on his left arm throbbed with pain. Maybe it was still trying to grow back. Perhaps it was just his racing pulse that exacerbated the phantom pain. Maybe the bony hand wanted to be let loose to fight back. The bandages had come loose and unraveled onto the garage floor, soaking up grease and blood. Outside, Cody could hear the hooks banging against the flagpole like an annoying clock chiming, clicking away the seconds, tracking his last moments. The wind blew gently through the garage door, bringing the scent of spring upon its breath.

And Cody smiled.

"Something funny fuck-face?" Levi asked.

Cricket went for a hammer, "Maybe we should knock that smile off his face." But a subtle hand gesture from Levi directed him to drop the tool.

Cody brought his knees up, pulling his feet closer until he squatted. It pained him to do so, but he mustered the strength anyway. He decided there was a chance after all. A chance to survive, get past all this and be with Daisy again. The lilacs reminded him of his flower, Daisy. He saw her smile in his mind and felt her love within him. He took a couple of deep breaths so he could speak.

"You made a mistake killing Michael, Levi. You're going to pay for what you did."

Levi just smirked. "How's that? Michael can't save you. No one can save you. Your whole family is dead, and you're all alone."

Cody propped himself a little taller, "You killed my brother Michael. But you didn't kill my only brother, asshole."

Levi heard a click behind him, and when he turned, AJ Timmons stood with a shotgun pointed right at Levi's chest, "Get away from him, you piece of shit, or I swear, I'll put a hole in you so big there won't be anything left to autopsy."

Levi took a few small steps to Cody's right and kept his hands in sight.

He wasn't scared of what the shotgun could do; he was pissed about the interruption. He stayed calm, hoping AJ wouldn't unleash the buckshot into his torso.

"Timmons, this has nothing to do with you. Be smart and walk away before I take that shotgun and shove it up your ass," Levi braved a half-step toward AJ, but AJ raised the gun level with Levi's head. The aggressor stopped midstep.

Outside, an engine rumbled, and Cody recognized the V-8 Ram Rebel TRX. The truck tires squealed with fury, followed by a rattling sound and the horrific sound of clanging and scraping metal.

"Go see what the hell's going on!" Levi barked at Cricket and Amos.

The two bikers followed his command and ran through the interior door, across the store, and out the front door. Once they rounded the corner outside and passed the gas pumps, they saw AJ's truck pulling away, dragging two motorcycles behind it like tin cans.

Alyse Burns was behind the wheel of the TRX. She had one hand out the window with her middle finger prominently displayed and screaming an obscenity no one could hear over the roar of the engine.

River Kelly, AJ's new love interest, sat in the passenger seat yelling, "Go, go, go, go!"

Daisy Torrez occupied the back seat. She wanted to scream but was breathless from the adrenaline rush. Her grip on the front seats was so tight she nearly ripped the fabric. She kept her head down, frightened that the two men pursuing them on foot might have guns and start firing away.

The truck spun up the old overgrown road. Amos and Cricket chased on foot but stopped after forty yards. They knew their pursuit was hopeless and gave up. Alyse saw the two men stop running in the rearview mirror, illuminated only by the truck's taillights.

Amos watched the truck's brake lights turn brighter. He was bent over, his hands on his knees, and gasping for air. He stood, waved the Ram 1500 off, and walked a couple of small circles to catch his breath. Neither of the motorcycles was his, so his concern for their retrieval faded quickly. He squatted on his heels, rested, and waited for Cricket's reaction. He was too tired to speak and saved his breath for whatever might happen next. He couldn't remember the last time he ran that far. He couldn't remember the last time he ran.

Cricket had ceased the chase as well. He stood huffing, but not nearly as much as his hulking Road Baron brother. He fetched a pack of short Marlboros from his pocket, knocked the top of his Zippo lighter, and sparked the butane. He exhaled the smoke in a slow, deliberate breath. It enveloped him like he was wearing it. He took four drags from the cigarette before he started walking backward. He flipped Alyse off with both hands, even though she probably couldn't see his gestures from that distance, then turned and began a slow jog back to the store.

Alyse stood outside the parked truck, ready to jump behind the wheel if the men came after them with a vehicle. River Kelly walked to the back of the Ram and unhooked the chain that secured the two Harley-Davidsons. Daisy stayed in the safety of the truck and watched out the back window, too scared to move. She wished she was as brave as Alyse and River. She wanted to run down the road to jump into Cody's arms. But all she could do was cry and hope AJ's plan would bring her lover back to her.

30
WORTH IT

AJ stepped cautiously behind Cody, keeping the twelve-gauge shotgun pointed at Levi. Levi backstepped to the workbench, keeping his eyes locked on the gun's owner.

AJ pulled a small pocket knife from his pocket, unfolded the blade, and snapped the zip-ties that held his best friend. "You okay?"

"Yeah, I'm fine," Cody lied. "Thinking about going dancing when this is over." He wobbled to his feet and tried his best to stand straight. The pole that kept him captive seconds ago was now his crutch. He leaned against it with his left elbow for balance. Every blow Levi and Cricket had landed hurt like hell. Every bruise swelled, making his joints hurt and burn with pain. He stumbled and started to go down to the floor, but AJ dove under his arm and pulled him up to take his weight.

"Let's get the hell out of here, pal," Cody said.

"What about him?" AJ was still pointing the shotgun at Levi.

"Leave him. He's going to pay for this, but not today," Cody said. Then, he stumbled, and his entire weight pulled on AJ. AJ fought the fall. His knees buckled in unison with Cody's, and the two nearly tumbled onto the floor. AJ held tight to his friend, refusing to let him drop.

Levi took advantage of the moment. AJ was off guard, the shotgun waving aimlessly. Levi gripped the wrench and, in a flash, heaved it across the room. The tool hit center mass, knocking AJ backward, and the gun fired. The small pellets missed Levi's head except for a few that perforated his left ear. Blood dripped down Levi's neck as he attacked before AJ could pump another round into the chamber.

Cody fell to his knees before the shot went off. When he lifted his head, he could see Levi in tackle formation. Levi and AJ collided like a bowling ball and pin, and the result was as expected. The bowling ball plowed through the pin and knocked him to the far wall. The air left AJ's lungs with a forceful grunt.

"I warned you, asshole!" Levi screamed. "You nearly shot my damn ear off."

AJ came up with an uppercut to Levi's chin and followed it with a jab to the bridge of his nose. The big biker was unfazed, even though AJ's punches had some sting. Levi started to throw body shots at his lightweight opponent. Ribs broke under his power, and AJ struggled to breathe. AJ began to fall, his knees giving out like bendable straws. Levi grabbed his skull and bounced it off the cinder block wall. After the fourth bounce, AJ Timmons blacked out, and Levi let him collapse to the floor.

Cody had watched in horror as his best friend took the abuse. He forced his body to respond to his commands, dove forward, and came up with the shotgun. He struggled to regain his stance, but managed to get back into a standing position.

He gripped the pump with his right hand, threw the gun upward without letting go, and pulled back down hard, then up again. The action pumped a shotgun shell into the chamber, readying the Mossberg for lethal business. He moved his right hand down to the stock, gripped the wood tight, and kept his index finger on the trigger.

He steadied the gun's barrel with the bloody growth at the end of his left arm. The blood-soaked and greasy bandage dangled from his wrist.

"You won't do it. You'll go back to prison if you do—for life." Levi said calmly, staring Cody down.

"It'll be worth it, you piece of—" Pain interrupted his words. Before he could pull the trigger, the hot sting of metal pierced his flesh and shocked his system. His entire back spasmed, and he lost control of his motor functions. Then he felt the pressure release as Cricket pulled a six-inch knife blade out of his back.

Cody's knees buckled again. He twisted around to see the face of betrayal holding the blood-covered knife.

31

STARRY NIGHT

Cody was prepared to hit the floor hard. He was falling away from Cricket and could see Levi to his right in his peripheral vision. The shotgun was still clasped in his hand, but Cody's fingers refused his command to shoot. He wanted to point the gun at one of them and fire— *take one of the bastards with me.*

But he didn't hit the floor. He felt two large arms catch him and cushion his fall. Amos McGrath let Cody down gently with his left hand while grabbing the shotgun with his right. Cricket stepped forward, ready to jab Cody again, but his right arm suddenly disappeared in a blast of blood and gunpowder. His arm was gone from the elbow down and the force of the blast dislocated his shoulder.

He glanced at Levi—frozen in time. Then his eyes fell to Amos, kneeling over Cody with the shotgun leveled, smoke pluming from the end of the hot barrel.

The pain bit him like a viper, lightning fast and unstoppable.

As Cricket let out a deafening scream, Levi bolted out the overhead door. He knew he would be Amos's next target. He knew he needed to get away. He shot around the back of the building, his heavy boots stomping hard through thick grass. Amos's truck was hidden between the store and a row of thick pine trees behind the building. The keys were in the ignition—the keys were always in the ignition—and Levi fired up the old Chevy and sped away. Gravel flung from the tires and peppered the exterior of the building.

Cricket rolled around on the floor, blood puddling under his torso, spewing from a stubby arm that ended at the lower end of his bicep.

His once attached hand lay in the parking lot outside, with only a few inches of the forearm bones attached.

"Drop your weapon!" A voice called from outside.

Amos couldn't see the source of the voice but knew they could see him in the well-lit garage. That would give him a disadvantage in a firefight. Besides, he'd had enough of the violence for a lifetime. He set the shotgun down gently and raised his hands.

Bourbon entered the door and into the light with his pistol drawn and the hammer in the firing position. "Cody? Cody, are you okay?"

Cody was too weak to talk or respond. He writhed in pain, more concerned for his unconscious friend lying six feet away. He pointed to AJ. *Get AJ. Help AJ, please!*

"Jesus f'n Christ!" Bourbon said. "Looks like a friggin warzone in here." He kept the gun pointed at Amos, "On your belly. Now!"

Amos complied. He pointed to Cody, "He's been stabbed. He needs a doctor."

"Oh, damn," Cricket shouted. "Fuck him. I need an ambulance, man," Cricket shouted. "I'm going to die!"

"Shut the hell up," Bourbon demanded.

Flesti came in behind Bourbon; her eyes went straight to Cody. She ran to his side and immediately put pressure on his stab wound. "Can you walk?"

Cody was able to murmur a few words. His voice was raspy and weak, "Don't worry...AJ...help AJ." Flesti ignored his plea. Cody pointed at the big man lying on the floor when he spoke, "Bourbon...Bourbon, he saved me. It's okay." Bourbon gave Amos a stern look, "That true?"

Amos only nodded. He worked to get to his knees and pointed at Cricket with his chin, "He stabbed Cody. I blew his friggin arm off as he came at him again. Holy shit, I blew his arm off." The tough guy's stone hard shell melted away as reality set in, and a few tears rolled over his cheeks into his beard. "Jesus, oh, Jesus, I'm sorry. I didn't mean to hurt anyone." He realized at that moment that shooting a man was nothing like throwing punches. He hated himself for what he'd done to Cricket but hated Cricket more for what he'd done to Cody and Michael Savage.

"It's okay, son," Bourbon said to Amos. "Just relax. We need to help these three men. Can you help me? Can you do that?"

Amos gave a slight nod when he stood. Bourbon's nerves went haywire when he realized the man's enormous stature. But Amos slumped over to Cricket, pulled a rag off the bench, and tied it tightly around the mangled arm to stop the bleeding.

"Gotta phone, kid?" Bourbon asked Amos as he looked over at AJ.

Amos reached into his vest's inner pocket and showed it to Bourbon.

"Give it here," Bourbon demanded. He dialed 9-1-1 and ordered an ambulance to their location: three victims, one in serious condition and two in critical.

Bourbon came to Flesti's side and whispered, "I don't think they're all going to make it. We need to get them to a hospital—fast."

"Not all of them," Flesti said. She turned to Cody, "Can you stand?"

Cody nodded, but in truth, he wasn't sure. He was barely hanging on now but only wanted Bourbon and Flesti to save AJ.

"We have to get him to the lake—to the water. It's the only way he'll survive," Flesti said.

"What? No," Bourbon argued. "We have to get these men to the hospital."

She took Bourbon's hands in hers and locked eyes with him. "Bourbon, I'm asking you this one time. Trust me. Trust Cain Lake. Cody's bond with the lake is stronger than anyone else I know. I can feel it."

Bourbon would have dismissed the plea as utter nonsense from a crazy woman who lived in the woods, but lately, he'd seen things he couldn't explain. Things that defied nature. Things that defied science, and now he believed there was something special about Cain Lake and Cody Savage. Besides, he wasn't very optimistic he'd survive the long journey to the ER.

Convinced, Bourbon said to Amos, "Help me get him up."

Amos lifted Cody by the armpits as Bourbon ducked under and braced his wounded companion. Bourbon and Amos each took a side to hold Cody upright. Cody moved his feet, trying to walk to the lake to humor Flesti's request. What did it matter now? He was a dead man. The wound in his back was deep and deadly. He knew that. So he could die in the hospital, in an ambulance, or floating face down in Cain Lake.

It didn't matter now.

His effort was frugal, so Bourbon and Amos did most of the work. They dragged him across the dark parking lot, over a grassy knoll, and to the lake's edge. Years of erosion, waves, and wakes, left the shore craggy and broken. Cobblestones, the size of cantaloupes, took most of the brunt from the waves, but the larger waves were too stubborn to be held back. The shore was beaten like a dirty rug, over and over, breaking down fiber by fiber, day after day.

Flesti followed close behind and then scooted ahead when they reached the water. The two big men guided Cody to waist deep water and laid him back. He didn't float, so Flesti supported his head. Cody stared skyward. His watery eyes smeared the stars and moon within his sight. He was lost in a Van Goghesque world, swirling with the paint, feeling wet and smudged like oil on canvas. It was a beautiful starry night to die.

As he stared at the vast night sky, little stars appeared from below, swirling like a reflection of the night sky and magnifying it a millionfold. All of them blue. All of them focused on Cody Savage. They darted in and out, feeding on his pain and suffering. It had been weeks since the micropods had fed on human affliction. And this was a feast.

Cody heard screaming from the direction of the garage. A familiar voice called his name as it approached. The water splashed around him. The micropods disappeared as Daisy ran into the lake. She panicked and pushed through the water's resistance to reach Cody. She screamed his name, and he called back to her as if he was trying to reveal his location. She pushed Amos to the side, not intimidated by his massive form, and cupped Cody's face in her hands.

"What—" She stuttered. "What happened?"

Bourbon spoke for him, "He was stabbed—in the back."

"We need to get him to a hospital," Daisy yelled.

"No," Flesti said. "He won't make it there in time. He needs this—the lake water."

Daisy knew Cody's secret and how his hand was growing back, like a lizard's tail regenerating. She also knew it seemed to accelerate when they were at the lake. She thought it was crazy but also knew it to be true.

Reluctantly, she put her trust in Flesti's plan, gave her a nod in agreement, and let them continue.

The micropods returned one by one, and then one-hundred by one-hundred. They came in like sharks taking a bite just for taste and returned quickly to stay for the full course. They fed on Cody's energy and pain and before long, it was nearly impossible to single out one of the organisms. The water glowed with an eerie blue light the size of a truck, surrounding around everyone in the water.

Cody's attention deviated from the stars to Daisy's brown eyes. It was easier to see her now with the ambient light from the liquid world below. He smiled and put his right hand behind her head, pulling her closer. With their foreheads pressed together, they waited. She waited for the healing to begin, while Cody anticipated his death. He wasn't lucid enough to understand what was going on.

Amos began to freak out at the scene. It was the first time he'd seen the phenomenon. It was the first time he'd seen Cain Lake's secret. "What the hell? What the hell is happening?" His voice was high, and the words came fast. "What are those things?"

"Relax, son," Bourbon said. "They won't hurt you."

Amos wasn't convinced. He sprinted to the shore and out of the water. His pants, soaked from the thighs down, had a few streaks of blue, glowing light. He began slapping his legs as if fire ants were crawling up his jeans. The micropods were stubborn, but eventually, their light faded and died.

Alyse and River were at the garage, tending to AJ. There was little they could do for his head trauma except wait for the ambulance. It wasn't long before they heard a siren in the distance approaching their location. They were sobbing over their unconscious friend, and River even interlaced her fingers and prayed.

Both men were fading—teetering on the verge of death. Both men were surrounded by loved ones. Both men needed a miracle to survive.

32

WASHING MACHINE

Simpson, what the hell is going on?" Hassett shouted into her phone. Deputy Simpson's ear burned from her tone. His phone was barely receiving a cell signal, so he needed to stay in one place.

"I'm not sure," Deputy Simpson replied. "I heard shooting—"

"Where are you?"

"Uh...In the boat."

"The boat? What are you still doing in the boat? Get your ass to shore and find out what the hell is going on. I'll be there as soon as I can."

"Well," Simpson said. "That might be a problem, boss. The patrol boat shit the bed. Can't get it to fire. I think it's the—"

"I thought you were a mechanic? Fix it."

"Yeah, I'm working on it, but I don't think it's fixable—not out here. I'll use the trolling motor to get back if I have to. Don't want to be stranded out here all night, floating around with a corpse." He looked at Jesse Lewis's body lying on the bottom of the boat and shuddered. *I don't get paid enough for this creepy shit.*

"I'm sure Bourbon can give you a hand. The two of you should be able to figure it out."

"Well, that's the second problem, boss. Bourbon and the hermit lady jumped overboard. They're swimming across the lake in a blue—. They're swimming across the lake."

"What the hell do you mean? Why would they jump off the boat?"

"Because it's not running," Simpson shook his head because he wasn't sure how to explain the events unfolding without sounding insane.

There was a long pause on the line. Sheriff Hassett finally responded,

"Just get to Parson's Store as fast as possible. I'll meet you there." She clicked the disconnect button without a chance to say another word.

Simpson took the cowl off the boat's engine and studied the components. He couldn't see the problem but was sure it was the diaphragm.

He had heard the gunshots at Parson's as if he'd pulled the trigger himself. It was amazing how well sound carried across the flat, placid surface of the water. He heard the shots, some yelling, and then a woman scream. He could sit here all night and eavesdrop on half the town. The whispers—and sometimes shouts—skipped across the lake's surface like a well-thrown flat stone.

He finally gave up on diagnosing the engine. It was dark. He couldn't see what he was working on, even if he could fix it. He went to the front of the boat, hooked the trolling motor terminals to a battery, tilted the shaft down into the water, and turned the little electric motor's speed control as high as it would go. The twelve-volt motor hummed as it began to push the boat through the water. He moved at a pace equal to a brisk walk. He felt like a turtle in a race, but as long as the battery stayed charged, it would get him to the abandoned gas station.

*****

Deputy Simpson pushed the motor to its limit and arrived at his destination in eleven minutes. He twisted the throttle to the stop position and glided gracefully parallel to the cobblestone shore. He was sixty yards from the edge of Cain Lake, where one man stood on the rocky beach, and three people stood in the water. The people in the water surrounded a man floating on his back.

The same glowing water that had carried Flesti and Bourbon across the lake illuminated the shoreline. Simpson wasn't sure if it was because it was darker now, but the lights were a hundred times brighter than before. The blue light had been gentle while carrying the two swimmers, but now it churned, bubbled, and agitated in the shallows like someone dropped a powerful flashlight into a washing machine.

Simpson powered up the boat's spotlight and rotated it counterclockwise toward the shadowy figures circling the washing machine.

190

He instantly identified Bourbon and Flesti but not the others.

"Simpson, turn that damn light off!" Flesti shouted.

Simpson obliged and pressed the power button to the "Off" position as if he were taking orders from the sheriff herself.

"Who's shooting?" Simpson asked. "Is everyone okay?" His voice was almost a yell like he was competing against the sound of the washing machine. But the truth was it was just his adrenaline and police training. No one replied to his questions. They were all focused on the figure floating in the middle of the machine. Simpson couldn't identify the guy, but based on his conversation with Bourbon and Flesti earlier, he knew it must be Cody Savage.

He tried to call Hassett and give her a description of what was going on, but his phone had lost its signal again.

He contemplated driving the boat away from the scene, toward the middle of the lake. Maybe he could get a signal there. But he needed to save the trolling motor's battery and Sheriff Hassett wanted him at Parson's Store when she arrived. She'd be there soon and hopefully witness the strange event occurring with her own eyes.

Bourbon took three steps into the deeper water and faced Deputy Simpson. "Simpson, just give us a minute, please." He glanced back to the man floating in the blue water. "We just need a little more time. Don't start the boat, and keep your distance. This man's life may depend on it."

"Who's life, Bourbon?"

Bourbon didn't answer. He went back to the circle of friends holding Cody above water. He returned to the miracle.

33
CLAIRVOYANTS 

Cody was cold. So cold. He fought to keep his eyes open but was losing control of his body. Van Gogh's stars dimmed like dying fireflies. Daisy stood over Cody as he floated on his back, forcing her blooming smile that she was famous for. She stayed positive, giving Cody hope. But the flower wilted as Cody went unconscious.

Cody's clairvoyant ability was working again. He knew he was in a dream state because he could no longer feel the cold or pain. He stood in a room so large that the walls were out of sight. The ceiling was ugly foam panels with metal supports, like the drop ceilings he remembered from high school. The floor was similar to smooth black marble with a faint reflection. There was nothing but a void in every direction.

He walked, not knowing where he was going or what direction he was traveling. He just walked, expecting to see someone in danger. That's how it always worked; his ability to see people in danger.

He hated it. He hated seeing the things he'd seen. His psychic insight didn't help him save his brother. He had been chasing an illusion—a phantom—a dead man. And what did it get him?

Daisy would be furious with him.

He was beaten and stabbed.

AJ was possibly dead or dying.

Levi Thompson had gone too far. He needed to pay for what he'd done to Michael and AJ. Cody knew he had to pull through. There was no giving up.

"Can you see me?" A voice called out, echoing off the walls that didn't exist. It was a tiny voice—a child. Cody had hoped he was alone, but the owner of the voice was proof that his visions were still occurring.

"Do you need help?" Cody called out.

"No," The voice answered. "You do."

"Where are you?"

"I'm here," The voice was immediately behind Cody.

Cody spun 180 degrees and looked down at the child—a boy, of Indian descent, with a round face and brown eyes looking up at him innocently. Cody knelt, "Roshan? Ro, what are you doing here?"

"I thought you required some assistance, Mr. Cody," Roshan said. He was standing with his arms behind his back and smiling—something Cody had never seen him do. He'd seen Roshan earlier that day at Shari's office at the morgue, drawing more pictures to hang on the wall. But what was he doing here in Cody's vision? How was he speaking? He'd never spoken a word in his life.

This isn't real. This isn't possible.

"I created this illustration for you," He held a sheet of paper twelve inches wide by nine inches tall. "I didn't possess all the correct hues to create a triadic color scheme, so I just rendered the image with split compliments." He said it as if he were a little disappointed in himself. "I've got to have mom purchase more art supplies."

Roshan handed the drawing to Cody. It was more detailed than any picture he'd drawn before. Cody could smell the fresh markers and ink on the smooth hot press watercolor paper. Everything was outlined with black ink like a comic book panel and colored with marker. The image depicted a man and woman pushing two children on a swing set. It was clear the subjects were he and Daisy. Daisy was wearing a yellow dress and looking at the man beside her, who smiled back. She was pushing Sammy. Cody recognized his ballcap with the embroidered star on the front—a souvenir Alyse had bought him from a day at the mall.

Roshan had drawn Cody in a purple shirt and blue jeans. He was pushing a little girl on the swing. The girl on the swing looked away from Sammy with an expressionless face.

The images on the paper began to move like a Disney animation. Daisy pushed Sammy, causing him to swing higher and higher, while

Cody just gave the little girl a slight push to create some momentum.

"Is this the future?" Cody asked Roshan.

"It was, but I drew this last week," Roshan answered. "Your actions have consequences. Your decisions are rash, and your behavior is reckless. This was the future—last week."

Ro took the drawing from Cody, pinching it in the middle with both hands. He then tore the image down the middle and handed half back to Cody. Cody stared at the torn paper. In the drawing, Cody now stood alone at the swing set. The color and the ink had all turned to shades and tints of gray, creating a monochromatic depiction of Cody's future.

Roshan held up the other half of the paper. The little girl was now in Daisy's arms. Sammy stood beside his mother, holding her hand. They were all smiling—happy without the other half of the picture. A subtle shadow formed across the paper, moving slowly toward the family with no dad, like a snake in the grass.

Cody reached for Daisy's side of the drawing, hoping there was some way to put the two pieces back together and make it whole again. But both sides turned to ash instantly with no flame or heat. Gravity took hold of the ashes as a light zephyr carried them away before they could settle to the floor. The image was gone and impossible to fix.

Cody spun to his left and then back to the right, "Ro? Ro, are you still here?"

"I have to go, Mr. Savage. You have to go too."

"Can you see the future, Ro?" Cody ran toward Roshan's voice, but it echoed all around him. Cody ran in small circles, trying to hone in on Roshan's location. But, the voice was only a voice—as intangible as the wind.

"Ro, where is Levi Thompson? Can you tell me?" Cody was frantic now. Roshan had shown him a glimpse of the future. He sensed that, although his mind conjured this place, his interaction with Roshan was real. While Cody's body lay submerged in Cain Lake, his mind was free to wander and interact with another clairvoyant. Cody thought he was the only one with this ability, but now he knew Roshan's secret. He'd have to decide whether or not he should reveal that secret to Shari.

Roshan whispered something before he faded out of the dream-like state they were visiting. The room darkened as if a custodian, hiding behind a curtain, shut down the lights. Cody felt cold water against his skin, and the frigid sensation returned. Voices, muffled by water, talked in monotone.

He opened his eyes to exit the psychic episode. With the support of Daisy, Bourbon, and Flesti, he floated on the surface of Cain Lake.

Gravity pulled Cody's feet to the bottom of the lake, and he stood. He was in waist-deep water. A feverish burn enveloped his body and steam rose from the lake's surface. He welcomed the heat as it suffocated the cold sensation gripping him. The pain in his back disappeared. The bones in his ribs felt whole again. He let out a guttural growl as he caught his breath. It felt as though he hadn't breathed in hours.

Daisy threw herself at him, wrapping her arms around his burning body. The heat was nearly uncomfortable to her, but her grip was unbreakable. She finally relaxed, tears soaking her cheeks, and whispered, "Are you okay?"

There was a blue glow in his eyes, and Cody nodded that he was fine. He kissed her as his body temperature returned to normal. He'd never been so happy to see her, but his concern was diverted to thoughts of his best friend, "AJ? Where's AJ?"

"They took him to the hospital," Daisy said. Alyse and River are with him. He's going to be okay, but he was still unconscious." In truth, she had no information on AJ's injuries or condition, but she needed to ease Cody's mind.

Bourbon was staring at Cody's left hand, speechless at the sight. Flesti just stood there with a satisfying smile on her face. Her faith in Cain Lake's power had been put to the ultimate test, and her adamant decision to bring Cody to the water was justified.

Cody raised his left fist from the water. He stared at the hand that had returned. His bewilderment was no less than anyone else's. Then he turned toward shore and began taking long, powerful strides toward shore.

"Where are you going?" Daisy asked, afraid of the answer.

"I'm going after Levi. He's going to pay for what he's done."

"Hold on, son," Bourbon said.

Cody stopped in ankle-deep water.

"Levi took off in the big guy's truck," Bourbon pointed to Amos, sitting on the bank watching the episode unfold. "He could have gone anywhere. Probably skipped town."

"He didn't," Cody said. "I know where he went. Roshan told me."

Bourbon was the only one who knew whom Cody spoke of. "Shari's boy? How the hell—Oh, never mind. I'm done trying to make sense of all this shit." He began following Cody. Daisy and Flesti followed behind, and they all reconvened on dry land.

"Bourbon," Cody said, "Would you make sure Daisy gets home safe?"

Bourbon didn't hesitate, "Nope, 'cause I'm coming with you."

"I can't let you do that, Bourbon," Cody said.

"You can't stop me either, kid. Levi's done enough. He killed your brother and possibly Andrew Mills. He made a mess of you and AJ. This fucking shit ends tonight, one way or another. Either we get him, or he gets us."

34

THE BARN

Cody and Bourbon put AJ's pickup truck to work, taking the corners thirty mph too fast.

"It's like deja vu, isn't it, Bourbon? You and I, on our way to stop another madman?"

"It sure is, kid," Bourbon answered. He was sitting in the passenger's seat putting his boots back on after retrieving them from Simpson. "Let's hope it goes better this time." He rolled his shoulder, thinking about the bullet that nicked his shoulder blade the night they went after the Sin-eater.

Cody flexed his strong left hand, "Yeah. Let's hope."

They headed north toward the church. Cody drove the Ram to the intersection by the church and only hesitated at the stop sign. Two black streaks crossed the road, a reminder of the night they pursued Jesse Lewis and Charlie Archer, in permanent rubber. And there would be a reminder of this night, as well, because Cody floored the gas pedal, and the two rear tires scribbled marks across the blacktop in a swooping arch. White smoke engulfed the large wheels like two ghostly hands trying to hang on. The hands lost their grip as the truck peeled away, taking the left-hand turn with a screech. Cody worked the steering wheel to the left and back to the right, taking the turn nearly out of control.

They drove until they passed Jesse Lewis's house. Jesse's house was dark. Remnants from the burned barn were still there. The barn's skeleton—thick wooden beams, charred by fire—still stood erect in the location, difficult to see against the night sky.

199

Cody slowed the truck to a crawl and killed the headlights, stopping eighty yards from Annabel Thompson's farm. The house was dark—unusual when Annabel was home.

"Doesn't look like she's here," Bourbon said. "That's good."

"Barn lights are on." Just like Roshan said. The kid was right. "That's where Levi is waiting."

"Waiting?" Bourbon asked. "You think he knows we're coming?"

"I fucking hope so," Cody said. "I hope he's in there shitting his pants right now. But I think he believes I'm almost dead, so he'll have his guard down."

"Somehow, I doubt that. Levi's always been stone-cold—nothing rattles his cage," Bourbon checked his pistol, ensuring the cylinder was full of ammunition. "My guess; he's not alone in there. He's probably drinking a beer and watching us through the window. Expect the unexpected, son, 'cause you've been through enough shit tonight."

Cody gave a little nod, keeping his eyes on the barn. He opened the vehicle door, stepped outside, and closed the door as quietly as possible.

Bourbon mimicked his move, feeling the cool night air against his sunburned skin. It was refreshing and painful simultaneously. He rechecked the house to make sure the lights were still dark. He was glad Annabel wasn't home. It was Sunday. If she were home, she'd be absorbed in a Mary Higgins Clark novel by the window with her reading light glowing over her head. No light. No book. No Annabel.

The two men stepped lightly up the road. An outside light on the barn glistened from the dew forming on the grassy lawn. The spring peepers were singing away somewhere behind the building. The scent in the air made Bourbon feel at home, and he half expected Annabel to appear on the porch to greet him, but the house remained serene.

Cody and Bourbon broke into a light jog once they were a hundred feet away and took cover behind an International tractor that served as a giant lawn ornament. The tractor hadn't run since Bourbon and Annabel met, but it was her father's tractor, and she refused to sell it.

"Let me go in alone," Cody whispered. He wasn't armed but didn't think Levi would be either. He was sure that if Levi wanted a fight, he'd prefer to beat Cody to death rather than let a gun have all the fun.

"I'll give you ten seconds," Bourbon replied. "Then I'm following you. He's probably on the second floor—in the hay loft. You take the stairs on the south end. I'll take the stairs to the north. We'll approach from both ends of the barn."

There was no time to argue, so Cody agreed. He stepped out from behind the tractor and headed for the man door. It was solid steel, rusted from years of weather, but the hinges were greased like a bacon pan. Cody pulled the unlocked door open. It swung silently until there was enough space for him to enter.

He could hear a radio playing softly somewhere in the barn—possibly the hayloft. And voices. Levi wasn't alone. He'd called for backup all ready.

That was fast. It's only been thirty minutes since he left Parson's Store.

Cody turned left and walked down the center of the barn, flanked on both sides by cow stalls. Four lights were mounted on the ceiling. The air was filled with dust, the scent of dry hay, and manure. A lone cow occupied one of the stalls. She watched Cody intently, hoping the human would stop to scratch her neck. Cody obliged her, barely stopping, but he couldn't resist Pearl's big eyes. He dug his fingernails behind her left ear and then a quick scratch between the eyes. He left the cow's stall and followed the lights to the other end of the long barn.

Above Cody, footsteps scuffed along the ceiling as hay dust fell through the cracks in the boards. Someone was walking on the second floor. He held back a sneeze and kept moving until he entered an open area the size of a three-stall garage. It was an area for parking farm vehicles and storing tools, but now it was primarily full of antiquated equipment that was no longer used.

In the corner of the space, to Cody's left, a blue and white 1956 Mercury car was covered with a thin tarp. Dust, as thick as a penny, covered the tarp. The bottom third of the wheels, with whitewall tires, revealed themselves where the tarp fell short. They were low on air pressure and tread but still looked drivable. The tarp was too short to cover the entire hood of the classic vehicle, revealing the airplane hood ornament mounted to the front.

The car's ornament reminded Cody of the day Michael recieved the

L-shape scar on his arm. He'd crashed his bike into a similar symbol on his dad's old Chevy.

Cody touched the shiny plane and wondered why so many car manufacturers used an airplane as a hood ornament. Did it make the car look faster? More futuristic? Or did the shiny plane represent the future of the industry? He decided it was a moot question, which he'd probably never have an answer. He moved on.

Past the open space, a small room to the right stored the saddles and tack for the horses. It had a large open window with no glass that faced into the barn. A dim light illuminated the interior, reflecting off the soft leather and rivets of the saddles. Once Cody reached the tack room, he climbed the stairs that ascended to the loft above.

The steps were dark, but an incandescent glow from the loft emitted just enough light for Cody to make his way. It was hot and stuffy from the day's heat, fifteen degrees warmer than the air outside. Cody felt the thick air fill his lungs. The walls were lined with stacks of baled hay that had probably occupied the space for decades, brought up when the farm was populated with more cows, horses, and sheep. Now, it was Annabel Thompson's hobby farm.

When he reached the top, he saw Levi standing in the middle of the barn. The second floor was open from wall to wall, with heavy hemlock beams supporting the entire structure. Two large windows, void of glass, were built into the barn's gable ends—perfect access for birds, bats, rain, and wind. There were bales of hay stacked on the north side, which Cody hoped weren't blocking Bourbon's access. More bales lined the walls on both sides.

The two men that had met Levi there were Duke and Aaron Bristol. They were cousins, not brothers, but the two men could have passed as twins. They were only months apart in age, and both resembled their father's side of the family. Cody had seen Duke at his house with Levi, but he'd never met Aaron. The pair had a reputation as skilled fighters—even though most of their fights were with each other.

They were all turned away from Cody. Levi stood in the middle of the large room, pointing a loaded crossbow at a paper target attached to a wall of neatly stacked hay bales at the north end. Bourbon would have a hard time entering the loft without being noticed.

Levi shouldered the weapon, took aim, and controlled his breathing. "We may have to go back and finish that pretzel stick, AJ Timmons." He pulled the trigger, and the bolt fired too fast to watch. Cody heard it hit the target at the other end of the barn—seven inches off center.

Cody ducked behind a large empty crate. He had no idea what it had been used for, but it was perfect cover for now.

Duke Bristol pulled another arrow from the quiver he was holding and walked it to Levi. "Sounds like you messed that kid up good. Think he'll talk?"

"Oh, he'll talk. So we'll need to shut him up permanently," Levi fired a second shot—five inches low from the bullseye.

Aaron Bristol stood up from the cooler he was sitting on and took out a cool can of beer. "Is that why you had us meet you here? You want us to take care of him."

Levi put his hand out to Duke, who handed him another crossbow bolt. "You two deal with Timmons. I heard an ambulance head for the store, so he's probably in the hospital. No way he's conscious, but I won't be able to get within a mile of that place. But you two will be able to walk right in. Make it quick and clean, though."

"What's in it for us?" Aaron asked. "I mean, I'm not putting my ass on the line for nothing."

"Gonna cost you a grand," Duke said. "Each. And that crossbow."

Levi was prepared to pay them both five thousand each, but he let their stupidity and mouths cheat themselves. "Deal. I'll give you a grand tonight and the rest after Timmon's funeral."

"What about Savage?" Duke asked.

Levi fired the bolt into the dead center of the target. "I'll finish Savage myself. If he survives the night. Last I saw of him, he'd been stabbed in the back with a six-inch knife."

Cody stepped out from behind the crate. He didn't conscientiously make the move; his legs just reacted faster than his brain. There was no way he'd let the Bristol cousins near AJ. "I'm not that easy to kill," Cody said. "And I don't think you're the man who will do it, Levi."

"What the hell?" Duke said, recognizing Cody from their encounter earlier that day. He wasn't a big guy but he looked fit under his thirty-pound belly. Maybe a former athlete who spent weekends drinking beer after his minimum twenty-minute workout. He had a clean shaven face with a broad nose and blond hair that backed away from his eyebrows too far for his age. Cody mentally aged him to be in his early thirties. The third man, Aaron, could have been the first man's brother. The two looked like fraternal twins.

Duke turned to Levi, "Dude, are you filling us with shit?"

Aaron chimed in, "Doesn't look like you hurt him too bad." He laughed a little and stood. "Should have let us deal with this problem to begin with, Levi."

Duke laughed, "Hell yeah, we'd have done it right. Ain't no walking away from a Bristol beat down."

Simpletons.

"How in the hell?" Levi finally said. "No, fucking way. No fucking way you're walking after the hurt I put on you. This is some kinda trick." He threw the crossbow into a pile of baled hay. "And you're stupid enough to come here?"

"Guess you're not as tough as you think, Levi," Cody said. "As for me? Well, I'm full of surprises." He stepped within ten feet of all three men and just smiled and braced himself for the attack that was sure to come.

"Where's Cricket?" Levi said.

Cody rubbed the spot on his back where the knife went deep. "He's been taken to the hospital. He'll live. Take him a while to get used to living with one arm, but he's alive. I'm sure once he's charged with all the felonies you two have committed, he's going to squeal like a newborn puppy."

Levi stepped closer. "I took my time tonight. Relished the beating Cricket and I gave you. You made a big mistake coming here alone, Savage. I would think your 'psychic ability' would have warned you about that."

A gun clicked behind Levi. Bourbon had his pistol drawn and pointed straight at Levi's back. "He's not the only one with back up, asshole."

Levi recognized the voice without turning around, "Goddam, Bourbon, you still carrying that Smith & Wesson six-shooter?"

"Yup, and it's pointed right at that hollow shell where your heart is supposed to be. Shall I put a hole in it and find out if there's anything in there?"

Levi turned his attention to Bourbon, "I thought you were the famous sheriff that never drew his pistol? What happened to that?"

"I'm not a sheriff anymore, and you're worth the bullet."

Cody cracked his neck. The popping was loud enough for everyone to hear in the silent loft. "Well, what's it going to be, Levi? Are you coming with us, or we gonna do this the hard way?"

Levi pulled his vest off and set it on the crossbow's case. "I've never taken the easy way. I ain't about to start now."

"Good," Cody said.

Confident that Bourbon would never pull the trigger, Levi darted at Cody like a bull. The big man was surprisingly fast. He kept his momentum, and Cody tried to sidestep the lunge. But he was too late. Levi wrangled Cody in his arms and pushed him back ten feet. He lifted the lighter man off his feet and plowed him into the floor like a football lineman tackling a quarterback. The old floorboards and beams collapsed from the weight of the two falling men. The room filled with dust and hay as they disappeared through the hole.

Duke and Aaron started for the stairs that Cody had climbed, but Bourbon fired a shot into the far wall. The sound echoed through the barn, stirring the few animals below and a half-dozen pigeons nesting in the rafters. Bourbon pulled back the Smith & Wesson's hammer to rotate the cylinder and align the next bullet with the barrel.

"Hold on, boys, you've done nothing wrong so far," Bourbon yelled. "This fight is between the two of them. You interfere, and you'll be aiding and abetting a felon. I don't think I have to explain what the consequences will be."

Duke looked to Aaron, "Not if we eliminate any witnesses."

35

DUST & HAY 

Cody and Levi busted through the floor to the first level of the barn and landed on the roof of the 1956 Mercury sedan. Their weight caved the metal top several inches in a cloud of dust. The windows popped, and shards of glass collected in the thin tarp covering the vehicle. Cody rolled to one side of the Mercury and landed feet-first on the concrete floor. Levi had fallen off the opposite side with a little less grace.

They stood in the open area of the barn. The drop through the floor would have been nine feet if the car hadn't broken their fall. Tools were displayed along the wall behind the vehicle—hung and forgotten; garden tools, shepherd's poles, hoses, saw blades, and lumber. All were dusty but orderly. The smell of mildew saturated the room as loose hay and dust floated to the floor. The anomaly in the room was a yellow and black garden tractor recently washed and parked eighteen feet across from the classic Mercury. The metal and rubber shined even in the dim light, contrasting against the dusty wood walls and rusty tools.

Levi moved to the back wall and pulled a pitchfork from its support. "You're not leaving this barn alive, Savage." He twirled the pitchfork in his hand. "And neither is the old man."

Cody gave him a little laugh, "The 'old man' might be the one you should worry about, Levi. He's a tough sonavabitch."

They both moved around to the front of the car; Levi held his weapon. Cody held nothing but a grudge. Levi jumped forward, thrusting the pitchfork at Cody. Cody dove high—higher than the tool—grabbed the fork with his new left hand, and landed a powerful right fist into the bridge of Levi's nose. Before Levi knew what hit him, Cody landed on his feet, spun counterclockwise, and knocked the pitchfork handle out of Levi's grip with his right palm. He held the stolen weapon with his left hand and continued his spin. He and the fork spun 180 degrees, stopping only when two prongs pierced Levi's thigh.

Levi grunted in pain. But took advantage of the position to wrap his meaty arms around Cody's neck in a reverse chokehold. Cody pushed backward hard, and the two men backed up fast and slammed into a wall. The barn shook; more dust and hay rained from the ceiling through the cracks above.

Levi's grip was constricting but not deep enough to choke Cody out. Cody knew that Levi's arm could slip under his chin and crush his windpipe or a carotid artery if he struggled too much.

"I'm going to pop your head off like a friggin cork, dickhead?" Levi grunted through clenched teeth. His rugged arm was tightening around Cody's neck and impeding blood flow to his brain. Cody quickly felt the effect it was having on his concentration. He sucked thick air through his lips, trying to stay conscious. The room went silent, and even the dust seemed to float upon the air currents in slow motion. He felt like he'd been drugged. He only had a few more seconds before his knees would give out.

Cody grabbed Levi's arm for leverage and kicked both feet higher than his head. As his legs fell back to the floor, he kept his body in a V-shape and rolled forward. His weight and momentum were too much for Levi to fight. Cody used the energy to throw Levi over his shoulder, and the big man fell to the concrete like a wet hay bale.

*****

Upstairs, Bourbon had his pistol drawn on the two cousins. He wanted to put it away; secure the weapon inside the leather holster on his ribcage. But his arm wouldn't obey his mind. Tremors vibrated his hand and affected his aim. His forehead felt damp as his breaths for air turned to short huffs.

A shadow appeared in the high window of the barn, sleek and tiny. Bourbon could feel the shadow's gaze upon him for a moment, and then it dove to a thick hemlock beam that formed a rafter. Poe cawed at Bourbon and flapped his wings as he bounced side-to-side. The crow was focused on the ex-sheriff.

A voice whispered in Bourbon's head, *"Pull the trigger."*

No.

"Pull the trigger and rid the world of these monsters."

No. "Get out of my fucking head, Flesti."

Flesti's voice grew, *"They are sinners, Bourbon. Make them pay."*

Bourbon fought the pistol and the betrayal of his own hand. He felt like a puppet in the hands of a cruel child. He'd been afflicted by Flesti Thaed—the puppeteer.

"Damn you, woman! What have you done to me?"

The two cousins were confused by Bourbon's behavior. They didn't know whether to attack or run from the crazy man talking to himself. So they watched for a moment, observing his actions, trying to make a decision. They looked back and forth to each other in indecision.

"Get out of here," Bourbon yelled to the men. His concern had altered—scared that he might shoot the Bristol cousins in cold blood.

The two men hesitated. Duke took one step toward Bourbon as if he were testing the man's intentions. Bourbon's hand tightened, and he shouted the warning again. Then the shot rang out as Bourbon lost control of his trigger finger.

⁕⁕⁕⁕⁕

Downstairs, Cody heard the gunshot rock the barn loft. The sound was muffled by the thick layers of hay that lined the upstairs walls but still loud in his ears. He was gasping for air, and his legs felt heavy under him. He was on his knees, the rough concrete digging into his skin, as a hand grabbed a chunk of hair at the crest of his skull.

Levi had already recovered from the fall and was determined to finish what he'd started. Big fists began to rain down on Cody's head and face, and he knew it wouldn't take long for Levi to knock him out cold again. For a split second, he wondered if he'd pass out and wake up tied to a beam again or if Levi would finish the job with the pitchfork. Maybe, he'd

209

never wake up again. Perhaps this time tomorrow, he'd be laying in the morgue next to Michael.

He endured the blows for a moment to catch his breath. Then the unexpected happened.

Not now. No. Dammit, no.

But the unwanted vision came despite his opposition. This time, the dream came without water against his skin. This time, there was no lake to stimulate the psychic hallucination. This time, it was born from the fear of possible death.

To this point, Cody's visions had been dark, as if he'd been watching TV with the brightness and contrast settings turned too low. But this vision was blinding with a white light that stung his eyes. He covered them with his forearm but slowly peeked over the top. He wanted to view what was so vital that it interrupted his murder.

Willa stood in front of him. AJ was to her right. Daisy and Alyse were to her left. They began to speak in unison—a chorus of moral support—but they all had their own words.

"Stand up."

"Don't give up now."

"You're stronger than this."

"You have to win."

Over and over, they cheered him on, but how could he win this fight when he couldn't control where he was?

I can't beat him.

"You can."

"You must."

He's too strong. He's too fucking strong.

"But you're better."

The voices went silent for a moment. Cody was still on his knees as Willa approached him. She placed a hand on his shoulder and knelt in front of him. Her eyes were like a warm blanket covering him in a storm. And then she spoke, "Levi's changed. He's not the brother I loved. Stop him before he kills you."

For a moment, Cody sensed absolute peace and reached out with his new left hand to touch her face. Her cheek felt as warm as her smile.

She reached for his hand and their fingers interlocked. She held it firmly as she spoke, "You're different now. You're not the same man you were yesterday. I love you, and I believe in you."

Willa pushed Cody's glowing left hand back at him. "You've been given a gift." She stood as another figure approached—his brother Michael.

Michael reached for Cody's right hand as he looked down at his big brother. "Your better than him. You're better than all of us. Now, go kick his ass."

Cody snapped out of the dream. He wasn't sure how long he'd been catatonic. It could have been one second or two minutes. He could feel the blows still coming, and his face starting to swell. Blood ran from his nose and mouth, and swelling skin put pressure on his left eye.

He sprung to his feet in one quick motion, not even sure how he did it. But Levi didn't stop swinging. Levi stepped back, cocked his right arm like a musket hammer, and swung with everything he had to deliver a final knockout blow.

But the punch never landed. Cody's regenerated hand caught the fist as if it reacted in defense of its own volition. Cody threw an uppercut with his right elbow. He could hear Levi's teeth smash together. The big man stumbled back, wobbled to his left, and straightened like an angry pitbull. He stabilized himself with his right hand against the fender of the 1956 Mercury. The airplane hood ornament was pointed at Cody—at Levi's target.

"Why won't you die?" Levi grunted with his next attack. He pushed off the hood of the classic car. He had the musket hammer drawn again and fired when he was within range.

Levi's biggest mistake was always aiming for the head—going for the tenth round knockout. The head was a small, elusive target that moved with speed.

Cody ducked the predictable punch and slid to his left. Levi's momentum made it easy for Cody to hit his ex-brother-in-law in the abdomen. The air left Levi's lungs from the blow. Breathless, Levi spun 180 degrees while trying to catch Cody's jaw with an elbow. Again, the head was his target. That, too, missed.

Levi charged again like an arena bull zeroing in on a matador. The bull and the matador locked horns and began pushing against each other. At first, the heavyweight bull prevailed, shoving Cody backward.

Cody's pain dissipated, and he began to stall Levi's thrust. Levi struggled harder to move his smaller opponent.

Cody felt a surge of strength in his legs and arms. He thought it was the adrenaline spike in his blood but came to the realization that it was the supernatural influence of Cain Lake coursing through his veins.

They spun again—horns unlocked—and Cody hit Levi with a left punch to the chest. His hand glowed with power in the dim barn, and the blow was so forceful that Levi's feet left the ground. He flew backward eight feet before colliding with the '56 Mercury. Cody heard the metal hood crunch like a soccer ball hitting a van door. Levi stood limp against the front of the vehicle, stuck like a bird being hit by a train, but he didn't drop to the ground.

The look on Levi's face was pain or fear—Cody wasn't sure which. Maybe it was both. Levi didn't move. He was frozen in place as if he'd turned to stone. His rock legs finally crumbled, and he fell on his knees to the concrete floor. The car's hood ornament was blood-soaked chrome. Two inches of the plane were broken off and lodged in Levi's back, resulting in a couple of cracked vertebrae and a pinched spinal cord.

Cody knelt beside Levi, grabbed the back of his shirt collar, and moved close enough to whisper in his ear. "Hurts like hell, doesn't it?"

Levi was hapless to defend himself. He was on his stomach, pulling himself toward the door with his elbows while dragging his useless legs. He gasped for breath as fear and panic set in.

Cody picked up the pitchfork. He twirled it a couple of times in his hands and raised it above his head, tongs aiming for the base of Levi's neck. He heard one of the ghost voices like before, but this one was different.

The voice screamed, *"Do it. Stick the goddamn snake in the neck."*

The voice was Flesti's, but hearing her in his head instead of his ears reminded him of the day his parents died. The voice had the same tone and accent as the one that urged him to close the garage doors. Flesti's voice filled his mind and memory as if he were simultaneously living in the present and past.

Levi's neck was exposed. The opportunity was present. Cody pulled the farmer's tool back further—the blow had to be potent. His aim needed to be true. He wanted to stop himself, but dammit, the voice was loud now.

"This is for AJ, asshole," Cody spit the words through gritted teeth.

A meaty hand gripped his shoulder softly. "Don't," Bourbon said with a buttery tone. "Don't do it, son. He's finished."

"He has to pay for what he did," Cody said, uncertain if he was speaking his words or Flesti's. He held the pitchfork high.

"There's no honor in this, Cody. He's finished. You're finished. Don't throw your life away for this piece of garbage."

The pitchfork fell to the floor beside Levi, ringing like a dead tuning fork. Levi collapsed in the same manner but with a different sound.

Bourbon heard the two Bristol cousins drive away from the scene. They had come to their senses and decided not to push their luck against the man with the pistol.

Poe was cawing outside, but his squaking grew faint as he disappeared in the dark.

Bourbon used Levi's phone to call Sheriff Hassett. "Sheriff? I have Levi Thompson in custody in his mother's barn. Savage? No, no, I haven't seen him. We parted ways after we left the lake."

36

AJ

Cody raced away from the barn in the AJ's truck while Bourbon waited for Sheriff Hassett to arrive. He took the corners like a NASCAR driver at Watkin's-Glen Speedway, keeping the wheels busy gripping the road. A million scenarios raced through his mind. He pounded angrily on the steering wheel, blaming himself for AJ's condition.

Cody stopped at the red octagon at the intersection of Grandview and Lake View. He stared at rubber tire marks that wiggled parallel to the yellow line. The entrance to the church and cemetery was to his right side. He hesitated before transferring his foot from the brake to the accelerator pedal. This was the last place he'd seen Willa, whether as a spirit or a hallucination. He hoped to see her now, even if just a glimpse, but Willa was nowhere to be seen. He felt crazy for even thinking she would appear.

He punched the gas with his right foot and cranked the steering wheel counterclockwise. The V-8 engine torqued the wheels into motion, and Cody sped to the hospital. He could see flashing lights approaching down the road and over the horizon. Sheriff Hassett was on her way to Annabel Thompson's barn to arrest Levi. Cody jumped on the brakes, slowed the truck to a crawl, and pulled into a random house.

Sheriff Hassett zipped pass in her Jeep without giving the truck a second thought. Cody waited a few more minutes until an ambulance passed that was tracing Hassett's tracks.

Cody backed out of the driveway and continued his race.

*****

When Cody entered the hospital's waiting room, AJ was still being assessed by the doctors. Alyse Burns and River Kelly sat nervously on a puffy couch.

Alyse's knees bounced as the stress of the wait consumed her. She wore a ring on each finger of her left hand, and she was twisting the one on her left index finger. She was nervous. Cody had learned to read her mood by whichever ring she fiddled with. It was a subconscious habit of hers.

She jumped to her feet when Cody was within range for a hug. She fell into his arms, and the two ex-lovers embraced for a long time. Tears fell from her chiseled cheeks onto Cody's dirty shirt. She pulled away and studied the fresh black and blue lumps around his eyes.

"What happened with Levi?" Alyse asked.

"He's in custody," was all Cody said.

Alyse just nodded while biting her lip.

Cody gave River a quicker hug and sat between the two beauties.

"They're performing a CAT scan now," Alyse said. "The doctors are worried about swelling on his brain."

Cody ran his new fingers through his thick blond hair.

Alyse stared at the hand for a moment and then whispered to him as she nodded at the hand, "Did that really happen, or am I hallucinating?"

Cody nodded while he practiced flexing his new fingers.

"You've got some explaining to do. When all of this is over, we need to have a conversation."

"Is Daisy here?" Cody asked, trying to change the subject.

"No, she wanted to be here but needed to get home before it got too late. Didn't want her mom to get worried, and she needed to hug Sammy."

"I'll be lucky if she ever speaks to me again. She warned me not to go looking for Jesse Lewis. She was right. Look what's happened because of my actions.

"You can't blame yourself. Levi brought all of this on. Levi's responsible for AJ, not you."

Cody wasn't convinced.

River was silent. She seemed too upset to talk to anyone, so she just sipped a shitty coffee from the vending machine and stared blankly at a soundless television mounted on the wall airing an episode of The Golden Girls.

They waited for almost an hour in semi-comfortable chairs while reading the subtitles on the TV. None of them found the Golden Girls funny tonight. None of them wanted to laugh. The sitcom was nothing more than a distraction from the dire news they dreaded. They were tired from the day's events, and they were tired of waiting.

*****

The doctor finally entered the waiting room. Cody, Alyse, and River, jumped from their chairs to greet her. She wore what every ER doctor wore without a stethoscope or a clipboard. She introduced herself as Dr. Wexler and gave them AJ's diagnosis.

They fell back to the couch as their legs waivered. River cried, so Cody put his arm around her to console her. Alyse buried her face in her hands to hide her emotions.

AJ was in a coma. The next twenty-four hours would be crucial to his condition, and all they could do was wait.

The three friends alternated turns visiting the patient and taking turns falling asleep in the lobby chairs, but they never left the hospital.

37
HUGH JACKMAN 

Hassett was relieved that her suspicion of Deputy Simpson was misplaced. She felt stupid for believing he was capable of the brutal murder of Michael Savage and Andrew Mills. It had been three days since she put the cuffs on Levi Thompson, Amos McGrath, and Jeremy "Cricket" Morrison. All the evidence had been submitted and reported, and Jesse Lewis had been buried.

Jesse's funeral was a quiet event. A handful of mourners were present, but few seemed to be sincerely mourning. Their appearance originated from curiosity rather than concern. The former pastor of Stoneville had betrayed his congregation's privacy and exploited their sins. They wanted the closure, to know Jesse Lewis was dead and buried, so they could move on with their lives.

Jeff Bourbon was one of the few. His motive to attend was out of respect because he respected everyone—even criminals to a degree. He too wanted closure, and the assurance that the Sin-eater was gone. Stoneville's nightmare was over; the Sin-eater's wrath had ended.

Bourbon shaved his beard completely. It was the first time he'd seen his clean face in decades. The local barber—a kid in his twenties with curly hair and a ton of tattoos—gave him the best haircut he'd ever had.

Sheriff Hassett leaned against her patrol vehicle outside the cemetery during Jesse Lewis's funeral. She watched from a distance, worried someone with a grudge might appear to disrupt the event. She'd seen it in Chicago—gang-bangers retaliating by desecrating graves and deceased rivals' bodies. But this wasn't Chicago. There were no gangs, and the residents of the small town let cool heads prevail.

Bourbon left the funeral after the final prayer and walked down a narrow road through the cemetery. The elevation provided a stunning view of Cain Lake with a blue sky and serene water. Whatever violence or crime occurred in the streets of Stoneville was imperceptible from here. He enjoyed the vista momentarily, took a deep breath, and began his march toward the attractive sheriff standing at the gate. She barely recognized him as he approached her.

"How's the knee?" She asked as he shyly made eye-to-eye contact.

Bourbon made a small circular motion with the afflicted joint, "Good as new. In fact, I feel better than ever."

Hassett smiled and stepped closer, "You look good, Bourbon. I didn't realize there was such a handsome man under all that hair. You look like Hugh Jackman when you clean up."

"Is he a football player? Don't get much time to watch TV."

"Wolverine?"

"From Michigan? A college player?"

She laughed. "No. Hugh Jackman, the actor. You don't watch many movies, do you?"

"Job's kept me pretty busy for the last couple of decades. Sometimes Annabel and I would watch the holiday classics, though."

Annabel. Jo Hassett had heard all about her at the office. Bourbon and Annabel were the town's power couple, inseparable even though they spent little time together. She wondered if he'd return to her now that Jesse Lewis was dead and his hunt was over.

She didn't know the truth—how Annabel Thompson was a target of the Sin-eater because of her hit-and-run accident that killed Charlotte Archer. The truth had died with Archer.

"Well, maybe you could buy me dinner sometime, and I'll take you to a movie."

Bourbon blushed a little. He hadn't been interested in another woman in years, and the only time a woman flirted with him was to get out of a traffic ticket. He agreed to take her to dinner some night. "Maybe, but first there's something I need to do. And then I'm going to be out of town for a while."

"Going back to the lake?"

Bourbon nodded. "I spent weeks out there focused on finding Jesse Lewis. Now that he's been found, I need to go back and find myself. Do a little fishing. Hike the peaks. Find the man I used to be before the law took over my life."

"Whew," Hassett said, "I was afraid you'd want your job back."

He stared at the badge on her hip, "You can keep the job. It looks better on you."

Hassett gave Bourbon a hug—partly to console him for all he'd been through, partly because she respected him. But mostly the hug was because he was a good person and she knew few people like that anymore. He was a breath of fresh air in a world filled with assholes and frauds. Bourbon was genuine and kind, strong and ethical, with morals of stone. She couldn't help but be attracted to a man like that. But she also knew he'd go back to Annabel. Their love was undeniable and unbreakable. She secretly wished she wouldn't accept him.

"I'll call you when I get back in town," Bourbon said.

"Leaving today?"

"Yeah. I just have one more thing to do."

"Me too," Hassett said.

"Oh, what's that?"

She looked at the few people in the cemetery. Then her eyes darted to the lake beyond the church and over her shoulder toward Stoneville. "I've got to figure out who killed Jesse Lewis. My money's on Cody Savage. Once we get the ballistics report on the pistol he was carrying, I'll know for sure."

Bourbon stared sternly at her, "Savage didn't kill Jesse."

"Well, that's your opinion. I'm going to get the evidence and the facts. Whoever is responsible is going to be brought to justice."

"Well," Bourbon said, "Good luck with that."

38
ONE LAST THING 

Bourbon's hands trembled as he pulled into Annabel Thompson's driveway. The usually cool ex-sheriff was like a teenager driving up to pick up his prom date. He had no expectations of the conversation about to ensue but hoped the scenario in his head was accurate. It had been three weeks since he last saw Annabel. Three weeks for her to miss him, hate him, or forget him.

The sun was high, still warm behind the thick clouds that dotted the blue overhead. The birds were always singing during the day. The crickets and frogs sang in unison at night. He always loved arriving at her farm, but today he was too distracted to take pleasure in the beauty of the Thompson farm.

The farm was unusually silent. Four cows gathered at the fence closest to the house, kept away from the green yard by three rows of barb-wire. A crow perched on the barn's weather vane, but Bourbon knew it wasn't the pesky Poe that had followed him the night Cody defeated Levi.

Even the flighty chickens and roosters seemed lazy, lying on the ground rather than pecking away at the yard. An eerie calm settled over the hobby farm, which was satisfying. Bourbon had seen too much violence here three nights ago and was sorry for bringing the mayhem to Annabel's door.

He climbed the porch steps and faced the screen door. His thick knuckles were about to tap when he noticed her silhouette at the dining room table. The door squeaked softly. The house was dark—all the blinds sealed tight, curtains drawn shut, and not a single light on in the house. She stood out against the kitchen's white tile, where she sat by herself at a small round table.

"Annie?"

She didn't answer, so he softly called her name again.

The house was immaculate, like always. The decor hadn't changed since the last time he visited—modern simplicity contrasting rustic accents. The scent of a cinnamon candle brought back memories of the two cooking breakfast every Sunday. It was his favorite time of the week.

"Why are you here, Jefferson?" Her voice was sleepy and slow, and Bourbon wasn't sure if she'd just woke up or needed to go to bed.

"What are you doing sitting here alone in the dark?"

"It's peaceful."

Bourbon went to the window, pulled the curtains back, and cracked the blinds a little. The horizontal beams of light contoured around her body and across the table. They illuminated a faint haze of smoke that enveloped the tired woman at the table.

"I think you know why I'm here," Bourbon said.

Annabel was stoic, which was unusual for the usually charismatic woman. Bourbon expected to receive a hug, but she seemed distant and annoyed by his presence. He was glad because he hadn't come with good news.

She leaned forward, tapped a cigarette to dislodge the ashes, and took a long draw from the other end. It was the first time Bourbon had ever seen her smoke. She leaned back and exhaled away from him.

Bourbon's voice cracked slightly, "I'm sorry it's come to this."

"Come to what? My life being destroyed? My kid's gone? Our love...," She stopped herself, took a drink of water, and swallowed hard as if trying to choke back her following words. "Just go home. Don't worry about me. I'll be fine."

"That's not why I'm here. I mean, of course, I'm worried about you. I can't stand what all of this has done to your family. I'm sorry what it did to Levi."

"None of this is your fault. What's done is done, and everyone has paid the consequences."

"Not everyone. Not for everything." Bourbon dug into the cargo pocket of his pants. His hand came out in a fist and placed a small object on the table. There was no mistaking it. The beam of light piercing the window reflected off the brass finish of the .30-30 gun shell. It was absent of lead or gunpowder and as hollow as he felt at that moment.

Annabel didn't say a word. She just stared at the empty cartridge, conceding to his accusation.

"I believe this is yours."

She didn't deny it. "I always said you should have been a detective. How'd you know? 'Bout every other hunter in this county owns a .30-30 rifle. How'd you know it was mine?"

Bourbon sat back in the dining table chair and crossed his right leg over the other, "It wasn't just the shell. I went up to that rock—where you had the perfect view of Jesse Lewis. The shooter was lying down to make that shot, but if they had moved one foot to the left, they would have had an even clearer shot. Why shoot through the trees? Why not move over and shoot through the clear opening?" He was glaring at her now—his eyes cold and frozen.

Annabel took another drag from her cigarette without answering or saying a word.

Bourbon continued, "Because that would have meant crushing a rare flower. Only Annabel Thompson would go out of her way to avoid hurting a delicate lady slipper—one of the most endangered orchids in the state. So you stayed to the right and let the flower be. Am I right?"

"They were my mother's favorite, you know?"

Bourbon wasn't done. "Before I checked the shooting position, I walked up to the trail where Cody heard a four-wheeler. The four-wheeler tracks were no doubt yours. How many miles have we ridden on this farm, leaving those very same tracks behind and following them back home again?" His icy stare began to melt, and water balanced delicately on his lower eyelid. "I bought you those tires because I liked the aggressive tread. I didn't want you to get stuck again in the back field's mud. Remember?"

Bourbon's tears were contagious, and Annabel's eyes melted in a similar fashion. Then she took a deep breath and composed herself.

"This would have been over with, Annie. All of this was behind us. I was coming home to you. I was coming back to us. Jesus, I missed you."

"Over for whom, Jefferson? Over for whom? It would have never been over for me, dammit. I lost my daughter to your deputy. I have physical scars from the night that madman Jessie Lewis attacked me in his barn. Do you have any idea how that haunts me?"

She was nearly yelling now. Her words were slurred as if rage or alcohol affected her ability to form words. "Then Levi gets a hair-brain idea to draw Jesse out of hiding by becoming the very thing I hated. My own son—a sinner. I couldn't let him kill Jesse Lewis. I couldn't. I knew what he was up to, so I had to beat him to the kill. It was the only way to stop him."

Bourbon stood. He was speechless. He couldn't imagine how hard this had been on his ex-lover. He wasn't going to turn her in. Sheriff Hassett would have to figure this out on her own.

"I know Jesse Lewis hurt you," Bourbon said as he faced the window blind. "I wanted to kill him myself—almost did. But we're not killers. Or, at least, I thought we weren't."

"Didn't you kill your deputy? I suppose that was okay since you were doing your civic duty?"

"No, it wasn't okay. I was wrong to shoot Archer. He forced me. He tried to draw on me first, and if I hadn't, who knows what would have happened to Erika Poole. But I've had to live with that every single day since. It's haunted me every day since, and it will haunt me every day going forward."

Annabel snuffed her cigarette out in a small round ashtray. The smoke drifted lightly toward the ceiling and faded away.

"Now," Bourbon continued, "You'll have to live with the guilt of killing Jesse Lewis."

"No, I won't," Annabel said. She reached into her robe pocket and placed an empty pill bottle beside the brass bullet shell. "No, I won't."

Fuck! Fuck, fuck, fuck! Bourbon jumped to his feet. "What did you do, Annie? Why?"

"I won't go to jail—I won't—not for that goddam pond scum."

Bourbon stood behind her and wrapped his arms around her as if he could squeeze the overdose of sleeping pills out of her. "I won't let you die. You've nothing to hide. I promise, no one will ever know you did this."

"I'm sorry, Jefferson. But I need the pain to stop. Please do one last thing for me."

"Anything."

"Tell Cody," She stopped to cough violently. "Tell him, I'm sorry for all I've done. Tell him he was the best thing that ever happened to Willa."

"You tell him yourself, goddamit."

Her eyes closed almost completely.

Bourbon put his cheek to hers, "Fight this, Annie. Fight. We'll make this better."

She slumped forward in her chair. "I love—" She choked on her words. Coughed. Went blank. And then she passed out.

Bourbon called 911 and waited for an ambulance to arrive. It was the longest seventeen minutes of his life.

39
THE FUNERAL 

The memorial service for Annabel Thompson was the largest Stoneville had ever witnessed. She'd been a respected member of the community for almost two decades, accumulating friends, colleagues, and acquaintances almost daily. There wasn't a single person in town with a negative opinion of the widowed farmer with a steely work ethic. The medical examiner stated that she died from an accidental overdose of sleeping pills, but the whispers throughout the funeral home told another story. They said she'd lost everything, and her poor heart couldn't break into any smaller pieces. She finally succumbed to the pain of trying to keep all the fragments together.

Bourbon was dressed in his finest suit, which he'd worn to his father's funeral and Willa and Cody's wedding. It was the same suit Annabel helped him pick out, but he never figured he'd wear it to her funeral—maybe his own, but never hers.

Bourbon received nearly every guest who would speak to him. There were some people who blamed him for her death—leaving her after the trauma she endured from Jesse Lewis. He was okay with that. He'd never let them know the truth—how Annabel hit poor Charlotte Archer and set off a chain of catastrophic events. He'd never tell anyone how it broke her or that she intentionally took the pills. He'd bear the brunt of the rumors and gladly shoulder the blame. He could take the criticism, but he couldn't take Annabel's reputation being ruined.

A hand touched his shoulder, "So sorry for your loss, Bourbon." Daisy Torrez's voice was like another flower among the thousands. She was alone, dressed in a black mid-sleeve top and a sleek gray skirt. Her high-heel shoes made her three inches taller, but she still had to look up to meet him eye-to-eye.

"Thank you, Daisy, but it's the whole town's loss, not just mine."

"I know. Is there anything you need? Cody and I could bring you some dinner or something."

"Oh, God, no. All the town women have been bringing me food for three days. I'm going to have to go back to the woods just to lose weight. How's AJ doing? Any updates?"

Daisy's smile wilted a little, "He's stable. The doctors said the swelling on his brain has diminished, but he's still in a coma. They don't think he'll have permanent brain damage. Fingers crossed." She put her middle finger over her index finger to signify her hope.

"That's good to hear. Is Cody with you?" Bourbon asked. He peeked over her shoulder, expecting to see him.

Daisy told Bourbon how Cody refused to leave the hospital longer than a few hours. Usually, he just went home, showered, ate, and returned. They knew Cody felt responsible for what had happened to AJ, and they tried to convince him not to blame himself, but their encouragement was ineffectual.

"Poor kid," Bourbon said, referring to AJ. "How the hell did he know Cody was in danger? Or that he was at the old store?"

Daisy raised her phone and gave it a wiggle for effect, "Tracking app on his phone. AJ bought Cody his phone so they could keep in touch. AJ downloaded a tracking app the night they met Levi at the Fuel Line. I guess he knew Cody would get himself in trouble while looking for Jesse Lewis. He was so desperate to find his brother.

"But with the shitty cell service around Cain Lake, tracking Cody was hit and miss. He did the best he could."

Bourbon put the pieces together. "So AJ was keeping tabs on his buddy the whole time."

Daisy nodded. "I don't have all the details—just what I overheard AJ tell Alyse while we drove to Parson's that night. He was talking fast and driving faster, so he was kinda vague. Plus, I was hiding on the floor of the truck." Her mouth twisted in shame from her admission.

Bourbon listened to Daisy's description of AJ's plight to follow

Cody, but his eyes were fixed on the woman across the room who'd just entered. She wore a tight gray dress with a subtle pattern of chevron-like shapes contrasting against small swirls. The monochromatic design—dark, medium, and light grays—kept the dress quiet but stood out amongst the crowd. The woman in the expensive dress stood nearly a head taller than the other women. Sheriff Jo Hassett smiled gently at Bourbon and crossed the room, stepping inside his personal space.

He didn't mind.

"Good afternoon, sheriff," Bourbon greeted her.

"Please, just call me Jo. I'm not on duty right now."

Daisy's couriosity interrupted, "Jo? Is that short for Jolene or Joanne or something else?"

"It's short for Joe, with an E. My father was certain he was having a boy, so he wanted to name me after his father. He spent seven months calling me 'Joe' before I was born. He protested about giving me any other name. My mother refused to spell my name with an E on the end to make it more feminine."

Bourbon smiled for the first time in days, and Daisy took notice. She felt like an intruder, which was rare for a journalist.

"Well, if you'll excuse me—I have to get back to the hospital," Daisy said. "I'm going to bring Cody some lunch. I'll let you know if there are any updates on AJ."

They said their goodbyes and Bourbon and Hassett watched Daisy leave the funeral home. After a few more intrusions, Hassett resumed her conversation with Bourbon.

She asked him about his plans to return to Cain Lake. Bourbon told her he still planned to go back, this was just a delay, and now he needed the little retreat more than ever. "There've been too many funerals for my taste lately," he said. He didn't tell her about Flesti Thaed and how she might connect to everything around Cain Lake. Bourbon felt violated by Flesti's assault on his mind. He nearly killed Jesse Lewis at the lake because she was talking inside his head. Then she seemed to be in control at the barn, almost resulting in the death of the two cousins, Duke and Aaron Bristol.

Bourbon came to the realization—there was no denying it

anymore—that Cain Lake and the micropods that filled it were affecting people on some abstruse level, both psychologically and physically. He considered the lake a miracle of nature and God, but Flesti Thaed could somehow control people affected by the micropods. Maybe she was controlling Annabel when she swallowed those damn pills.

Sheriff Hassett sensed the weight on Bourbon's mind. She touched his shoulder, and Bourbon felt himself lean toward her. The tilt of his stance was less than an inch, but he could feel himself pulled toward her, like the opposing ends of two magnets. Her light perfume entranced him momentarily, and he found himself staring at her lips.

Bourbon tried to focus on their conversation, "Any luck? With your investigation?"

Hassett folded her arms across the dress's pattern, "Not much. Amos McGrath and Cricket both lawyered up. McGrath seems to be cooperative. We have the video from Cricket's phone."

"Video?"

"The night Levi tortured Cody, Cricket filmed the entire thing with his phone. We recovered it at the scene. The whole thing was recorded, up to the point when McGrath fired the shotgun. The phone's battery must have gone dead at that point."

"I want to know who killed Andrew Mills," Bourbon said. "I was friends with his family—"

"We'll find the person who did it," Hassett said. "My money's on Cody Savage."

"What? No. I told you, there's no way Cody killed Andrew. He's not capable of murder."

"Who knows what people are capable of," Her voice was low. She stared at the open coffin at the front of the room.

Bourbon leaned away, the magnets now repelling each other, "Sheriff, I know Cody. I knew Andrew Mills. There's no connection. No motive. Andrew had to be another one of Levi's victims."

"Maybe," she said. "But Cody was carrying the pistol that killed Andrew Mills. Cody claimed he borrowed the gun from Jeremy Morrison, but I think he bought it illegally. Besides, he violated his parole. I've got the District Attorney working on a search warrant for his house.

Gonna see what else we can dig up. I thought Levi killed Jesse Lewis, but Amos McGrath says he was with him at Parson's all afternoon. So, I'm still not sure who killed Lewis. Maybe Savage killed them both."

"Now you're way off base."

She uncrossed her arms and placed her hands on her hips, "You know something I don't?"

There was no way he would rat out Annabel for killing Jesse Lewis. Her crime was going to the grave with her, and it would go to his grave with him when the time came. "Maybe I killed Jesse Lewis. You know I was out there hunting for him."

"Don't try derailing this investigation. Lewis was shot with a high-powered rifle, but the caliber was smaller than that hand cannon you carry. Don't try to cover for Savage. I think Savage is more dangerous than you realize."

He is dangerous, but mostly to himself.

A few women from Annabel's reading group interrupted Bourbon and Hassett's discussion.

"Thank you for coming, Jo. I hope to see you again soon." Bourbon turned away from the athletic new sheriff, ending their conversation.

Bourbon kept his eyes on Jo Hassett, eagerly waiting for her to depart the funeral service. He excused himself from Annabel's friends and made his way to the back of the funeral home, down the hall, and out the rear entrance.

He stood near an empty dumpster, pulled out his cell phone, and called Daisy Torrez.

She answered on the first ring, "Hey, Bourbon, what can I do for you?"

"Get Cody out of town as soon as you can."

40

EPILOGUE

River Kelly left the hospital in tears. She made her way across the parking lot—her phone had been buzzing for an hour. She ignored the call ringing her Android phone, even though she'd been anxiously awaiting it for a week. The caller would have to wait until she reached the privacy of her vacation rental.

She climbed behind the wheel of her Nissan Pathfinder, pulled out of the parking lot, and headed to the other side of town. She parked in the driveway of her father's rental house, a red bungalow nestled on a hillside overlooking the serene river bay. She climbed half a flight of stairs with heavy legs, pulling her exhaustion up each step like a rucksack full of dead weight. Her tears dried in streaks down her cheeks, partially covered by running mascara. Her red hair splashed over her ears and shoulders, bouncing with each step and blowing gently across her face in the evening breeze that crossed the bay.

The neighborhood was quiet and peaceful, and she enjoyed the serenity of the shaded porch before entering the side door. She took a deep breath, sucking in the fresh Adirondack air, and let it out slowly to compose herself. There was nothing more she could do for AJ but wait. She hoped he'd be out of his coma by the time she had to go back to work, or she didn't know what she would do. She would have to return to school a week before the fall semester commenced and prepare for the incoming students. She loved her job as a physical education teacher but was in no hurry to start the next school year.

The phone buzzed once again. She picked it up without looking at the caller's identification.

"This is River," she answered.

"Hey, River, this is Pat Wells," a voice announced.

"Hello, Patrick."

Patrick Wells was the dive master for the Albany volunteer Search and Rescue Team. He was seeking a couple of volunteer scuba divers to search Lake George for a missing kayaker. River politely declined, reminding Pat she was still out of town and had other obligations. He understood, thanked her, and disconnected the call.

She walked to the kitchen and made herself a platter of nachos with ground beef, salsa, and banana peppers. Her mind was locked on poor AJ, lying in a hospital bed, unable to feed himself. She felt too guilty to eat, so she covered the platter with cling wrap and stuck it inside the refrigerator. Her hand clasped the neck of a cold brown bottle instead. She twisted the top off the Michelob, walked barefoot to the deck, and plopped in a deck chair. The vista was beautiful but tough to enjoy alone.

She sniffed a little as her nose tingled—the sensation warning her she was about to break again. She poured some of the beer down her throat to dilute her sorrow.

A motorcycle roared down one of the side streets, tearing the placid scene apart. The engine was obnoxious, and she could feel the decibels pounding away at her eardrums. Several large dogs began lamenting the bike's trespass, protesting in deep-throated growls and barks. A murder of crows, fleeing from the noise pollution, scattered through the trees beside her, regrouped in flight and traveled across the water to find solace on the other side of the bay.

River wished she could fly with them to escape the motorcycle's intrusion. It reminded her of the night the rogue Road Barons had beaten her boyfriend nearly to death. She remembered the sound of metal scraping the gravel as Alyse dragged the bikes behind AJ's truck. She remembered seeing AJ lying on the concrete floor, limp and unconscious, with blood running down his neck and chin. She remembered the ear-piercing sound of the sirens as the ambulance transported AJ away.

She also remembered Cody Savage, healed by his devoted friends, that stupid lake, and then walking away like nothing had happened.

Why the fuck didn't they help AJ? Why couldn't he heal in the lake?

She threw the nearly empty beer bottle to the rocky slope that led to the river's edge. It shattered like her temper. Then she calmed herself with a few deep breaths. She'd have to clean the mess before her father, the District Attorney, found it.

The phone rang again. This time, it was the call she'd been waiting for, and she was finally ready to talk.

She repeated her salutation as she accepted the call, "This is River."

"River? Hi, I've been trying to reach you. This is Dr. Claxton from the University—"

"Yes, yes, Dr. Claxton. I'm sorry I missed your calls earlier. I had a little emergency to tend to."

Dr. Claxton was cruising in his sixties, with a voice worn raw from years of educational lectures. "Oh, I see. I hope everything is all right. I'm calling about the artifact you found, of course."

River jumped to her feet and made her way inside to escape the noise of the wind, traffic, and barking dogs. She opened her duffel bag and retrieved a thick roll of leather fabric.

"This artifact is quite beautiful," Dr. Claxton said. "Where did you find it?"

River didn't answer immediately. She lay the fabric on the oak coffee table and gingerly unwrapped her prize inside.

Dr. Claxton continued, "I mean, I'm sure the pictures you sent don't do it justice. I'd love to examine the piece in person. Will you be back in town soon? We could do lunch, perhaps. If you brought it to my lab, I could do a more thorough study."

"So, what is it?" River asked. She unraveled the fabric, revealing a stone knife with crude carvings on the handle. There wasn't an ounce of metal in the blade or hilt, as if the entire thing had been carved from a single piece of a rare stone. It was light blue with a marbled texture throughout. The blade and handle were only differentiated by a slight ridge wrapping around the circumference.

The blade was about six inches long, with sharpened edges on both sides. It held its edge quite well, sharp enough to cut skin with minimal pressure. River had learned that the hard way, slicing a two-inch-long gash in her palm the day she found it. The handle was the same length as the blade and tapered on the end to point. A hieroglyphic carving adorned the handle—a triangle with three wavy lines on each side.

Dr. Claxton continued, "It appears to be Native American in origin. Probably carved from chert, but I've never quite seen a sample like this."

"Chert?" She grasped the knife's handle with her right hand and examined it closely.

"Chert, yes. It's a type of sedimentary rock, like flint, composed of cryptocrystalline quartz. The blue is rare; I've never seen a sample of that hue. I assume you found it near water? It's amazing considering your location."

"Why's that?"

"Chert normally formed in ancient oceans, but there have been discoveries of the rock in saline alkaline lakes. The sample you possess could date back to the Jurassic period."

River stared at the knife, barely hearing the old professor's words.

"I'd like to study it in person," Claxton continued. "Maybe under a microscope. My colleagues might be able to use radiometric dating to determine the age, and an anthropologist I know could identify those carvings. Are you interested in selling it?"

"No. I don't think so, Dr. Claxton," River said. "Thank you for your help." With that, she pushed the disconnect button. An eerie calm came over her. She heard whispers in both ears, muffled and indistinct, and felt a tingle of energy ascend her right hand. The tingle originated from the stone knife she gripped tight as if it were vibrating at high speed.

She closed her eyes, just to feel the energy, but when she did, visions of Cain Lake began to overwhelm her mind. She saw the blue micropods swirling in darkness, like the day she found the knife. She also saw Flesti Thaed, Cody Savage, and a mysterious female with blood on her hands.

The micropods swirled again, erasing the image, but it was soon replaced by another; a little girl wearing a dress.

The girl was about twelve years old. The dress was of simple homemade design like the ones she saw in old drawings of pioneer women. She was standing on a plank that jutted out over the water. In her hand, was the very same knife that River held now, and her hands and dress were covered in blood. The image flickered. The micropods swirled once again, and the vision ended.

River dropped the dagger onto the coffee table but immediately felt the urge to pick it back up. She resisted momentarily, then opened her hand and thought about gripping it again.

It was a beautiful knife.

Without warning, the blade spun ninety degrees, like a magnet's needle, until it pointed away from her. It flew up and into her hand under its own power, and once again, she was gripping the weapon.

She screamed as if she thought a ghost had lifted the knife and put it in her palm, but there was no one there but her. She threw the knife this time—further and harder—and it stuck into a framed canvas painting of Cain Lake at sunset. She felt shame for damaging the canvas. Her father would be furious. She instantly regretted the impulsive move.

Before she could move across the room to extract the knife and access the damage, the blade returned to her like a living boomerang. Her reflexes responded, like a snake striking without thought, and she easily caught the knife's handle.

She wasn't sure what the weapon was, or where it came from, but it was hers now.

She cracked a venomous smile, and heard a whisper in her ear.

"Make them pay. You have the power now. Show them who you are," the female voice encouraged.

She walked back to the deck overlooking Cain Lake, held the knife out, and pointed to the water. She made a slow sweeping motion from right to left and thought about poor AJ in the hospital.

"They're all going to pay. Cody Savage and the Road Barons are all going to die."

THE END

THANK YOU

www.TerryFisherBooks.com

Sign-up for announcements and notifications
about my next book
CAIN LAKE 3